A Variety of Chains

By

Christine Blackthorn

SINFUL PRESS

First published in 2016 by Sinful Press.
www.sinfulpress.co.uk
Copyright © 2016 Christine Blackthorn
Cover design by Deranged Doctor Design
The right of Christine Blackthorn to be identified as the
author of this work has been asserted in accordance with the
Copyright, Designs and Patents Act, 1988.

A CIP catalogue record for this book is available from the
British Library

ISBN-13: 978-1-910908-05-1

This book is a work of fiction. Names, characters,
businesses, organisations, places and events are either the
product of the author's imagination or are used fictitiously. Any
resemblance to actual persons, living or dead, events or locales
is entirely coincidental.

For Kathryn

ErGer - Bloodhaven

The etymology of the word remains unclear but is most likely to be found in the old Breton language, from the phrase *er Gêr* - at home. It denotes a human with a curious and rare genetic mutation, allowing them to instinctively channel a wide range of energy strands from, and to, those with a physical or mental bond with them. This seems to be occasioned by a pheromone in the ErGer's blood, resulting in the creation of a sensation of 'home' and safety in those bound, therefore lowering their natural drive for self-preservation. Unfortunately, the same pheromone is also addictive to vampires and many otherworld species, leading to ErGer being drained of blood often before a bond can be fully established.

The ritual of bonding is a secretive one with many variants, but relies on the need to lower, or weaken, the ErGer's emotional composure to allow for an initial connection to be made. Bonding is rare and difficult to occasion; success is limited exclusively to the date of February fourteenth, based on the hormonal balances in the ErGer's body.

1

Sacrifice

She would, in all probability, die tonight. Though death might still turn out to be the more desirable outcome. Death or slavery. If it came down to that final choice, her preference was clear: she would always choose death. She had chosen slavery before and it did not agree with her.

None of this mattered if she could just save the life of three little girls by doing so. So, today of all days, on the one day she could lose her life to him, she entered the halls of the Lord of London voluntarily – as a sacrifice. On the streets, surrounding her, the Valentine's Day celebrations filled the air with a kind of manic desperation. She felt nothing of it. She did not even feel the icy tendrils of the rain drenching her too-thin charity shop coat, penetrating to her skin, burning. She had gone past the discomfort of life as she reached for the heavy glass door to the building, the cold within her matching the weather and her prospects for the future.

1

Neben Investments. Her eyes hesitated for a moment on the heavy gold letters splayed before her. Such a nondescript term but then she guessed it was hardly possible for him to write "Supernatural Court of London" onto his entrance, no matter how accurate it would have been. It did not pay to advertise - and really, it was not as if he needed it. Everyone who wanted to find him, needed to find him, did. Just as she had.

The door was heavy, the hinges stiff. Her hands slipped on the metal bar, the contact painful against her icy skin. It took her two attempts before she could push through into warmth – and noise. It washed over her, surrounded her, slid off her just as the rain had. Kathryn walked slowly across the hard marble floor as the voices fell silent and her presence began to register. She was ErGer. Her body held the power so many thirsted for. She felt them bristle, taken aback by her unwillingness to cower before what were the predators of their world. They did not matter. She had not come to see them. None of these, no witch or were, faery or shifter, would lay a hand on her tonight. They did not have that power. She had come to see their Master, to see the Vampire Lord of London, to die at his hand. And she did not care.

"Kathryn McClusky to see Lord Lucian."

The receptionist behind the heavy oak counter froze before her large blue eyes jumped to Kathryn's face. It would have been funny if anything so mundane still had the power to touch her. As it was, she just countered the wide-eyed stare, ignored the sudden silence in the room, and waited. Yes, Kathryn McClusky was here; the only unclaimed ErGer, the prize of the supernatural world, stood in this hall, bedraggled and wet, a pool of rain water dripping onto the gleaming marble floor. She had not been able to use her own name for more than a decade, but now she almost revelled in it. She felt their eyes on her, felt them salivate at those syllables where only seconds ago they would have ignored her in disdain. None of them was strong enough to try for her here in these halls. They would not dare deprive their Master of his prize. Out on the streets they might have, but then they would not have even realised what, or who, she was. That was why they stood here, in the foyer, the waiting room of the court where those without influence and full of pretensions congregated. Their avaricious looks, the calculation in the eyes she met, were nothing. She could not even muster any disdain for them.

"Milady."

For a moment she was enchanted by the song of Wales weaving its way through the curiously soft tones. The voice of a harper, a dreamer – not someone she would have expected here. A touchable voice, a dangerous voice. It took her longer to realise that it was aimed at her. The discovery was enough to wake the little self-preservation instinct she had left. It was never wise to ignore a vampire, especially not one like him.

He was an old one; she felt the pressure of age against her skin and saw it in the body that would have looked better in 17th century lace than 21st century cotton. Not that he was anything but stunning, with long blond hair and bright green eyes, high cheekbones and the physique of a swimmer – but there was an indescribable quality which proclaimed his clothes to be a costume, not worn naturally. Worse, his presence was strong enough to shake her, to penetrate her carefully cultivated distance. He remained standing beside her, and seemed to be willing to wait forever, bowing politely only when all of her attention had turned to him.

"Milady, I would be glad to take your coat."

His words made her aware of the gradually spreading puddle around her. Her body had become so insensitive to the cold that she no longer noticed the water slowly soaking through her thin clothes. Only his words reminded her of the icy rain and pulled her back from the brink of the emotional oblivion she had desperately tried to nurture in her mind. She was so unbearably cold, but she knew that it was slowly freezing her from within, not from without. With what was to come, it might not be an entirely bad thing to turn to ice. A shiver slithered down her spine.

He mistook her reaction, his voice trying to reassure as he continued.

"The Court will be more than happy to provide you with garments whilst your own dry."

No point in answering, no reason to explain. She just handed him her coat, but kept her scarf firmly wound around her neck.

"I am here to see Lord Lucian," she repeated.

The silence stretched. She bore his assessing glance as she had the avaricious ones before. There was no hurry. She knew this game too well. The news of her presence here would already have travelled all through the court even had the Lord been too weak, too stupid, to feel her presence in his halls.

4

And he was neither weak nor stupid. He would know of her arrival. Now she was safe. Nothing would happen to her until she was brought before him.

Silence can only stretch so far before it breaks, and he was the one to break it. With another courteous bow, the vampire waved her on. "I will gladly show the ErGer the way to the Great Hall."

The weight of his gaze never wavered from Kathryn, as if he were afraid she would disappear. It almost made her laugh. If he just knew that the chains which had led her here cut deeper than steel ever could. Too many chains to count, too many bonds to escape. When he gestured for her to precede him towards the elevators, she demurred, conscious of the whispered conversation restarting in their wake, so soft it could almost be felt more than heard.

With every step deeper into the building, Kathryn retreated further into the cold inside her, letting herself be taken by nothingness. He led her to an elevator and held the door for her. A silent presence at her side as they descended towards the real power. Did he expect her to speak? She doubted it. She could not help the involuntary start she felt when the doors eventually swished open and she was met by eyes identical to those of the vampire still beside her, his appearance the same down to the finest detail. As her brain re-engaged she realised that they must be twins, though the matching clothes seemed almost juvenile, something even her sisters had outgrown. The ten-year olds might choose to dress to demarcate their individuality from a sister who shared their features, but Kathryn was too aware of the strategic advantages a little game of mistaken identity could have. One would never know where the danger came from.

That realisation, the assessment of power politics, of advantage and disadvantage, the automatic recognition of danger, settled her. She was used to this. Her eyes slipped past the man beside her, glancing over the other shapes and shadows in the long hallway. If upstairs had been the waiting room to power, then this was its antechamber. Those upstairs had been mere flunkies; the eyes she met here were more predatory, more rapacious. These were those with an aspiration for power and connection, those just outside the sphere of influence, constantly squabbling, struggling and plotting to rise. But still, this was not where the true power lay. She stepped forward, a warm hand on her back steering her through it all. She ignored it.

By the time they reached a set of huge black wooden doors looming before them, she had let go of everything, including her fear, and nothing of herself was left. Only the cold. She would need it, for behind these doors she would play out the most important game of her life – she would bargain for everything and, at the same time, lose all. This was where all decisions had led her.

The doors opened into a large room, stretching away towards a dais on which sat an ebony chair so like a throne it was impossible not to let that image intrude. It was a clever mind game. Standing in the open doorway, a visitor would find himself at eye-level with the occupant of that chair. But to approach, one had to step down five steps, pass oak pillars and walk along the immense hall covered by a formal arched ceiling. With every step, the visitor would not only be aware of the chair's dominant position, but of the change in perception one's own downwards path created. The room was a power play in itself. Taking a step through the doors was like entering a cathedral built to honour not God, but one man alone, the man lounging nonchalantly in the chair on the dais - Lord Lucian Castillo Neben, Lord of London, and rumoured aspirant to the position of High Lord of the British Isles. And to his left, kneeling on the floor between two vampires, his head cruelly stretched backwards by a hand in his hair and a rope around his neck, was her older brother Paul.

Kathryn remembered the conversation with her daughter Anna just before she had left the dingy little rented room they had all taken refuge in for the last few months. The twins, her younger sisters, were more used to the vagaries of grown-ups coming and going, but Anna, at the tender age of six and often side-lined beside her aunts even though they were only four years older than she, was less forgiving.

"Mama, why do you have to go?" Those huge brown eyes, so like her own, had fixed on her accusingly. It had been hard to face that little frown today, when it would be the last time.

"I have to go and meet someone. Paul will be home soon."

"I don't want Uncle Paul – I want you. He is mean."

Paul had become mean over a decade of running, of constant fear and insecurity, had become so through the life an association with her had forced on him. He was the man who had tried to sell her only an hour before, the man she was going to rescue by giving herself up in order to save him.

The warning had come from an unusual source at her job in a run-down café on the south side of London – a torn and dirty piece of paper had suddenly appeared in her bag. Once unfolded, it read: "Your brother has asked for an audience with the Vampire Lord of London. The ErGer is being offered for sale. The Lord will kill your brother and find you. He is not in a bargaining mood."

Only that. A dirty piece of paper, with no signature, no way of knowing who might have put it there. Her colleagues, another waitress and the proprietor-cook, were both human and had no reason to know about her genetic mutation, about her status as an ErGer. They did not know how much the paranormal world prized her kind as a source of blood to feed a natural high. They knew little of how easy it would be to sell her, but Paul did. He had tried to do so three times before – and managed it once. So Kathryn never doubted the note. She feigned illness and though her boss grumbled, he let her go. He was a good man under the bluster and drink.

First she returned to their lodgings to check on the girls, whom she had left in Paul's care five hours before, and to say goodbye for the last time. Paul's action, as hateful as it was, gave her something she had not thought possible. It gave her the opportunity to buy *their* freedom, at the price of her own.

Now she let her feet carry her along the plush red carpet towards the dais and automatically her eyes fixed on her brother, calling to mind the loving boy she remembered from childhood and trying to find him in the face of this embittered, drunk man. He was five years older than her, had helped her hide the spinach under the salad, supported her in

8

the myriad little endeavours of childhood and held her as their parents lay dying – murdered so that their daughter could function as a power conduit for the local Vampire Lord who had been surprised to learn that the fourteen-year-old schoolgirl visiting the museum he had just opened was one of those rare creatures: an ErGer. The supernaturals had killed her parents but underestimated Paul, a thin and pretty boy of nineteen, who had grabbed his broken and bleeding sister after that first night and had run without ever looking back. She wanted to see that young man in those eyes, but she only saw hate.

Instead, she turned to the man who held her future in his hands. In truth she had nothing to trade. He did not need her compliance but she desperately hoped she might somehow bluff and persuade him to trade with empty cards. Her eyes met the brilliantly blue ones that considered her. Even from this distance she could see that he was tall. His hair was dark enough to barely show against the high back of the ebony chair; in contrast his skin had the pale clarity so common in vampires. A patrician face, elegant nose and generous mouth made him the most beautiful man she had ever seen, but the expression in his eyes made him the coldest. This was not a man blinded by arrogance; this was a clever tactician whose mind was sharper than the swords his guards wore.

The room was eerily quiet, though it was far from empty. Kathryn forced herself to take note of the other occupants – once her attention had been snared by the man on the dais it was not easily distracted from this. She wondered at first if she had interrupted a ball but quickly realised that the clothes, whilst formal and elaborate, were too casual. At best guess she decided she had stumbled into a formal audience, the concept of which would have made her smile at any other time. In her cheap clothing, dripping all over the expensive, lush carpet, she was less than the stepchild come to visit – she was a travesty; one they desperately wanted.

Two-thirds along the hall she halted, as was appropriate according to the rules of etiquette she had unwillingly picked up in her various captivities in different courts. The strength and evenness of her own voice surprised her.

"Lord Lucian, Lord of London. I come to fulfil my brother's vow."

Those blue eyes measured her before he rose from his relaxed posture to stand. "How would you know what vows were given here this night?"

"It is not the first time the offer has been made."

It hurt to admit it even through the barrier she had allowed to build around her emotions. The blue eyes bored into her, assessing, but their ice only aided the cold in swallowing her.

"His vow was not the one I have been seeking."

She was not sure she understood his meaning so remained silent. It had always been one of the more successful strategies when dealing with a vampire. If she did not speak she could neither give anything away nor anger him.

He stepped off the dais, his movements prowling and predatory, testament to both his intent and nature. The blue shirt moulded to his physique as he moved, leaving little doubt that this man was neither soft nor weak, and the tight black trousers left even less to the imagination. Kathryn knew she should be frightened of him but could not find the emotion, not even when he was so close that she had to raise her head to meet his eyes. She had gone pleasantly numb, huddled in her internal fortress of ice.

"What do you seek?" Her voice seemed to come from far away.

"Your vow. The promise you will give yourself to me, body and mind. The assurance you will not try to escape, not tonight, not ever. The oath not to resist bonding to me and my court."

"I cannot guarantee a bond."

She felt the need to clarify this, to ensure he was aware of the conditions, though in her experience vampiric arrogance would brush away that physical requirement, which neither of them would have any control over. Her voice was toneless as her eyes flickered back to Paul. A pale hand under her chin halted the movement and forced her face back so that her eyes were caught by his blue ones again.

"Let that be my concern. From you I want the assurance that you will not actively or passively resist the bond when I take your body or your blood."

Her nod was jerky, but she had known that this would be the price demanded of her this night, whether it be given voluntarily or taken by force.

"To seal the bargain I insist on a Blood Oath."

The words meant nothing to her. She had no idea what a blood oath entailed, her education in the etiquette of vampiric courts and supernatural society woefully deficient, limited to what she had discovered for herself. All she had ever been taught was pain and how to kneel to her Lord. Fortunately, she knew how to phrase a question without betraying her ignorance. Something in her face, or perhaps her continued silence, prompted him to elaborate.

"A vow sealed through an exchange of blood. You must swallow one mouthful of my blood voluntarily, and the promise is considered unbreakable even under threat of death."

Again she nodded; it was a condition she could fulfil. The idea of taking blood had never bothered her particularly; actually it was less troublesome in her mind than eating meat, as the blood donor, human or animal, rarely died as a consequence of the action. Compliantly she watched him take a silver knife from his belt and slice the pad of his thumb before offering it to her mouth. Kathryn tried to lick the welling blood, steeling against the metallic taste. But as she opened her mouth he forced his thumb deep into it, only stopping a hairbreadth away from making her gag. Instinctively she tried to pull back, to remove the intruding digit, but his other hand came up to cradle her face, holding it securely in place.

"One mouthful, ErGer. Take one mouthful and swallow."

She stayed, held in place not only by his hand but by his commanding eyes, hot and intense on her face. In them she saw an iron will not used to bending to anyone or anything, and an intelligence too cunning for her to be safe.

The fingers of the hand holding her to him gently stroked over her cheek. He was not satisfied with her passive

12

acquiescence; he wanted more from her, so much more. "ErGer, you need to draw my blood, fill your mouth with it."

She tried to pull more blood from his wound, and his eyes closed, his whole body tensing as if in pain. At a second draw, his mouth dropped open in a groan. She let his thumb slip from her mouth, intensely uncomfortable with the situation. No matter who he was, no matter what he was planning to do to her, she did not enjoy hurting another being. There was not much decency left in her life, but she wanted to hold onto what there was.

His eyelids were heavy as he met her gaze again, and when she licked the traces of his blood from her lips, she thought she heard an echo of a moan. When he spoke, the silky voice with which he had demanded her Oath had dropped deeper, was tinged with hoarseness.

"Your brother has gambled heavily in my clubs. For a second and third promise I will forgive his debt and allow him free passage from my lands."

"How much?"

It did not really matter, they had no money. Twenty pounds would be too much for Paul to pay, but she had to ask, even if it was just to make a senseless point as a sop to her pride. They both knew she would agree in the end, but she had long since learnt not to show weakness, not even when she held a losing hand, though her bravado was severely deflated by his answer.

"Just over fourteen thousand pounds."

Oh, Paul! Her eyes closed in defeat, but she could not stop herself from confronting this clear manipulation of her brother's gambling addiction head-on.

"You let him play that heavily intentionally?"

"Of course." There was no apology in his tone, not one ounce of regret. He had played his gambit and won, and he was not ashamed of it.

"What promises?" Her voice had lost all expression again.

"For one, you promise under Blood Oath that you will not try to escape my hold in any other way either." It was easy to nod to this; suicide had never been in her nature, and she had already given that promise in her own estimation.

"The second?"

"You promise never to lie to me."

The second request puzzled her, but she accepted the newly cut thumb that was lifted to her mouth again before she had even given herself time to consider. It was hard for her to think of what she might lose by promising not to lie to him, especially as her answer was a foregone conclusion. This time it was after only one pull of her mouth that he gently withdrew his digit from her with a dry, self-mocking chuckle.

"I see the promise as sealed," he said.

"So witnessed." An amused voice startled her and she realised that one of the blond twins had approached them from behind without her noticing. She silently scolded herself – it was stupid to forget the dangers beyond the one facing her.

"Kieran," said the Lord of London without lifting his eyes from hers. "Would you be so kind as to throw our guest out. Gently though, he is the brother of your Lady."

"With pleasure, Milord."

He bowed to her too, and panic rose, pulling a rope around her throat and taking her breath. She needed to ensure that the terms of the agreement were understood by both of them.

"You promise to let him go, consider his debt as paid and allow him to leave London freely?"

"Yes."

She was missing something. He had given in too quickly, had won too easily. Her mind scrambled but she could not find the hook.

"Don't you have to take my blood too, for your part of the promise to be binding?"

Suddenly his eyes burned hot, and his voice dropped so low that she could feel it in the pit of her stomach.

"Believe me, you will bleed for me before the night is out."

His words dried her mouth and she held her breath for a moment. But it was not only fear that made her gut clench.

As her brother was dragged past her, she searched for something positive to say, a last goodbye, a reminder without giving away the secret they were harbouring. In the end, the only thing she could find was a plea.

"Please look after them!"

He laughed nastily. "They will be better off without you anyway."

It hurt, but he was almost certainly right. They could finally stop running without her. As her eyes followed the last link to her former life being unceremoniously dragged from the room, the clock struck ten – two more hours before she would lose her mind.

Before her brother had even been dragged from the room, her attention had been recaptured by the simple expediency of the Lord of London's finger returning to her cheek and guiding her gaze back to his. He waited until her attention had returned to him, and only him, before he offered her his arm as if she were a visiting dignitary and not his new pet. She hesitated only a second, and even then she did not know why she risked his displeasure in such a small way. When her fingers came to rest lightly on the soft fabric of his shirt, keeping the touch to an absolute minimum without denying him her obedience, an almost imperceptible tremor ran through her – the only outward sign of her despair – and though he did not react, she feared she had just given him more power over her. As if he needed it.

Without resistance she allowed him to lead her through hallways and anterooms, deeper into the warren that would be her prison, and perhaps her grave. She wanted to feel alone, but her mind could not blank out the overwhelming presence of the man beside her. With every move, his body brushed hers; with every breath, his scent invaded her. She felt the warmth of hard muscle under her hands, felt the heat of his body slowly beat against the coldness of her skin, and though she'd had endless practice, she struggled to let the ice of her mind consume this tangible link. He did not speak, and so she remained mute as well.

Kathryn did not even try to commit their path to memory – she had promised not to escape and was bound by her own word as securely as a chain would have done – instead she bowed her head in resignation and followed his lead. It was said many ErGer did not survive being claimed, and of those that were said to have bonded, the provenance of that claim was based on the continued increase in that Lord's power. Only their Lords knew what physical or mental state they survived in, few ever being seen again by anyone outside their courts. In all her years she had never met another, had never even met someone who had seen another ErGer, though she had to admit that her interaction with the supernatural world was by design as limited as possible.

Eventually they reached a hallway with a single door at its end which he politely opened for her to enter. She realised that she had made a step back in time, had entered a place that had been imprinted so much with the character and presence of this man that she might as well have walked into his den. The room was vast and seemed to be hewn from the very bedrock under the foundations of the building. She had not realised that this was even possible so close to the river.

The rough walls were covered by luxurious wall hangings of burgundy and emerald, depicting scenes of hunting, war and conquest, and yet, it was not a brutal place. A huge fireplace blazed at the far side of the room. Two armchairs, deep, inviting and majestic, were arranged on either side of it with a table between them. Only two other pieces of furniture adorned the rest of the large room – a heavy-set dark chest of drawers and a huge four-poster bed, piled high with pillows in the same hues as the wall hangings.

The power impressed on her by the colours and textures was so controlling that she stopped just inside the door. The door closed behind her with a soft snick, shutting out the world and leaving her alone with the owner of this place, and of her life. The sound did not frighten her; there was no finality in it. She had left all hope for escape long before she had entered the building. Her captor passed her on his way to the fireplace, where he let his body glide into one of the chairs, and pinned her with his piercing eyes. She met them unflinchingly – there was nothing he could do to her that had not been done before, save death, and that was the only thing she was sure he would not give her.

His voice held no emotion, no excitement as he spoke.

"Undress."

2

Need

She pulled her green cotton T-shirt, still damp and clinging unpleasantly to her cold skin, over her head without hesitation, only pausing for a second to look for somewhere to put it. She was not used to being careless with her clothes, as money was precious and her almost six foot two inches made things hard to replace. But then she tossed it on the floor; she might not need it again after tonight.

Each and every Lord and Lordling who had captured her over the last ten years had informed her gleefully that they would keep her chained and naked – not because her body pleased them, but because it would mean they, and their people, would have instant and constant access to what it could provide. She unsnapped her jeans and piled them on top of the shirt. Her bra and panties followed.

Her scarf was last, apart from the wristbands she had no intention of removing. Her hands hesitated over the cheap

19

fabric she habitually kept closely knotted around her neck. The scars marring the skin of her neck were hideous and graphic, but had strangely excited the last Vampire Lord Paul had sold her to. With trepidation she pulled at the tight knot and let the cloth drop from her throat to the pile of clothes on the floor.

He did not appear to react at all as she stood there naked but for the two broad wristbands. She fixed her eyes on the pattern of the dark red carpet at her feet and wondered fleetingly if it was red to hide spilled blood, then pushed that thought into the cold too.

"There is wine on the chest. Bring it here." His voice was still calm and expressionless.

"I am not your servant!" she said without thinking, regretting it the moment the words left her lips.

The silence of the room wrapped around her like a heavy chain. She refused to look at him. Instead, her eyes were drawn to the glass on the chest and the dark, red wine – almost as dark as blood.

"There are three young girls in the room your brother is entering just now."

He did not have to say more. The words cut through her, and she closed her eyes in pain.

"How do you know about them?"

"I have known since you entered my territory."

They had arrived in town only three months before, and she had been relieved and happy that they seemed to go undiscovered for such a long time.

"Why did you not come for me then?" Why had he

20

allowed her to have that hope? To be free for another three months when the outcome had been so clear?

"There had not been any need before tonight."

No need to bring her in before the only night each year on which a bond could be established.

She had already started to move towards the chest when he spoke again.

"The longer you obey me, absolutely, the longer they will be safe."

No contest. She was defeated.

The glass was large and her hands unsteady when she carried it to him. He took it wordlessly and placed it on the table, the light of the fire playing through the liquid. Even though her attention was on the wine as she stood naked in front of his chair, she felt his eyes playing over her scarred and too-thin body.

When she finally looked at him she was surprised to see his gaze was not fixed on the marks other men, other vampires, had left on her, or even on her breasts, which were the only part of her body where their constant hunger seemed to leave little sign. No, his eyes were on her face, and met hers with an expression she could not identify. She expected him to speak, or drink from the glass she had brought him. Instead he reached for her hands and pulled her closer, close enough for her feet to touch his, and then, nudging her legs apart, pulled her even closer. When her legs touched the velvet upholstery of the chair, he transferred his hands to her knees.

"Kneel."

21

Her mind was not fast enough to translate the order into action, so he applied light pressure to her legs and guided them up on the chair. The fabric of his trousers was less soft than she had expected, more cotton than linen. It scraped along the soft skin of her inner thighs, his scent, his warmth, his presence touching her. She found herself straddling him, his hands around her waist, settling her to sit on his lap. His large hands spanned her thin waist so that his thumbs met over her belly. Not sure where to rest her own hands she let them come to lay on the armrests.

The black wristbands stood out in stark contrast to her pale skin. He released her waist and lifted her right hand for closer inspection, found the simple closure that held the band in place and pulled it off. However much she tried to control her reaction, her whole body still jerked. He had revealed her ultimate humiliation. These were not the scars left by countless teeth tearing into her, like those found on her neck. Her throat bore marks of her resistance, her fight, easily hidden from the world with a playful scarf, but the marks on her wrists were the result of chains as she fought, ripping her flesh to the bone in a desperate attempt to escape. They were marks of shame, of fights lost with herself. He said nothing, not as he removed the other band, nor as he settled her hands back on the armrests and his own around her waist.

"Pick up the wine and take a sip," he said.

"I don't drink," she replied.

His eyes remained expressionless, as was his voice when he spoke again. "It was not a request."

Absolute obedience for the safety of the girls.

22

She reached for the glass and took a small sip. As she tried to put it back down, his hands tightened on her waist and brought her attention back to him mid-movement.

"I am thirsty, too."

She offered him the glass, but he shook his head. "My hands are full."

To illustrate this fact he began to trace little half circles over her belly with his thumbs. She tried to offer the glass to his lips but he shook his head again.

"Not like that." There was a hint of amusement in his eyes and a twitch to his lips. Instead, she tried to offer her wrist, but that simply made him raise an eyebrow.

"How then?" She felt the desperation in her own voice and tried to suppress it while making the cold return.

"Take a sip and hold it in your mouth."

She was starting to have an idea where this was leading. She tried to lean forward to feed him the wine but his hands kept her from him.

"Set down the glass first, then let me drink from your mouth."

Carefully she put down the glass before leaning forward. In her haste and nervousness she parted her lips before touching his and spilled most of the wine down her chin and his neck. She froze in terror, aware of the strength in the hands around her waist and the sharp teeth entirely too close to her. His lips parted and his tongue snaked out to lazily lap at the liquid dripping down her lips and chin. Only when he had cleaned her thoroughly did he allow her to move back enough to meet his gaze. Her eyes fell to his mouth and the

23

spilled wine that painted his neck and shirt red. Small droplets were still caught in the evening shadow of the beard along his cheeks.

"Clean it!"

The first flick of her tongue was tentative at best, barely a touch, but when he moved his head to allow her more access she became bolder. The taste of his skin, mixed with that of the red wine, filled her mouth – unidentifiable, subtle and strange. As her tongue reached his neck, his arousal grew impossibly large beneath her, pressing against the folds of her sex through only two layers of clothes. She shied back – feeling stupid immediately. It was inevitable where this evening was going to lead. For an ErGer to bond, the mind needed to be broken open as only sex could – and her own body would force it soon enough. In her experience, he had shown more patience than any other. Every Lord who had ever acquired her, either because her brother had sold her to them or because they had tracked her down, had taken her blood and body within minutes of their acquaintance. What was the point of delay? A bond with an ErGer doubled the Lord's power levels, as well as giving him and his dependants a more elusive advantage, a feeling of home, of safety and wellbeing rarely found in a predatory society. All they needed to do was break her mind with blood or sex.

He had not moved at all as she shied back, still presenting his neck for her tongue and holding her waist between his stroking fingers, but his eyes were hot and burning. Kathryn bent to return to her duty. As she nosed the soiled shirt out of her way to reach his collarbone, a knock sounded on the door. She gasped, and his hands softly guided her back upright. She felt her breath coming faster, but she could not help it; she knew this was the moment when his people would come to hold her down, to await the time when they could take their turns with her body after he was done with her. If she was lucky, she would not survive the night.

"Enter!" he said.

She heard the door but did not dare turn. No matter what lay behind, the largest danger remained firmly in front of her. With the sound of each approaching step the speed of her breathing increased. She did not want to show fear, but it was impossible to suppress the rising terror. In those deep blue eyes a new emotion rose, something close to confusion. She felt the tightness of her chest foreshadowing the rising hyperventilation she could not control.

"Milord, everything is arranged to your satisfaction," the newcomer said.

She cringed at the sight of the pale hand setting a plate piled high with cheese and grapes on the table. A man stepped into her field of vision and she realised it was one of the twins. One man – she could survive one. Her breath calmed, the involuntary shakes of her body abating from one moment to the next. Kathryn felt their eyes on her, felt their answering tension, their vigilance. Not even the smallest twitch, the smallest change in her body, escaped their notice. Only with the relaxation of her fear did she feel the men relax their intense concentration.

"Thank you, Brandon."

"My pleasure, Milord." He bowed to his liege and then, to

her surprise, to her. "Milady."

She did not hear him leave and knew the manner of his arrival had been intended to calm her fears. The sound of the latch was loud and somewhat final as it fell closed.

"I am still thirsty."

His demand brought her back to the task at hand, sharpened her concentration, her mind on him anew. She reached for the glass and took another sip into her mouth. As she leant close, she was frightened her nerves would betray her, that she would again spill the wine too soon – but before she had the chance, he closed the distance between them and opened his lips beneath hers. When she let the wine run from her mouth into his, she felt him swallow, felt his tongue lap at her lips, never forcing its way into her mouth. When she moved away he did not hold her back, though his tongue licked over his own lips as if to savour the last drop of wine he could.

"Take another sip."

She did and held it in her mouth whilst setting the glass down again.

When she turned to him, he grinned almost boyishly. "Now swallow," he said.

The smooth and heavy wine slid down her throat, pooling comfortably warm in her belly, where his fingers stroked hypnotically. She was not used to alcohol. It was not a good habit to acquire when you were constantly on the run – as Paul was a good example of. Even with only these two sips in her she felt a warm languidness rising in her joints.

"Choose something."

He indicated towards the plate with a movement of his chin. She wanted so badly to take some cheese. Cheese was expensive and therefore a luxury in her world, a luxury which was normally saved for the children. But she was afraid that she would not be able to keep it down so she reached for one of the grapes, but it was taken from her before she could raise it to her mouth. He held it between his long fingers before offering it to her lips.

Holding his gaze, she tried to take the fruit from his hand, the cold sweetness a counterpoint to the warmth of the fingers that held it. He refused to let go, forcing her to bite the ripe grape in two. Juice spurted down his hand, the smell somehow weaving seamlessly into the basic nature of his presence in the room. She was so mesmerised as she followed the path it took along his skin, she swallowed her half of the grape without due attention to its delicacy.

He waited patiently, not even the bat of an eyelash betraying any reaction. He simply offered the other half of the grape to her lips. This time she savoured the taste of the fruit. When she had swallowed it he held his fingers to her mouth.

"Clean them."

Her tongue caught the sticky trail across his palm from fingers to wrist. His skin had a salty taste, almost smoky and, to her surprise, his hands showed signs of callouses.

"All of it," he insisted, clearly dissatisfied with her ministrations.

His hand was warm and heavy in hers as she took it. The skin between his fingers was so much softer, his taste so much stronger. It exploded in her mouth, mixed with the sweetness of the fruit. It would be so easy to get lost in this simple task, to forget what was going to come. To do what she was told, even though she expected some form of punishment each time she moved. She had long since learnt not to expect reason for punishments and cruelties.

He simply sat back in his chair, watching her with those enigmatic eyes, the long limbs below hers spread in studied relaxation. When the last traces of stickiness had disappeared, his eyes were blue slits and his breath was coming in pants. She had no idea what she should do, what reaction might provoke him, so she simply waited. Gently, he extricated his hands from between hers and returned them to her waist.

"What will happen in an hour?" he asked, his question catching her by surprise.

Her eyes flickered to the clock on the mantelpiece and she realised with shock that it was only just over an hour until midnight, until her biological clock would throw her into hell. She sucked in a breath.

"What will happen in an hour?" he repeated.

She was not entirely sure how to respond. Did he want her to tell him how to bind an ErGer? She thought that it was common knowledge among vampires, and she was unsure how the bond worked from their side. The sex and blood seemed to be clear, but she did not know the mental component. She could tell him what she did to try to keep it from happening but was not sure how much that would help as she had promised not to resist. And in all this there was the question of whether she wanted to answer at all.

She had given her word and that was pretty much the only

honour she had left in her life. "When you take my—"

His finger came to rest on her lips, halting any further words. A wry smile stretched his lips without letting even a glimpse of his fangs peek through.

"I do not need instruction on what to do, I am well informed there. What will happen to you?"

That was a harder question to answer, and for a moment, she almost hated him for asking it. Could he not leave her one last piece of dignity? A bitter laugh escaped her lips. Dignity? She had not had any since she had turned fourteen and been recognised as an ErGer.

"My memory is a bit spotty in places but apparently I fuck everything in sight."

Her answer was deliberately crude, her voice dripping with all the hate and disgust she felt for herself and those who forced her into this existence. She did not see him flinch, save for a rise of his eyebrow as he stared evenly back into her blazing eyes. She could barely stand it, the even gaze, the lack of any blame or disgust in his expression. It undermined her bitterness. She squirmed in his hands to escape her own thoughts.

"What happens?"

Kathryn could not meet his eyes any longer, her equilibrium severely threatened by his matter-of-factness. Her front teeth started to worry her lower lip and her hands started to dig into the soft velvet of the arms of the chair. He captured her chin and turned her face to meet his eyes. His thumb ran over her lower lip, gently teasing it free from the abuse her teeth inflicted on it. He held her there, ensuring she

29

knew that he would demand her compliance.

"What happens?"

Low, slow words. His voice still held no anger, not even demand – simply a calm confidence in her ultimate submission to his will, in her ultimate answer to the question. As she spoke she could not look at him. So she let her eyes flicker over the room, coming to rest again and again on the clock: *10:49pm*.

"I don't know," she admitted.

"What do you know?" He was relentless in his pursuit of information.

"I have only been held captive once on February fourteenth. I…" She was lost for words, her mind too full and too blank at the same time to answer. Her breath came faster, its panicky edge audible in the silent room.

His voice broke through the mounting terror: "What happens when you are not held captive?"

She could answer this. Holding onto that thought, the necessity to string words together, helped.

"I find an abandoned building, lock myself in and hope to hell that no one finds me before the day is over."

She met his eyes with a challenging look of her own and that is how she saw his eyes flicker down to her wrists. Suddenly she felt deflated again, felt obliged to clarify, "No, not from those times, not from any of the cellars."

He nodded, not pressing any further. She was almost grateful for the small amount of privacy he granted her with his lack of pursuit, for the small amount of self-respect he allowed her.

"What happened last February in Tirana?"

Of course he knew about that. She was too tired to worry about this now. Her eyes became empty as she let her mind wander back, and she heard her words before having made the conscious effort to voice them.

"We had been in Albania only two weeks, freshly arrived from Rome, when Paul handed me over to the Lord of Albania for one million <u>leke</u>. It sounds so much, but it was barely over six thousand pounds."

She sighed, lost in her own thoughts. "It was February first, thirteen days before St Valentine's Day, thirteen days in which he thought he could break my mind and prepare me for a bond. By the fourteenth I was weak and ill, and yet, at midnight, the Need arose. Apparently I screamed from arousal whilst he kept everyone away from me. Only then did he give me to his court. He believed by the time they were done with me, their seed would have sensitised me enough to his for a bond to be inevitable. I do not know how long they had me. I don't even know when he took their place. I suddenly felt him in my mind, taking even that. But he was not strong, and his concentration slipped. I don't know what I did – it was as if, in that moment, he showed me where his mind linked to his body, and where I would have to cut. So I did. I cut that link with my mind and felt him scream and wither."

Kathryn waited for him to judge her too dangerous, to see she was best contained and killed before she posed a threat to him personally. She waited with hope, but the blow never came.

"How did you get away?"

"The weaker of his court died because they had not been emancipated from him, and even the older ones were disoriented. I just walked out, found Paul and the children, and left town."

He nodded thoughtfully.

"Take another grape."

He said the words as if she had not just told him she had killed a Vampire Lord in cold blood. Her eyes were drawn to the plate, but she could not convince herself to reach for any of it. When he took a grape instead, she tried to speak. "No."

A frown marred the beauty of his face and she tried to qualify before it appeared as if she wanted to disobey his order. "I don't think I can."

The beginnings of censure on his face smoothed and he nodded, pity in his eyes. His hands began a gentle massage of the tense muscles lining her spine. Slowly, her back started to relax, little by little.

"Have you ever made love?" he asked.

She looked at him, exasperated. Had he actually asked that question? How often she had been found and caught, how often she had been raped? Had she ever had sex? Had he not been listening? Obviously she had had sex before. He must have seen her confusion and clarified his question. "I want to know if you have ever given yourself to a man without force?"

She winced, uncomfortable with the distinction, but there was no way to avoid giving the answer, locked in by her own promise.

"Tell me about it."

There was not much to tell. Her eyes flickered to the clock again: *10:53pm*. Now she had noticed the clock, it was impossible not to fix on the slowly moving minute hand. It was too much to hope he would not notice her preoccupation, but it still surprised her when he sighed and frowned at her. She froze, too aware of the dangers his anger could pose for her.

"Get up." His hands pushed her backwards, forcing her to her feet. Kathryn stood still before him, tense and resigned, her legs stiff after kneeling on the chair for so long. There was only an hour left, but truly she suspected her time had just run out. She expected him to rise, to move the evening to its inevitable crescendo, but instead he relaxed back into his chair with a studied nonchalance.

"Go to the chest and open the top-right drawer."

She turned, and with every step she took away from the fire, the cold of the room slipped over her skin and soul more firmly. An hour ago she would have welcomed the numbness it brought to her mind, but now there was only cold.

The drawer slid open almost silently – a well-made and cared for piece of furniture. Unfortunately, she could name too much of its varied contents. There were whips, restraints, dildos, nipple clamps and more leather than she could even try to identify. Finally, the numbness returned, enveloping her in its comforting embrace. She was only one step away from being able to put her body on autopilot and leave it to have done to it whatever he wanted, and judging by the contents of this drawer, the last step would come soon.

33

"Take the blindfold," he said.

The words whispered over her skin, chasing tremors up her spine. The voice was close, a sensual caress, whispered only for her ears, reaching her on a wave of his power from the other side of the room.

"Bring it here."

She saw the simple strip of black satin but she could not reach for it. Her hands had clamped so hard on the rim of the drawer that she was worried her nails would leave marks on it. The mere thought of reaching out, of loosening her grip to reach into the drawer with the instruments that meant more than just simple pain, suddenly exceeded her strength. She could take the pain; it was the degradation that defeated her.

"There is nothing in this drawer you will get to feel tonight other than the blindfold."

His voice was reassuring, and she might have felt better had she not also heard his almost silent after-whisper: "Not tonight."

In the end, it was the ominous bells of the clock on the mantelpiece chiming *11.00pm* which made her finally reach into the drawer. The chimes were lashes against her mind, imagined pain or remembered. It helped to distance her mind from her body. The cold, the place to hide when her life descended into pain and humiliation, came closer, promising solace. It made it bearable to turn to him and take that first step back to the fireplace. The Lord followed her every movement with his eyes, watching, analysing, cataloguing – but even his intent blue gaze had no power to reach her anymore. It was almost midnight.

She handed him the black cloth and waited, resigned and calm. He picked up the wine and, playing with it against his lips, met her gaze over the rim. Then he took a sip, set it down and reached for her.

Lucian pulled her back into the kneeling position straddling him and she came unresisting to his hand. He played with the blindfold, running it through one palm, then the other. Kathryn expected him to raise it to her eyes at any moment.

"Tell me about the first time you had sex."

This must be the most confusing man on the planet. Her eyes were fixed on the cloth slipping through his hands, its movement hypnotic, only managing to disengage her attention from that sight as he stopped moving.

Unhurried, he waited for her to meet his eyes. "You are entirely too fixated on the clock. When I choose to initiate your bonding is not your concern – it is mine. All decisions are mine now. You have nothing to decide regarding your future. Here and now, I want your attention on me, and as you seem to be unable to give me that, the blindfold is a tool to ensure your cooperation. If you are distracted again, I will take your ability to see the clock away. Now, tell me about the first time you had sex."

"You could have turned the clock around." She was unable to stop herself from blurting out inconsequentialities, even at the danger of angering him. She could have kicked herself.

"I could have, but it would be so much less enjoyable." With a lightning-quick move he played the soft fabric over her stomach.

It sent an electrifying shock through her, the smooth silk strangely cool against her heated skin.

"Tell me!" He snapped, each word enunciated precisely and a demand in its own right. This first sign of temper, first sign of anything but the maddening calm he had displayed until now, was comforting. Kathryn knew about anger, and demands, and it was the lack of either which had kept her so off balance.

It was not a big deal to answer; it was not as if she had a reputation worth protecting. "We were living on the streets. One of the girls, Heroise I think, was sick, really sick. It must have been Berlin. I cannot remember where Paul was. I had found a spot in a corner of a parking garage and scrounged some cardboard and blankets for warmth. This man in a suit saw us and offered me two hundred Euros for sex with one of the twins."

For a moment she was back there, back in the dirty structure, the rattling breathing of the sick child a terrifying soundtrack. Kathryn had listened with fearful horror to each cough, her mind scrambling madly for a means of finding medication and food for the children. She had been glad of that man in the suit, had been glad when he had approached them.

"I told him no. So he offered me one hundred Euros for the use of my body." Kathryn shrugged, wincing when his hands, which had placed the blindfold on the arm of the chair and returned to her waist, clamped ever tighter around her small frame, tight enough to hurt. She guessed Paul had not told him about that part of her life. That was surprising – he told everyone else wherever they went. It was astonishing with what depths of depravity she could surprise people. She faced him squarely.

"I am a whore."

He did not flinch as she had wanted him to. "Yes," he replied. "As have I been… at times."

It surprised her. She did not even react to his hands softly starting to massage her waist with gentle, soothing circles.

"Have you ever had sex just because you wanted to?"

"Two or three years back," she confirmed. "I was working as a waitress in a little café close to the University of Strathclyde. He was another waiter, a student, and I decided that I wanted to try it once for myself. He was nice, younger than me and really nervous. He made dinner, and there were flowers."

She had to smile, and looking down, found an answering smile on those enigmatic lips, mirrored in those blue eyes.

"Did you enjoy it?" His voice was a mere whisper as he held her gaze.

She shrugged. "It was nice." His tongue wet his lips, a quick movement that left them with a sheen of moisture in the flickering firelight. She could not look away, caught in the unaccountable desire to taste his skin in turn.

"Did you achieve an orgasm?"

She shook her head slowly but added with a wistful smile, "It didn't matter. It wasn't really about that."

"Just the closeness." His voice was as soft as hers. She nodded again and they shared a moment of perfect understanding. His hands were stroking up and down her back in slow sensual strokes; at each upstroke he applied a little pressure, moving her mouth a little closer to his with every touch.

"Have you ever had an orgasm?"

"Once, I think."

This qualification made his lips twitch, a quick spasm so close to hers. She was now close enough that it was hard to concentrate, hard to focus her eyes.

"You think?"

She felt his breath on her lips, tasted it. "One of Paul's friends. He let us crash with him… in exchange for… After a while he took his time. He even bought a book about what women liked. In the end, sex wasn't that bad. It made me feel strange though."

"Did you enjoy it?" She was now close enough to feel the movement of his lips against hers.

"Not sure."

She was uncertain if she managed to say the words before his mouth covered hers, but decided it did not matter. His soft lips stroked over hers, sensitising them to the touch, the taste of him, before she felt his tongue gently painting the seam of her mouth, playfully caressing the corners. Unexpectedly, her own lips parted under his, allowed him access. She waited for the invasion, for the rough stab of his tongue to overwhelm hers, for that sense of revulsion, suffocation. Instead, she only felt gentleness as he continued to play his lips over hers. The devastating tenderness left her confused and unable to react. Warmth seemed to intrude at his touch where there had only ever been cold. She angled her head, chased that warmth. When he moved back, her lips were wet and swollen, her breath short.

"Did you like that?"

She did not know how to answer. She had never felt like this before, was not sure she wanted to. Her numbness was all shot to hell with this one touch, one taste.

"Darling, you promised not to lie." It was a soft reminder, the endearment's gentleness adding to her confusion. Kathryn still did not know what to say as he cradled her head and brought her lips closer to his again.

"Did you like it?"

The whispered words were punctuated by soft nibbles against her lower lip and she realised that her promise not to lie might be less innocent than she thought.

"I don't know."

She felt him smile against her lips. "That's all right. We have time to practise until you do."

"We have no time." She answered before thinking and again knew she should have just shut up.

He pressed a hard, closed-mouthed kiss on her lips and set her back on his knees. The grin lighting his face was not gentle – it was pure wickedness as he picked up the blindfold from where it had fallen.

She tried to protest, "I did not look at the clock!"

The soft blackness of the cloth surrounded her and his answer was whispered into her ear as he fastened it behind her head. "No, but you concentrated on something other than me."

She never had the chance for another look at the clock.

3

Taken

The blindfold changed all, made her feel everything so much more keenly. It disoriented her in a way she had not thought possible. Sensation and sound became her only fixed points – his touch and his voice.

"Do you feel the warmth of the fire on your skin?"

She felt the waves of heat on her right side, not as warm as the body underneath her, but pleasant and gentle. She luxuriated in the warmth and almost forgot to answer him. Her nod was languid, and she could feel the smile in his voice.

"Do you like it?"

She nodded again.

"Speak. I want to hear your voice."

One of his hands moved up her back and massaged high up on her neck, buried beneath her hair. The feeling was incredible, each movement of his fingers pushing warm waves through her. Her hair became heavier, and she let her head rest against the massaging hand. Her muscles softened under the sensual onslaught and she sank into his touch.

"Do you like that?"

She might have forgotten his injunction to speak if her neck had not reached the point when nodding would have taken too much effort anyway.

"Yes."

Her voice was breathy, thin, strange in her own ears, though he seemed to take no notice of it. She felt him move underneath her, felt the silk of his shirt against her breasts as his lips began to caress the soft skin of her shoulder. She did not even tense when his lips played over the horrific scarring on her neck. It was hard not to stretch to allow him more access. Even after the most recent scars had healed, her neck remained one of the most sensitive parts of her body. His tongue dipped in the indentation at her collarbone.

"Do you like that?"

"Yes." She was tempted to tell him how stupid that question had been but managed to restrain herself, though she suspected her tone gave him some inkling as to her sentiment. Again she felt his lips stretch against her skin, a smile wide enough to be noticed. He travelled farther south and slowly moved her body, his arms firmly supporting her, leaning her farther back. When his tongue flicked her nipple, she had to hold on tight, had to clutch the armrests in order not to fall backwards.

"Do you like that?"

"No."

She didn't. The languid relaxation was being overtaken by

tension, the threat of a disruptive wave of heat tightening her muscles one by one. Before the sensation could shake her mind back to full awareness, he left her nipple and pressed a soft, open-mouthed kiss between her breasts, the silkiness of his lips raising goosebumps on her arms.

"Put your hands on my shoulders."

The command made her tense, no matter how skilfully his stroking fingers strove to pull the blanket of relaxation back around her. Was he crazy? Didn't he realise that she would fall?

"Put your hands on my shoulders."

She shook her head vehemently.

"Kathryn, do it now!"

It was the first time he had used her name, and the tone left no doubt that he expected to be obeyed. She let go of the armrests and reached for his shoulders for support before realising it was unnecessary. His hand under her neck, the other massaging the skin at her lower back, were easily able to support her weight. He let her feel it, let her rest on his strength, his support, his control, whilst pressing small, leisurely kisses between her breasts. Then he bit her. Not painfully, not even strong enough to really make her feel his teeth, just a reminder of his presence.

"Do you like that?"

It took her longer to consider this question. She was not entirely sure she knew whether he meant the bite or the fact that he held her weight. In the end the distinction did not matter. The answer to both was the same. "No."

She felt his chuckle. His mouth moved up the crest of her

breast in slow strokes until he was able to engulf her nipple with the heat of his mouth again. She did not like that at all. The way it made her belly tense and her body tingle – she did not like that she liked it.

With slow, deliberate pulls, he drew her nipple deeper into his mouth – sucking, nibbling, stroking without letting up. There was a moan and she did not realise it was her own until it had already left her mouth. Her nipple slipped from his mouth with a soft, wet sound, and he gathered her body close. Her arms slipped naturally over his shoulders and his breath stroked her cheeks.

"I liked that," he said.

She felt herself being lifted, her legs losing their support, and she yelped. Instinctively, she clamped her legs around his waist. She did not fall. His arms were bands of steel supporting her underneath her thighs and across her back. He laughed out loud, a deep, joyous sound with a melody woven through it. He loosened his grip as if to let her go, for only a millisecond, before his arms tightened around her again.

The sound that escaped her lips almost held alarm, though strangely, she never doubted her safety. When she felt his muscles tense to do it again, she laughed and slapped him lightly on the shoulder. "Stop it!"

They both froze. She could not believe that she had slapped, however playfully, the Vampire Lord of London.

"Did you just actually raise your hand to me?"

She was terrified. There was something in his voice she could not read, and that panicked her.

"I believe that deserves punishment," he said.

43

Before she could worry further, her mouth was claimed by his. This was not a gentle kiss; it was a taking, a no-holds-barred plunder reaching to her toes. His taste exploded through her, and when her tongue was invited to come play this time, it did so instinctively and gladly. She felt herself bedded on velvet, covered in his strength and warmth, whilst his mouth kept on feeding on hers, not letting her come up for air.

When he finally paused, they were both panting. He gently pushed the blindfold from her eyes and allowed her to see him crouching over her like a panther protecting his prey. Her arms and legs were still wrapped around him, and in the sudden light, she was embarrassed. She let her arms and legs slip to the bed. His eyes were no longer expressionless, instead they held a fire more terrifying than any cruelty.

Slowly, he lowered more and more of his weight to rest on her until she could feel his hard and still clothed limbs against her nakedness. His arousal was unmistakable as it rested in the embrace of her body, only separated from her skin by the fabric of his trousers. His hand stroked down, over her hip to her knee, before he hooked a hand underneath it and brought it up to his waist, opening her further to him.

She wanted to blame the hour, so close to the fourteenth, for the wetness soaking his trousers, but knew that would not be entirely honest. Her body was wet with arousal and spasms of pleasure were tightening her womb. He started to roll his hips, stroking the fabric over a part of her that she had not realised could become so sensitive. With each stroke of his body against hers, something tensed in her a little more. His lips started to play with hers again, teasingly stroking over them and then nipping her with lightning speed. She needed something she did not know she needed, and with every second it seemed to come closer. The sound ripped from her throat was between a moan and a sob – and it stopped him in his tracks.

His brow came to rest against hers on a moan. "There is nothing I want more than to continue this so that when I ask you again if you have ever had an orgasm, you are in no doubt at all, but unfortunately now is not the time. Now is too close to midnight, and it would be careless of me to lose control."

He stopped and let his words sober her as fast as a bucketful of cold water would have. She remembered her only purpose here was to serve his power. She met his gaze. The only regret she felt was for the disappearing chance to finally figure out why sex should be anything but torture, but even that was only a small twinge. She knew that maybe it would be better if she never figured that out.

He cradled her face, stroking her cheeks softly. "I do not intend to be careless with you."

His eyes closed, and for a long while, they just lay there, sharing the air between them. The physical closeness of another being at rest felt surprisingly nice. She liked his smell; it reminded her of rays of sun through a forest canopy with hints of lemon. That thought made her smile and he kissed her nose in response, not disturbing her peace, simply acknowledging it. But she could feel the waves of desire rising and knew that she would soon be swept away by her hormones.

He must have felt something too. "How long now?" he asked.

She swallowed hard and dry. "Not long."

He kissed her softly once more, as if in goodbye, then rose up and straddled her thighs. With this one move, he changed from man to Lord, and when she looked at him, he was no longer the gentle stranger looking back at her but the ruler of one of the largest regions, and he was surveying his territory. He raised her right hand to his lips and kissed the pulse point softly. She expected a bite, and saw awareness of the knowledge in his eyes, but after a second kiss, he slid his hand under the pillows and pulled. She saw the dark red restraint appear in his hands, and this was the moment when any trace of hope in her withered and died.

As he slipped the restraint over her wrist and tightened it, she nevertheless tried to say, "I promised not to fight."

Even to her own ears her voice was reedy and thin, barely comprehensible, but she did not doubt that he would still hear her. His hands came around her face again, softly stroking, but there was pity in his gaze. He kept his palm against her cheek, hesitating, contemplating. In the end she could feel the reluctance with which he let go to reach for her other arm and restrain it. Then his hands found her face once more, his fingers stroking away the tears welling from her eyes.

"Kathryn, the restraints are not to keep you from fighting me, they are to keep you from hurting yourself."

She refused to acknowledge what he was saying.

You said yourself you do not remember exactly what

happens during the fourteenth. Desire is a powerful sensation and this is the best way I can think to protect you."

His eyes were intent on hers, as if he wanted to convince her of the truth of his words by sheer force of will. Unfortunately, she had been shackled too often. With a soft kiss, he got off the bed and restrained her ankles as he had her hands, never letting his eyes stray from hers. Only as she lay splayed on the dark red fabric did his eyes wander over her body, taking in every inch in slow appreciation. When his eyes returned to her they were burning.

"Beautiful."

She was not and never had been. As a child she had been chubby and too tall, now she was painfully thin with skin so pale and covered in scars. Her hair, once her only vanity, was long and red, but had long since lost its lustre. She was not beautiful, not even pretty, and so she knew he lied. She let her head fall to the side, shutting him out. A millisecond later he had moved back to straddle her with his hands forcing her eyes back to his.

"You are beautiful."

She felt her face lose all expression before closing her eyes, shutting him out in the only way still available to her. She felt his sigh and the words that were whispered against her skin as he kissed her gently.

"We will have to work on that."

He sat up again and she felt him move over her. It was impossible to keep her eyes closed, not knowing what was happening. When they blinked open, she saw him drop his dark blue shirt over the side of the bed.

Beautiful was not a word that did him any justice. His shoulders were broad, the muscles in his arms as well-defined as those on his abdomen. There was no mark, not even a hair on him – the only touch of colour was his dark nipples, inviting her touch. Her mouth went dry and she was dimly aware of his pleasure under her gaze. He let her look while his hands returned to her waist to once again stroke soft circles over her sunken belly.

"I love the way you watch me."

She saw the truth of this in the dark joy with which he studied her. It was not vanity; it was a by-product of the skin-hunger humans developed. It was the knowledge that the person looking at you wanted to touch what they saw. She had never seen it in anyone's eyes before. They might have stayed that way until the hour of midnight took her reason but a soft knock sounded. She bit her lip as he called whoever was there to enter.

As two sets of footsteps came closer, she knew that she would come to hate him over the next few hours. No matter how irrational it may have seemed from his point of view, it did not change the fact that she still felt betrayed. The likelihood of a bond was higher if her mind was less sharp and her emotions pushed to their limits. Trust was an option but not the most convenient or expedient one.

As the twins came into view, she reminded herself to relax. It was only two men, only two. In the end, she would remember little of tonight anyway. She felt the numbness return and welcomed it.

"Look at me."

She did. There was no reason not to meet the blue eyes now; she knew her own would show only emptiness. He frowned, stroking her cheek as if he was trying to reach to her through her skin.

"I do not know what is going on in your head but Kieran and Brandon are not here to hurt you. They are here to make sure that I do not hurt you, no matter what happens after midnight."

Kathryn did not react, ignoring the frustration she could see was building in him. She felt pressure inside her head, felt him try to enter, but she was ErGer. No vampire could enter her mind without a bond.

"I will take some of your blood now," he said, just when she thought he had given up. "Just enough for my mind and body to be able to recognise yours. It will help to keep you safe."

Why was he explaining anything to her? Her blood might not be able to give him power before midnight, but it would still give him the addictive high, the feeling of absolute belonging and wellbeing only an ErGer could provide. She had almost been drained for that reason before. It was a surprise that he had not taken blood already. In her experience, no vampire, male or female, could hold back; they came again and again. The hand on her cheek softly pushed her head to the side and bared her neck. The twin on that side crouched down, bringing his eyes level with hers.

"Look at Kieran."

His lips were already touching her neck when he spoke these words. She tensed in anticipation. Kieran reached one hand to her head, softly stroking over her hair before holding her in place as Lucian's mouth fastened on her throat. She could not suppress the jerk of her body.

"Shh, just a small bite. He won't take much. It shouldn't hurt."

Kieran's voice was so different from Lucian's, calming still, but with a hint of a Welsh lilt rather than the clipped notes of the Queen's English. She concentrated on that as she felt the jaw move against her, the tongue lap at her blood, and he was right: it did not hurt until she felt Lucian suck... then pain started to bloom. Kieran's eyes flickered upwards and she felt the bed move on the other side. She tried to turn her head but the hand in her hair held her tight.

"Lucian," Brandon warned from the other side of her.

At the admonishment the lips on her neck stopped moving, and she felt one last stroke of a tongue over her neck before cold air hit the sensitive skin. The hand on her head was lifted, allowing her to turn her face.

Lucian's eyes had turned so dark, their blue was barely visible, and his lips were unnaturally red; he looked almost drunk on her blood. In fact, he was drunk on her blood. Then the clock sounded midnight; February fourteenth had begun, and almost before the last chime had sounded she was consumed by sexual desire, stronger than ever before. There was no slow development, the arousal went straight to a level indistinguishable from pain. She screamed.

She was aware of the frantic movement around her, but it did not matter; she was being torn apart by her own unquenchable need. Lips met hers and tried to extinguish some of the raging flames but it was like a thimble against a bush fire. She still took it eagerly, fed on the mouth touching hers, but the taste in her mouth was not the one she expected, and that frightened her enough to turn her head away. She heard herself keen, felt her body lift from the bed with a spasm of need, sobs rising in her throat when she was finally pierced, giving her the relief she needed.

Her moan was swallowed by a different mouth, a taste she needed, finally filling her awareness. Her world disappeared into sensation, into lips and hands playing over her, into flesh and teeth penetrating her body and an ever-increasing awareness of pressure on her mind. But the pain kept returning.

Pinpricks of seepage slowly appeared in the walls that protected her, and the awareness of him entered her mind in a million places. She felt the awareness as if it was an insinuating trickle of thick liquid, tasting uniquely like him, slowly covering everything, reaching into that aspect that was uniquely and absolutely herself. But there was no escape; he was filling her mind and her body; there was no way out. So her mind-self cowered, hunched in a corner of her being, hiding its face against figurative up-drawn knees, covering its head with its arms.

But his mind reached even there; covered her, surrounded her – and then stopped. Just stopped. Not waiting precisely, not hesitating, but in expectation of something. Her inner self uncurled, too curious at the sudden quiet, and he flowed into her. With every breath she took him in and her awareness changed. She felt him for what he was, for who he was, just for a moment. Then the almost painful acuteness of him faded, became something more common; the deep knowledge of a friend, the intimacy of a lover. He left tiny little hooks in her mind-self.

Only then, with him a part of her, did her mind bridge the gap to her body, became aware again of where she was, the tangled sheets surrounding her, the unrestrained arms, the sweat and blood drying on her skin. She felt the ache in her muscles and the million little bites decorating her. And she saw the blue eyes fixed on hers, the tear tracks on his skin and the utter exhaustion - but she also saw the joy. Then she felt him gather around her, first body then mind, and felt him push her past pain and awareness, exhaustion and sensation – deep into sleep.

Too surprised to fight, she went willingly.

4

Politics

It was almost impossible not to touch her as she slept. Some of that manic distance had fallen from her, but her amazing strength was apparent despite the fragility of her form. He spread her drying hair across the pillows, watching its light red begin to glow as the moisture slowly seeped away. He had no idea how long he had been sitting at the side of the bed, simply watching her sleep. It was not lust which held him here, nor even love or possessiveness – it was a strange protectiveness that infused his very being. He would have liked to say that it was the willingness of a man to protect his prize but he was only too aware that it was more than that.

When he had finally been able to give her the relief of sleep, he had been queasy and shaking. Nothing could have prepared him for the horror of the night or the intense self-loathing he felt. No matter that her body had screamed with sexual need, that she had reacted eagerly, or that his touch had given her relief. In the end, last night had still been rape.

"How is she doing?"

The voice came as no surprise. He had felt Kieran's presence as a comforting weight in his mind long before the other man had entered the room.

They shared the bond of friendship and blood, though they had originated from different Sires. It was rare for a vampire to take a blood bond with one not of their own lineage but both Kieran and Brandon had chosen to align themselves with him the day he had challenged for the London court. That had been more than a century ago – a long time to build a friendship, to love. He had come here for the power of the position, for what he could do with that power, the safe haven he could create. His Sire had been happy to send him, his power levels a threat to her own hold, and with him ensconced in London – one of the main European strongholds – her power within the Senate increased.

So he had come to London. The previous Lord was weak in mind and body, and conceded without much of a fight. The easy victory had been a problem in itself, inviting challenges from within and without. Throughout all of them, the twins had stood fast at his side, fulfilled the oath they had given that first day. Over time they had become friends, then occasional lovers when the loneliness became overwhelming. Now they would stand beside him as he fought one of the most important battles ever – the battle for this woman and her loyalty.

"Asleep." Lucian answered.

The hand on his shoulder was a reassuring weight in the dim room. It was so tempting to just lean back into the warmth of the other man. He resisted, not because of the strange aversion to touch modern men seemed to have developed, but because, somewhere inside, he felt he did not deserve the comfort.

"How are you?"

How was he? He looked at the woman on the bed. One red-blonde silky strand of hair had fallen over her naked shoulder, its colour brilliant against the extreme paleness of her skin. He stroked it away, luxuriating in the feel of her soft, velvety skin under his fingers.

He had held her after the madness of the ErGer, had held her throughout her bath, had supported her unconscious body with his own as his hands discovered each inch of her skin. She was breathtakingly beautiful and utterly terrifying. Her body held the marks of a thousand hurts, a hundred hands intending her harm. Too many bonds, too many frenzied feedings were imprinted on her form. The skin below her eyes was stretched and shadowed, her too-thin frame showing other signs of maltreatment and neglect. She had spent her life in fear and pain and bore the scars on her body and mind. In his world, she should be a treasure, and she had fallen into his hands at the worst possible time for him to show her.

"I don't know," he replied.

The answer did not even satisfy himself and he knew his friend too well to believe that he would let it pass. He was surprised when the other man simply moved a hand to his neck in a relaxing massage. For a while the only noise in the room was the crackle of the dying fire.

"Do you know why we swore allegiance to you?"

He had never asked why the two strongest members of the old court, those more able to challenge him, had not done so, had stood at his side instead. He remembered the day of the challenge well. A formal council-approved challenge required the challenger to take residence in the territory two weeks prior to the appointed date. This was to allow the current residents of the area to make a judgment as to whether or not they would be willing to live under the purview of the challenger were he to win. The existing members of the court could also assess and, often, threaten the newcomer. In the case of a challenge won, there was a six hour window in which the existing court could challenge on its own. And he had expected the twins, the court's champions, to do so.

Lucian had spent those two weeks in careful meetings, expecting every time there was a visitor to see one or both of the famed twins come to evaluate the interloper. But they had not come. He had still expected them to challenge and had prepared for it. The then-Lord of London, Augustine, had been their Sire, rumoured to have rescued them from the gallows before turning them – a bond of lineage, loyalty and blood.

They had stood at Augustine's side as Lucian entered the arena to fight, had held the greatcoat handed to them by their Sire and kissed him goodbye. Lucian had been prepared for a hard fight. Familiarity and habit often preserved a ruler in his power after a few hundred years, and Augustine's rule harked back to the Roman occupation, but one did not hold a territory without a great deal of personal power, aside from the power a Lord could draw from those linked to him.

He had watched the former centurion strip his modern clothes and reveal a body hardened by the battles along Antoninus' and Hadrian's walls. He had seen the experience and skill in the movements with which the other man had hefted the heavy gladius, the same sword with which he had fought as a human. But Lucian had seen the lack of practice in the minute slowness of the movements. This man had not wielded the weapon in earnest in a long time.

More damning was the tiredness he had seen in those dark eyes as they turned to him, that unmistakable fatigue many of the older ones developed without a bond to an ErGer. To live forever took more will and determination than most realised. He had come to London because rumours and whispers of a failing lord had reached his Sire, and standing in that arena, he had seen their truth.

A vampire challenge could be fought with physical and mental powers, but when he reached with his mind for Augustine's, he was not surprised to find the other man's shields wide open. So he had given the other man what he had desired, a death in battle, burning out his mind at the same time as beheading him. The court fell silent, watching the demise of a leader who had in recent years become cruel but had once given his followers something rare in a society dependent on strength: protection against outside threats. In that silence he had expected one of the two men to draw a weapon and utter the traditional challenge. He had stood ready, knowing that this would be the true fight for dominance and one not easily won. Both men had drawn their swords and laid them at his feet in anticipation of the blood oath. Even then it had taken him more than a moment to realise the gesture for what it was, and much longer to accept it as truth.

The support of these two men had made the transition within the court easier and had undermined the inevitable challengers from without over the years that followed. He had never asked why they had chosen to stand with him, in some way afraid of the answer. Leading a court was a lonely profession, which was why so many old ones, without the bridge an ErGer could form between the Lord and life, lost to the constant struggle to be strong. In those first decades, these two men had become an anchor, a touchstone of loyalty, the only company in which he did not have to play the role of the untouchable leader. By the time he had come to trust them enough to ask the question why they had given him their loyalty, he had also come to a point where an answer might have destroyed something fragile. For that reason, he had remained silent.

"No." Lucian waited for the answer, playing his fingers over the scarred and silky skin of the woman who had unwittingly and unwillingly become the very centre of all their lives.

"You asked everyone who came to see you what they wanted to become, what they wanted to achieve."

This proclamation surprised Lucian enough to turn from the sleeping body under his hands to the man at his back. But

Kieran was not paying any attention to him. His hands had dropped to his side and he was leaning against the bedpost, but his eyes, green and catlike, were fixed on a place far away, a time long gone.

"When you first arrived, after the challenge had been delivered to us by the council messenger, Augustine raged and raved. But when all his spies had come in with the information they collected, he quieted, became withdrawn, unwilling to react to any suggestions or plans we made for the challenge. We knew something was wrong, knew he had lost something… essential over the last two or three centuries. His outbursts, his distance, the cruelty… but we had looked away because we could not face the fact that we should have taken action."

Kieran's eyes suddenly found Lucian's, found and held, as if he wanted to imprint the next words on his friend.

"We should have stood against Augustine earlier. We should have protected the weak. When you came, we had come to the realisation our Sire would very possibly die, but that it might be a good thing after all. Initially, we planned to challenge you in turn, but then we heard the reports of those who had come to see you, not only the strong ones, but the weak ones too. You did not ask them for their skills, their power – you asked what they wanted to become. We live centuries and still we spend our time trying to preserve what we are, not becoming what we could be. You don't. You demand that we strive and develop, evolve and live. You give us the space to do that. No one has ever given her that opportunity."

In the intimacy of the dim room, the scent of the hearth a reminder of times they had exchanged pleasures and pains, friendship and sorrow, a realisation was exchanged – a reminder given, and a silent pact struck.

"She will make me vulnerable. It is the worst time possible to add her to the court. Even a month more, let alone a year, would have made us more secure. We are under suspicion by humanity, the fey are increasing their pressure and I cannot afford the weakness she will present to my power base as long as I have not got her power under my control. It would be only logical to break her mind."

Even as he said this most rational of comments his hand closed convulsively around the one of the sleeping ErGer. The gesture did not escape his friend's notice; a sardonic smile played along his generous lips.

"I think the more important question is: would you want it any other way, Milord?"

"No."

There was no doubt. He was not willing to give her up, to lose this feeling of utter life, of warmth in his soul, or the potential this woman presented for his life. What man would? Despite constant pain and flight, this woman had spent the last decade protecting the three people she loved. He wanted that warmth and that loyalty concentrated on him. Beauty was easily found, devotion a fleeting concept, but the ability for love despite pain was something so rare.

"No, I will never let her go, not even if I have to break her. I may be selfish, but I want this chance."

There was no surprise in Kieran's eyes as he gracefully

bent his knee before his lord, a dagger slicing his wrist and spilling drops of deep red blood down the pale skin of the offered arm.

"On this day, I swear fealty to and pledge my allegiance, my life, my loyalty in the service of Lucian, the Lord of London, and his Lady, the ErGer Kathryn, for as long as they agree to hold my oath."

It was an adaptation of the oath given to each liege lord, an oath he had sworn once already long ago. When Lucian took the offered blood, closed his mouth over the familiar and comforting taste, he did not simply accept the pledge of allegiance in the name of his mate, of Kathryn, but he accepted the pledge of a court to stand with them facing a future that promised to be challenging at best.

As Kieran rose he groaned, and for the first time Lucian noticed an uncharacteristic stiffness in his movements. A raised eyebrow was question enough.

"Brandon has increased the training intensity of your guards in expectation of the trouble your Lady might bring," Kieran said without rancour. "As a true woman, she is already making us pay."

This drew a chuckle from Lucian, who watched his friend carefully lower himself into the armchair.

"You can only be glad you were preoccupied with your lady. He will get to you as well. The man is mad, and paranoid to boot."

"Well, you should know. Have you told him your diagnosis?"

Kieran simply snorted. "I might hold degrees in medicine

and psychology but I am not suicidal enough to analyse my brother. He hits a lot harder."

And with that they were back in the easy exchange of friendly insults. But practicality had to intrude.

"How strong is the bond?"

"Weak. Her shields are formidable. I can feel her presence in my mind but that is the limit of my awareness as yet."

"You sent her to sleep."

"It was a crude measure, but it is the only influence I seem to have on her at the moment. And I suspect I overextended the push – I doubt she will rise without me aiding her."

"Good."

Kieran's matter of fact answer startled Lucian. He was rarely in favour of enforced unconsciousness as a coping mechanism, whether drug-induced or by the hand of a Vampire Lord.

"Lucian, look at her. She is too thin, exhausted to a degree I have never seen, and the only thing keeping her on her feet is her indomitable will. Sleep does not sound like a bad idea to start with."

Too true.

"How long until the bond strengthens to allow you to monitor her emotions?"

"I am not sure it will."

Here was the concern which nagged in the depth of his mind, finally voiced, finally acknowledged. The bond was almost insubstantial, and even that level of connection had taken all his strength to produce. She was not actively fighting him, but her mind was like a diamond cage, smooth surfaces and sharp edges with little traction to bind to.

"What do you mean?" Kieran's voice had sharpened, developing an undertone of concern.

"The bond is fragile, distant, strangely immutable." His hand had returned to stroke over her skin, to play along her smooth cheek. "It is not the same as the blood bond I share with the members of my court. It barely feels similar to one." His hands found her soft hair again, stroking and playing.

"What do you mean?"

"I have less emotional hold over her. I am not sure if it is a result of her being an ErGer or simply of her being who she is."

"Can you supplement it with a simple blood bond, at least until the mental bond grows stronger?"

"She is too weak."

"Lucian—"

"No!" He was surprised by the vehemence of his own words and tried to temper his tone as he continued. "She is physically too weak. I will not risk her health."

"Lucian, you risk her health by waiting. She is terrified and utterly lost. She needs the security the bond can give her."

"Kieran, you are a doctor. Can you, in good conscience, advise me to take her blood in the physical state she is in?"

"Can you in good conscience risk exposure to her without a deep bond? She is ErGer, she is addictive. For heaven's sake, *I* can feel her draw. I can only imagine how much stronger it must be for you. The only protection she has from us is that bond deepening to a level where you can monitor her."

"I will not risk her health," Lucian insisted.

"So what will you do?"

There was exasperation in his tone, and censure enough to warrant attention.

"I will find a way to reach her before it becomes necessary to force a blood bond."

"How? Lucian, I am your friend, but you are risking your own and your court's safety on this. As long as you cannot control that bond, you will be unable to control the additional power flow coming through her. If you were to be challenged, you would be vulnerable, unable to judge how far to reach."

"I will not risk her health, not without a concrete threat." There was nothing else to say; nothing that could be said.

It was some time later when the sound of the door opening broke the tense silence of the room, the light from the hallway introducing a perception of reality to the intimacy –Brandon's heavy tread along the floor a counterpoint to the atmosphere.

"Lucian is refusing to force a deeper bond with her." Kieran's eyes never left Lucian's as he spoke to his brother, a clear challenge.

"We will have to keep her separated from the rest of the court then."

The easy acceptance showed the difference between the two brothers. Kieran: the scholar, the thinker, the constant rebel, and Brandon: the force of nature, a supreme fighter, utterly unmovable and practical. Kieran tested and questioned his every decision, always in private never in public, but Brandon forced their attention to the practical aspects. The twins had become a perfect foil for his more ruthlessly strategic approach to the world. Brandon had stepped between them, as he often did, the mediator between two men who enjoyed the constant friendly wrangle for dominance. Contrary to his gruff and silent approach, he was the easiest, the most laid-back of the three.

"What are your plans?" Surprisingly, it was Kieran who asked.

"I will do my best to teach her to place her safety, her mind, into my keeping and hope she will choose to accept the bond."

"Trust takes time."

"Or ingenuity."

A predatory gleam filled him, ignited the hunter's instinct never buried deep in the psyche of a vampire. It was true – real trust took years to establish – but a human could learn that the loss of control was not synonymous with hurt, that dominance did not have to force, that submission could mean the safety to find freedom, if only for a little while. It was a dangerous game to play without the safety-net of a blood bond that would allow him to monitor her reactions. Fortunately, his sexual preferences and long experience in the art of dominance would be of good use.

Her hand felt delicate in his, pale twigs against his larger palm. He saw the skin stretched tightly over the knuckles, her fragile finger bones clearly delineated, thin scars visible along the tips, fingernails splintered – and still, below all that vulnerability, he could see the strong lines of corded muscle, the smooth outline of strength wrapping around her bones.

She was very much like her hand: fragile and full of indomitable strength.

Lucian lifted the hand to his lips, felt the brittle quality of her digits under his mouth, the taste of her skin already a calming balm on his very being. Under the enthralling scent of her, of her presence here, his perennially tense muscles relaxed with every breath.

"What do you see when you look at her?" Brandon asked softly, as if he did not want to break some magical spell being woven. It was an easy question to answer.

"Life, love... Family."

For weeks, months, it had been only a feeling, until he had met her, had felt her warmth and shared laughter, intimacy and tears with her in the span of a few hours. He had discovered that a desire, a dream so unreachable regardless of loyalty and power, had presented itself, ready to be grasped, if he only had the courage to take it.

He had ruled a court for over a hundred years now, had created a place of loyalty and relative safety for his own, a place to belong. But it was not enough, not for him. With every year, the realisation of something lacking had been growing, an ever-increasing sense of emptiness only disguised by intimacies shared and friendships found, even with the two men present. The dream of a family, a home, a haven in this world of constant demands and movement could not be denied anymore.

"I never wanted excitement and adventure." Not sure this would make them understand, he felt the need to elaborate. "I was a pretty child, the apple of my parent's eye, and spoiled rotten."

The chuckle in his words was dry and wryly amused in meditative memory.

"I was not really allowed to play outside. My mother had lost eleven children before me and limited any threat she could perceive. I saw the servant's children run through the orchard behind the house, waving their wooden swords and conquering the world. I was never tempted by their game, just their company. I did not want to leave. I dreamt of a home full of laughter. I saw a future that involved taking over my father's warehouses, marriage, children. I wanted a home."

The fire had burnt low enough to afford him an atmosphere of perceptive intimacy, its flickering light playing over the shining hair of his companions.

He saw that childhood dream, saw the country estate, and in its garden a red-haired woman holding a child. For a moment he was so utterly caught in the imagined memory, he could see the olive trees and hear the cicadas.

Kieran's quiet voice brought him back. "What happened?"

"The Plague."

The memory of that word still filled minds with horror; for many it was an almost genetic remembrance of a silent foe, deadly and unbeatable. For the three men in this room, three men who had seen its devastating swathe through Europe again and again, no more was necessary, and all three fell into recollections of lives taken and friendships broken by an illness that struck without warning.

Lucian remembered when the first whispers travelled through Granada; the first alarm spread faster than a wildfire, and panic eroded any perception of safety. He recalled the haste with which his mother had ordered the bare essentials to be packed to leave for the country, the expression in his father's eyes, that sweet, gentle longing with which he had always looked at his mother. The memory was bittersweet and he longed to have the same, to feel the same for another, with a power more painful by the years of forced forgetfulness. His parents had been loving, no matter that his father had been his mother's senior by almost twenty years. Their marriage had been contracted more by profit than emotion. By the time he was born, fifteen years after that union had first been announced, they had found what few people did: a quiet love, a deep familiarity, and a completeness.

His father had insisted Lucian take his mother to the country house before the city gates closed whilst he remained behind, seeing after the business. He had argued that there had been so many false alarms in the last few years, so many unnecessary flights from the city, that truly there was no need for him to leave too – especially not with a warehouse full of perishables to shift.

Lucian had worked as an accountant for his father's business, though spoiled and pampered as he was, he had rarely actually tended to his duties, spending more time with his equally rich and spoiled noble friends. But he had been happy to take his mother, to leave the city for the cooler, less expensive alternative after months of playing deep. So the day he rode out of the city, his mother in a carriage beside him, Lucian had laughed and clapped his father's shoulder, ignoring the gentle rebuke he had voiced concerning his way of life. He still remembered that last image, his father standing in the gateway waving as they rode out, the rhododendron bushes in full bloom. To this day he could not smell their sweet scent on the wind without tears rising to his eyes.

The Plague had followed them, gestating in his mother's body and taking most of them with it. Lucian himself had remained immune but had watched his mother's fast decline, had held her during those last moments, and had seen the light go out in her eyes. But by that stage he was already vampire.

Lucian never found out if his father approached his mistress or the other way around. It mattered little; Delphina had already been old then, and savvy. Money was power, and control over the only heir to one of the largest Christian trading houses in Europe was not something to pass.

The only thing he knew was that one evening, two days after they had reached the country estate, his mother had introduced him to a visitor, an acquaintance of his father – the most beautiful woman he had ever seen. Long, black hair, alabaster skin and eyes which burned into his soul. Two weeks later he had returned to his mother's side not quite human anymore, just in time to see her die, the last reminder of his family slipping away with her. By this stage he had already known that his dream of home and family were irrevocably gone – buried under an avalanche of Plague and blood.

He had never shared this with his friends, as close as they were. It was an almost unspoken taboo among their kind. Vampires lived in a predatory society, a feudal world in which the past became a weapon, the present a battlefield and in the future stretched the fog of constant vigilance. A society in which the only law was that of loyalty and recompense – the death of a vampire only incurring the need to replace or compensate his or her maker for the loss. It was a society in which the concept of a home was anathema, a family a collection of often deadly rivalries. Kathryn could give them more. Her blood, an addiction which tricked the mind into the belief of having found a home worth fighting for no matter what the Vampire Lord in question did. It was the cruellest nightmare and the sweetest fantasy. But it was not enough. In that hand, that fragile hand encased in his own, he held all his dreams, all his wishes.

"I see in her the potential for everything I ever wished for."

It was a relief when he actually said it out loud and admitted to the two men what his heart had been calling for. When he turned to meet Kieran's gaze, he was surprised to see a smile play around those beautiful lips. The shadow play caused by the dying light gave him an almost diabolical expression that was disconcerting.

"She will not make it easy for you."

"No." He knew that.

"You might lose her rather than claim what you desire. Will you be able to live with the despair of finding and losing a dream?"

"Better than never trying to achieve it."

"So what do you want from her?"

Lucian had to remind himself that there was a reason why

Kieran was such a good healer and spy. He was relentless.

"I want her love, her loyalty, and her life."

"You could have two out of the three by breaking open her mind to force a deeper bond." Kieran's voice was calm as he said this.

It was hard to control the fury rising in him at the suggestion, even though he knew Kieran only said it to provoke him, to let him confront an essential truth. Still, there was anger in his voice. "I want to bathe in her intelligence, play with her warmth, feel her emotion. I will not allow anyone or anything to interfere with that. I don't want to risk her being turned into a robot."

He felt the approval radiating from both men, a warm wave of confidence and support. It reminded him that families came in many guises, though theirs would blossom if he could reach the woman in mind as well as body.

"You have received a parliamentary subpoena."

Brandon's voice was calm and expressionless. The change in the room was electric, a tightening of minds, a readying to war by three men who had fought in more battles, physical and metaphorical, than was humanly comprehensible.

As Brandon pulled up another chair, a council of war ensued, similar to so many which had come before. But there was one change, one important difference as they surrounded the bed occupied by the sleeping woman: no one could have missed the focus all three held on her. As they spoke, her hand lay in Lucian's, his fingers painting absentminded circles over her skin. Kieran had reached for her drying hair, capturing it in a loose braid. On the other side of the bed,

71

Brandon's hand had found a resting place on the blanket covering her long leg. She had already become the centre of something still incomprehensible and unknown to her, and in many ways, to them.

"When?"

"You are requested to appear at a preliminary committee meeting three weeks from tomorrow."

"Kieran, what do your spies say?" Lucian asked after contemplating the information for a moment. "Have any of the other Vampire Lords been summoned?"

"We know that both the Lords of Leeds and Bristol are known to the government but neither has been approached, at least not openly. Until a few days ago I would have sworn that Carlisle remained unknown to the humans, but there have been some secretive meetings reported."

"Carlisle."

This gave them pause. The existence of the supernatural courts was more of an open secret to the government but most Lords worked hard to limit their visibility. Most had lived through at least one or two mob led witch hunts, and even though it was unlikely in these modern times of fast transportation and easy bribery that the strongest courts would be caught out by a mob, the weaker ones might. Even Lucian, as close as he was geographically to the government, had fought long and hard to preserve the anonymity of his court. At regular intervals human officials had tried to enter, or even control, supernatural politics but with only limited success. In reality, there had been little interest on either side – human and supernatural politics widely occurred alongside each other without the two realms ever touching.

The change had come, of all things, from the world of fiction. The sudden increase in novels and films portraying the supernatural in a favourable light had bred a very different public arena and had changed the power relations. The threat of what exposure would mean had diminished on the supernatural side but had increased exponentially on the human one.

No modern government could remain insensitive to public opinion, and so the current administration had chosen to consider the supernatural minority of their citizens in a different light. Known supernaturals or those with a connection to the courts had been approached; hints of secret registration policies and voting rights had emerged. Overtly, until now, the Courts had ignored all the attempts at communication. Internally, a hornet's nest had been stirred.

There had not been a Lord of the British Isles in centuries, an aberration in the power based politics of the supernatural. It had appeared that the British were a disagreeable lot, independent to a fault and leery of Overlords. So the supernatural courts had existed in an intricate power balance, peace widely preserved by a shared distrust to all and sundry. This had worked in isolation very well but was breaking down in the face of human interest.

Opinions differed wildly about what the reaction should be. Lucian advocated caution and careful entrenchment to preserve anonymity and safety. Declan, the Lord of Carlisle, on the other hand saw the time come to enter the light, and scrutiny, of humanity. For the most part, the other Lords leaned towards anonymity, but in a very human approach they were happy for the two front-liners, Declan and Lucian, to fight it out amongst themselves before taking a stand. The last few months had seen some troubling developments with instances of sabotage and accidental indiscretions, more than once leading to members of the London court coming to the attention of the human authorities. There was no evidence that led these instances directly back to Declan, but it was the logical conclusion to make. It also meant that Lucian had one or more traitors in his own territory. The fact that a subpoena had been delivered here and now, today, on a day when he was clearly emotionally and physically compromised by the recent bonding to an ErGer, was another indication.

But there was a second dimension to it. Humans did not realise that a court was so much more than simply a nexus of regulatory power for the supernatural species – it was a gateway. The reason why most courts were ruled by vampires was only in part because their nature was the most predatory, the most controlling, or because they were closest to humanity whilst having enough clout to control the non-human species. It was because the non-human species originated in the Other, in what had long ago been called the Summerlands. The fairies and elves, gnomes and ogres, dwarves and were-creatures were not human in origin; they were visitors or immigrants of what was beyond that door.

It was supposed that the human origin supernaturals, the witches and shifters, were the result of interbreeding. But not the vampire. Vampires had been a conscious design by some of the Other courts long ago. A Vampire Lord, in bonding to a certain area, became a lodestone, an anchor, for one or more Other courts, and made the transition possible. Traditionally, the Other courts ignored humanity and its doings, those Others living among them fitting in and hiding their peculiarities and powers. But this did not mean that human interest would not lead to swift and reciprocal interest from a dimension in which more immediate and cruel actions were entirely normal. Lucian was too aware that he was playing a power game on three battlefields, the human, the supernatural and the Other, and that he had brought into its midst a woman whose utter vulnerability and ignorance may very well form another threat.

With the bond weak, she remained a liability, distracting him and making his power unpredictable when he was walking a political tightrope that could have far-reaching effects. Kieran was right; it was logical to force the bond, rationally the right choice to take her blood and break her shields violently. But if he trusted in her strength and intelligence, he might secure a prize so much greater. A bond with an ErGer guaranteed a feeling of wellbeing in the court and produced unsurpassed levels of loyalty for the Lord in question. The love of a partner gave anyone, human or supernatural, something even more precious.

Eight months ago, when he had started to seriously research her, he had thought that the power gain would be enough for him. Now, having watched her courage and strength, he knew he would not be satisfied with less than her whole being. As the twins rose to find their own beds, he remained, steeped in contemplation and planning a campaign that had suddenly become more important than any of the political ones he faced.

In his ear he still heard Kieran's parting words of warning. "Be careful how far you are willing to go to force her compliance with your idea of a family. There are actions and threats no one can forgive."

5

Conditions

She woke to whispers, subdued laughter and a small hand playing with her hair. It was too normal, too familiar. Her mind screamed.

Kathryn had learnt long ago the way of vigilant awakening – do it fast, be ready to act, let no one know you were awake. Fourteen years of waking that way were ingrained; it mattered little that the enemy was too often equipped with senses superior to a human's and therefore rarely fooled. Sometimes, they let you have those additional moments of thought, that last instance of calm before another day of struggle and terror. Today she desperately needed those seconds.

It was the warmth that warned her. People got it wrong. The worst thing about poverty and homelessness was not the lack of food. It might not be possible to find much but there was often some. It was the cold, the unavoidable, constant pull of the intruding chill. Wherever they found shelter, even when they had enough money to rent somewhere, there was never enough warmth, never money for heating, and with three children any surplus blankets were spoken for. The best she could hope for, normally, were old newspapers. She was too warm for it all to have been merely a dream.

She opened her eyes to reality, just a careful slit. The girls were there... At first glance they were unharmed, even happy. Her field of vision was limited. She was lying on her side, a soft beige blanket pulled to her chin, but she could see the twins sitting cross-legged on the floor, both holding what appeared to be new dolls, though Heroise's old companion Jacque peaked its almost bald head out of her shirt. The warm weight along Kathryn's side could only be Anna, her daughter.

The child must have felt her move or had, with the uncanny instinct of the young, sensed her wakefulness.

"Mama?"

There was no way she could not answer that voice. Following years of habit, a tradition established before they could remember, the first signs of her wakefulness brought all three girls into her arms like quiet shadows in search of a moment of reassurance in a world which could too quickly change from safety to threat. Kathryn's eyes scanned the room for any potential danger as her arms held the children she had thought lost to her, as she breathed in their scent and felt the softness of bodies. She was grateful for just one moment to hold them and savour their closeness. She closed her eyes and just held on.

Too fast for Kathryn's peace of mind, the boundless energy which was Heroise would not be contained anymore and wiggled to escape her hold.

"Katie! Let go!"

The youthful scold was accompanied by a bony knee in Kathryn's gut, accidental and predictable, its companion hitting her twin, leading to the equally foreseeable squabbles and squeals of two young girls tumbling to the floor in an undignified tussle. Clutching Anna in shared exasperation, Kathryn realised they truly were alright.

Their skin was too pale, but it always was, and the smell of freshly washed hair infused the room with every move they made. It was braided in neat plaits down their backs, in a tidier fashion than she normally managed to impose on them or have them preserve for more than three minutes. Most importantly, the near-on constant shadows under their eyes seemed to be fading and their exuberance was not tinged with franticness. They were a colourful bundle in the bland room, their clothes new and pretty. It was clear that a well-meaning but badly informed adult had allowed them to choose their own wardrobe. Heroise's bright pink tutu over sunflower yellow tights clashed happily with the red and green frilly shirt, and Helena's combination of a blue princess dress over orange jeans was not much better, though at least it was a more pleasing colour combination. But it was time to face reality. Cradling her child close she turned to the man, the vampire, leaning against the doorjamb.

"Why are they here?"

He had been a presence on her mind before she had even fully woken, surrounding her with strangling ropes of awareness. Over the tumble of children she met the gaze of the man who was the largest threat ever to appear in their lives, a threat she herself had delivered them to. How could it have been different? How could she have thought for even one moment that she could manage to remove the children from the constant peril her life had become?

"They belong with you."

Calm and collected, his voice brought back the events of the night before, brought back the sacrifice she thought she had made.

"We had a bargain."

He raised an eyebrow at her tone of barely concealed fury. It shocked her too; moreover, it frightened her. She had long since learnt to subjugate her emotions to the need to survive, and though it was never wise to let an enemy see the terror in you, it was equally idiotic to let them see the anger they provoked. With the children here, she did not have the luxury of losing her cold-blooded common sense.

Anna was a warm, heavy weight on her hip as she rose, the move designed more to settle her own nerves than as a display of equalising power. He was vampire, and whether she were standing or sitting, if he attacked she would have no chance, but standing made her feel less vulnerable. It took her three attempts to resettle Anna comfortably, even the slight weight of the six year old was a strain on her perpetually tired arms.

"We had a bargain."

More collected now, her voice had evened out, settled. It was too late; a frown marred the beautiful features of the Lord. Her tension had communicated itself to the children, had snuffed out the laughter and play, replacing it with nervous vigilance characteristic of those who knew, at any time, their elders might be unable to protect them from an unexpected threat. It, more than anything else, broke her heart. This was what she had wanted to save them from; but as she watched the large, predatory body prowl into the room she could not even reassure them. The best she could do was put herself between them and the threat. She did not even dare to break the chokehold Anna had on her to put her down. Those unblinking eyes, blue and cold, drilled into hers, disregarding the little bodies cluttering the room; her best hope was for this state to continue.

"You bargained for your brother's life and freedom. He was entirely unharmed when he left."

He had almost reached them, his unhurried movements smooth but none the less threatening. Her arms had begun to shake, the burn in her muscles not entirely from the strain of carrying Anna. Kathryn knew her hold on her daughter was too tight, knew Anna's squirms indicated discomfort, but she was too frightened to let go.

"I bargained for their safe passage as well."

Her voice shook. She feared the hitch in her breath was not only audible to herself. It annoyed her more than she could say, though it was quickly swallowed by the choking wave of terror as the vampire reached for Anna. She was helpless and had to watch her daughter go willingly into his arms. For a moment she hesitated, and held onto the little life in her care. But his hold was secure, the sensation of clothes slipping through her hands an almost symbolic weight on her mind.

Her child, shy and distrustful on the best of days, went easily to him, allowed herself to be settled on his hip with an ease of familiarity which cut off Kathryn's breath. With every moment her mind painted new images of how this man could harm her child, right before her eyes. There would be nothing she could do to stop him. Panic froze her; her eyes fixed on the sight of his elegant hands on the dark green of her daughter's dress, cradling her with care. His pale skin was a stark contrast to the cloth, his gentleness emphasised by the utter vulnerability of the little girl in his arms.

As if from a distance she heard his voice but her mind was too terrified by the images it produced to hear the words. She watched him set the little girl down and her daughter join her aunts at his command. She saw the uncertainty, the fear with which all three girls looked at her not the vampire, and still there was too little air in the room. Everything was happening in slow motion, every sensation harsher as her mind seemed unable to even comprehend the smallest detail. Breathing was difficult, her lungs refusing to fill with enough oxygen, though the staccato sound of her efforts seemed impossibly loud. Cold sweat on her skin imitated the rising chill in her heart.

Rationally, she knew this was a panic attack, but the knowledge did nothing to calm her. She had never had one before and had been stupidly proud of the fact. Somewhere in her mind she had always thought her need to protect the girls had precluded any such emotional outburst. Now, when they needed her the most, she stood here frozen, useless.

"Heroise, please take the others downstairs. I need to

speak with Kathryn."

She understood enough to resent him removing the children from her presence, but realised it to be a kindness to the three girls whose world depended too much on her strength. She hated herself because she was physically and mentally unable to object, because she could not preserve the facade of calmness for them anymore. And she hated him for being the root cause of it all. She watched them dragging their feet as they left, the giggles and the joyful screams replaced by the uncertainty of children battered by grown-up decisions. It was the image of Anna's huge brown eyes as she looked back over her shoulder towards her mother which the blackness hovering at the borders of her vision almost washed away. It never got the chance.

"Kathryn!"

She felt herself being lifted, guided back onto the settee with irresistible force. She found herself on her back, looking up into that strong face, falling into his eyes. He loomed over her, cutting out the room, the light, the world until there was little more than his eyes. The weight of his hand against her chest, a pool of warmth over her heart, held her in place. It should have frightened her more, should have given her the last push to drown in the panic. Instead it gave her an anchor, a lodestone to come back to.

"Breathe, Kathryn. Deeply. In, out. If you cannot regulate your breathing I will have to push you into sleep again."

His voice, the tone more than the words, reached something in her. She felt his presence surrounding her mind, readying itself to take away her consciousness. She was aware of each time his chest filled with air, before the breath from his mouth stroked over her face. Instinctively, her own body adjusted to his, followed the even pattern. She had no idea of how long he held her like this, but with each needed breath, her mind was able to think a little clearer.

"It's not their fault. I did not resist the bonding."

The children were already here, there was little to lose by appealing to his sense of honour. He simply smiled, though it contained little amusement. Now that she was able to breathe again, had found at least the first rung of the ladder back to sanity, her mind was scrabbling to find a solution. Her focus was brought back to the man leaning over her by the impatient tap of an index finger on the tip of her nose.

"You did not resist the bonding and I have kept my word. I will overlook the challenge to my honour this once."

Anger coloured his tone, infused his eyes in what she knew well was a deliberate act. She understood the message. Ice wrapped around her spine, reached for her muscles and tendons, crystallising them in stone. There are some rules set not just in stone but in diamond among the courts, and a word of honour was one of them. If she were a vampire, he would be within his rights to challenge her to a duel in retribution for the insult. Something was wrong with her. She was not usually so stupid. She desperately needed to regain the disassociation of her mind, but nothing seemed further away than the familiar clarity of cold rationality.

"Please…"

She had no idea how to continue this sentence.

"Please what?"

"I did not mean to…"

His thumb stroked over her lips, taking with it the words she meant to say and leaving behind the taste of exotic spice which was so much the enigma of this man.

"Shhh. Yes you did, although I know you did not mean it as an insult. For the moment, that will be enough, and because it is enough I will explain without waiting for you to ask. You bargained for the life and freedom of your brother as well as the safety of the children. I gave you both. Your brother has left my territory well and in time; the children are safe."

"They should be with him."

With each word she took more of his taste into her, felt invaded, off balance. Her confusion was audible in her voice when she spoke and it annoyed her at a basic level. She was not this person. She wasn't emotional, or weak, or even indecisive. She had not been any of these in a long time and would not become that person now. There was still the children to consider and her strength was the only good thing left about her.

Kathryn tried to force him back to let her sit up. For a moment he refused, held her in place merely with the pressure of his hand on her chin, his finger stroking her lips. When he eventually moved and let her pull herself into a half-sitting position they were both aware that it was only because he allowed it.

"Sire."

Never before had she voluntarily used the formal title bestowed upon Vampire Lords, not even when her refusal had garnered her pain. It had been a matter of pride, which was often the only thing she had left. For the children, she would be happy to give even that.

"Sire," she repeated, "I am sorry the bond did not take but I can promise you I will hold to the agreement and remain in your court until either the bond takes hold or you decide you no longer want to pursue the matter. In a year you will have another chance."

What was a year for someone who could live for centuries?

"Please, Sire, let me contact my brother and arrange for the children to join him."

She had no idea how she would manage to bring this about but she still held her breath in anticipation of his answer. His eyes gave nothing away. They were the deep blue of a mountain lake when night fell, inscrutable and unfathomable. Deliberately she held still when his hand came to shape her face, his fingers tunnelling into her hair in a touch closer to a caress than an attempt to control.

"I very much doubt he would be answering your call. His income is dependent on him not doing so, and forgetting he ever had a sister."

"You paid him."

Not quite a question, not quite a statement. He chose to answer it nevertheless.

"Two hundred thousand now and a generous annuity as long as there is no contact between him and you or anyone connected to you, directly or indirectly."

It was too much to comprehend.

"He left without the girls."

"That was one of the conditions, yes."

It was as if his hand was the only warm point in her universe. She had no idea why the thought of Paul being gone hurt so much. Completely aside from the question of safety for the girls, was this not what she had accepted two days ago? Why did tears burn her eyes now? Why was there a lump of searing pain just below her heart where she once held the knowledge of safety, of love? But that feeling had left her long ago. It had died the day her parents had been killed. What withered now was only the memory of that feeling.

"He is my brother, my family."

"He was."

She knew he used the past tense deliberately. The only family she had left now was the girls.

"Why did you not let him take the girls?"

She tried for all the world to suppress the panic that threatened to rise again.

"Because you are wrong, little one. The bond has taken root. It will take time to develop but you are mine. And so are they."

She tried to feel this bond. She had thought it would mean a trail from her mind to his, an open wound, like a mental rope ripped from her, leaving her open to his every whim, painful and raw, but this was different. Where she normally felt herself end, there was now him, in all directions, an implacable prison of his mind surrounding all she was. It was a cage, encasing her being in a layer of burning ice and holding her in place for his pleasure. She pushed against the wall, not trying to break his hold but testing it. His lips twitched and amusement rose in those eyes holding hers. But it was the wave of warm desire whispering through her mind like soft fingers stroking over her breasts that made her stop. She understood the warning – her body and mind were his to do with as he pleased. He had no need to take them by force, to burden himself with another mind. He had all he needed here. He could take all the time in the world to break her.

"The girls are your insurance policy."

He did not react to her tone, not visibly, but his long fingers slipped deeper into her hair, stroked soothingly over the tense muscles of her neck. The sensation was mesmerising, creeping under her defences, trying to reach something inside her.

"They are safe, I give you my word."

"And will be as long as I do what you tell me to do."

"They are safe."

For a second she thought there might be another message under the words but she had long since stopped believing in fairy tales. She heard his sigh, felt it like a wave whispering over her mind, and knew that he was disappointed. It should not have mattered, should not have bothered her, and should not have hurt. She was good at disappointing people.

She had no idea how long they sat there in a strange relief of tension, or what broke the spell either. Between one blink of the eye and the next he seemed to shake himself from the hypnosis they had both fallen into, and as he moved back, the world came crashing down on her, returning her to her senses. In the distance she heard the sound of children's voices, music to her ears, and closer, the sound of dishes clanking against each other.

"Breakfast."

For a moment she thought he meant to bite her, and the grin on his face told her he well knew it. Then he winked at her.

"The bathroom is over there. You have five minutes before I come get you."

When she did not react right away, he turned her gently and gave her a little push in the right direction. Automatically she started to move. Before she had reached the indicated door his voice reached her.

"Kathryn?"

She turned.

"You will be safe here too, no matter how long it takes you to accept that fact."

That lie was not even worth the waste of a reaction.

Five minutes was not long enough to get her head on straight again, but it was enough to unaccountably find her own toothbrush and shaver in this strange bathroom. The room also contained a wide array of toiletry substitutes, all of higher quality, but she did not dare to touch anything. It was almost impossible though not to at least smell the ginger body lotion.

Just before last Christmas she had managed to get a job in a café in town, and on one particular day she had to take Anna with her because Paul had disappeared with the twins. It was a rare treat to spend some time alone with her little girl even though she was hiding in a corner of the store room so that no one would realise she was there. They'd had to walk home that evening because there was not enough money for the bus fare for both of them, and on the way they had passed a perfumery. In front of the shop was a stall with little cardboard tubs of tester lotions, and the smell had been heavenly. She had always been mad about scents and Anna had inherited the same fascination. Amused by their enthusiasm, the shop girl had given them each a little tub, and they had shared that secret indulgence for weeks, just the two of them. She did not dare to take any of the lotions here but she opened some of the bottles and raised them to her nose. The smell gave her the courage to open the door and leave the bathroom.

6

Danger

He had never seen anything as beautiful as the panic in the eyes of his ErGer, of Kathryn, the taste of the panic attack in her mind a visceral presence in the room. He had savoured it, loving the implications it held for them both, hating the strain it put her under. Humanity was a strange animal; primordial survival had taught it to suppress the adverse effects of fear until the moment of reaching safety. She was unable to understand it, but he knew. Her utter inability to act in the face of panic was testament of a subconscious awareness of safety. He just hoped they both had the time to let her rational mind understand what her instincts had already learnt before circumstance pushed him into forcing her.

Lucian was barely aware of the arrival of his seconds, Kieran and Brandon, or the arrival of the ordered food in the wake of his major-domo, Eric. Every grain of his attention was fixed on the woman behind the bathroom doors – her heartbeat, her breathing, an audible murmur to his vampire ears. She was physically and mentally fragile, a strong woman brought to the edge of her endurance. A woman who would, by the very nature of the bonding, have to be pushed even further. He cursed all those who had hurt her, had destroyed her ability to trust in others; worse, who had destroyed even the most basic trust she had in herself. He would have to step carefully, watch her every move, and get to know her better than she knew herself if he wanted to bring her through the full bonding intact.

"Luce."

It was hard to turn even a smidgen of attention away from the presence in the other room, away from Kathryn, but Kieran was shouldering the mammoth share of the court duties at the moment. More, as a trained medical doctor and psychologist, he was also supervising Kathryn's care and the care of the children.

"Kieran."

"The girls were worried. They said Kathryn became ill again?"

Children's logic. They had been told Kathryn was ill in order to explain the two days she had slept whilst her body, and his, adjusted to the initialisation of the bond. They had simply extended that explanation to account for Kathryn's unusual behaviour.

"Are they alright?"

It could not be easy for the girls to see the only stable element of their lives suffer. All three were smart and perceptive enough to realise something was wrong. It worried him. He would have liked to say his concern was for Kathryn and the unquestionable fact that she would be unable to settle into her new role if there was any doubt over the safety and happiness of the children. But he was simply not ruthless enough for that. Those children deserved more.

"They are as well as can be expected, though I believe they should see your ErGer again before long. I would like to bring them in before Eric takes them to the zoo. They are surprisingly well adjusted, used to sudden changes in their lives, but they depend very much on the ErGer for their emotional stability."

"Kathryn."

The correction was automatic, almost instinctive, and in the puzzled expression on his friend's face he saw the need to elaborate.

"Kathryn, her name is Kathryn. Don't call her the ErGer."

After a long moment, Kieran nodded, but something had changed in his eyes.

"Kathryn, then. What happened? How is she?"

Lucian's eyes returned to the door that separated him from his chosen and to the shadow moving below it as the only visual evidence of her existence. He did not need to see her. He felt her in his heart, his mind, his very essence.

"Panic attack. The first of many, I suspect. You warned me of them."

"I did not think they would start this early."

Kieran fell silent beside him but it was not the silence at the end of a conversation. Lucian waited him out.

"Luce, she might not be able to adjust to your life."

True – but it was not a situation he was willing to accept.

"Lucian, it might be kinder to force a full bonding now, hold her safe, and then use the years ahead to help her rebuild herself."

Lucian's snarl was near soundless and utterly vicious, its echo travelling as a wave of hot power through all linked to him. He felt the screams of pain, the shock and fear reflected back along the blood bonds connecting him to his court. It was the backlash which brought home how much the unsecured ErGer bond was affecting him. In his right mind he would never have let his anger slip, or allowed his emotions to find expression in a burst of raw power. He shut it down, cut off the ordinary, harmless flow of power emanating from him as a Vampire Lord and shored up the walls of his mind with sudden urgency. He was careful to allow only the links his vassals had to him to go unchecked whilst controlling his own to them. Only the newest bond that linked him to Kathryn was left untouched, and for a moment he felt relieved that the strong walls of her mind had protected her against his ire.

The shockwave of his fury had not only had a mental impact. Kieran had fallen to one knee under the pressure, holding on to the arm of the chair beside him, his head bowed, his laboured breath loud in the suddenly quiet room. For a moment Lucian hesitated to reach for his friend, not because he did not want to help but because he was unsure of the welcome his aid would receive. He expected to see accusation and shock in Kieran's eyes; instead there was only calm acceptance.

"This is what I mean, Lucian. You are not in control of your power as long as your link with her is as fragile as it is. With every passing second you are a threat both to her and the rest of your court. This is why an ErGer is bonded quickly. You need to take her mind, break it open and secure your control. Then you can help her rebuild herself. She is ErGer. Even now she is linked closely enough to you that you will have decades, centuries, in which to help her heal."

Lucian could not close his eyes to this truth or ignore the possible retributions of the actions his friend was forcing on him.

"Kieran, would you give me the same advice were you only her doctor and not my second?"

He saw the answer in the other man's face before it was even spoken aloud.

"No, I would not. I am your second and I have to speak as such. You are risking your own life and the lives of all your vassals for her wellbeing."

For the first time in decades of friendship and love, Lucian saw an emotion bordering on disdain on his friend's face and betrayal where he had only ever seen trust. It hurt, but it changed nothing. Kieran was wrong.

"You want me to choose the good of the many over the good of the one, is that it?"

"If you want to call it that, Lucian, then yes I do. It is your responsibility, your duty, to make that choice. A Lord stands to protect his court. You would not hesitate to sacrifice Brandon or me, or any other member of your court, to protect the weaker ones, but you are willing to sacrifice all for her; for the dream of a mate, a lover, a family. Your dream. I thought you were different from other Lords. I thought you would stand for those under your care."

The sneering derision was no longer hidden. It was a wild animal ready to rip Lucian apart. He knew Kieran's words were based on hurt and disappointment, but still his wilful incomprehension gouged lines of pain on his heart. This was his closest friend, his intimate, and for first time they were completely at odds.

Something broken hung in the balance between them and would be lost forever if Lucian was unable to reach out and rescue it. In his mind, the rising wave of aggression was barely contained. The part of him which made him a lord, which made him dominant, struggled against the chains he wrapped around his need to lash out, to reassert his dominance, in order to preserve a friendship too precious to lose. The red haze of battle settled over his mind, the automatic analysis of his foe's weaknesses, reactions and strategies taking forefront. Without conscious thought, he shifted, placed himself in front of the door to the bathroom, between his ErGer and the perceived threat. The only warning he had of the attack was the contraction of Kieran's pupils and the barely noticeable drop of his left shoulder. They had fought and trained together too often for either of them to be oblivious to the smallest warning of action.

Lucian was not entirely sure which of them would have won, but the question was never put to the test. The noise a whole tea set could make as it shattered on the elegant, wooden floor was amazing. Brandon's eyes were blazing, coldly judgmental in their consideration of his Lord and his brother. His tone was deceptive in its mildness.

"Let me assure both of you, I will be more than happy to beat some sense into your hard heads if either of you makes even the smallest move which could be construed as a threat. I can only assume you have taken leave of your senses for a moment and will rejoin the world of rational adults forthwith."

"Brandon—"

"Shut up, Kieran. Luce has the right of it."

Brandon never raised his voice, never showed any agitation as he spoke, and his tone seemed to be oil on the fire of Kieran's fury. All the emotion banked in what seemed to have been a festering wound came to the boil, and the cold calculation with which he might have faced Lucian was washed away under unrestrained rage. There was nothing human in the growl reverberating through the room as he turned to his brother.

Lucian admired Kieran's courage at that moment. Brandon might have been the most easy-going of them, the most laid-back, less powerful than either in terms of raw power, but when it came to pure physical strength and skill he would take them both down without breaking a sweat. Where Kieran's alpha instincts might have led him to carry through an attack on Lucian, another dominant who, in that moment of challenge, would not be a friend but simply a threat, he could not react in the same way to Brandon, his twin, and a man who easily accepted their dominance over him. Which might very well have been Brandon's intent.

"Both of you will shut up now and listen."

In that moment neither Lucian nor Kieran would have dared countermand Brandon, no matter who was dominant. Even an alpha had to recognise when he was being an ass.

"You are both wrong and both right." Brandon paused, an eyebrow raised as if to dare them to interrupt. Neither man was stupid enough to try.

"Kieran, Lucian is right. Would you expect him to sacrifice one of those children for the good of the court?"

"No, of course not. They are children; they have no choice, no protection. But she is different. She is an ErGer, a conduit for power to a court. That is what she is."

The anger in Kieran met the cold wall of calm that was his brother.

"How does that make her any different from one of the children?" Brandon asked.

It halted the torrent of Kieran's outrage. Brandon brought the point home, brutal in his rationale, slicing through all the churning emotions.

"Every single member of a vampire court chose the protection of life in a court over the dangers and the threats without the alignment to one of the powers. We make it our choice by accepting the protection it gives us, by making use of the resources provided by our courts, from the highest Lord to the lowest blood donor. An ErGer never chooses. Kathryn, this ErGer, has done everything to avoid the courts and to escape their protection. You expect Lucian not only to force her into a situation in which she has no choice, but rape her mind, take her power and then discard her when she is too much work? Is that truly the Lord you thought you swore allegiance to?"

Lucian was given no time to watch the effects this speech had on Kieran before Brandon rounded on him, no less cold and cutting in his assessment.

"You, Sire," The sarcastic emphasis on the title could have been cut with a knife, "have just proven to your whole court that in regards to this woman you have the control of a sixteen year old. As you are the noble bastard that you are and will follow the impossible task of trying to save your court, your love and yourself, you will bloody well have to learn some control again, not just as a man but like a new vampire with a sudden increase in power. So, just as the younglings in their first decade, you will have to practice control until you either stabilise your bond or have control of the fluctuating power. As Kieran is the only one who might actually survive it if you slip, you will have to practise with his help. If this should pose a problem for either of you, I will be happy to provide you with an incentive to get along."

It had been centuries since Lucian had felt this stupid. He was tempted to applaud the other man; not only had the dressing down been well deserved it had also been superbly delivered. One glance to the side made him wonder if his own expression was as repentant as the one on Kieran's face. He suspected it might be. They both stood there like little boys before the school master, ungainly and awkward.

"If you two are quite finished, we might be able to give the young woman who is about to come through that door the care and attention she needs and deserves."

"You sound like my old governess." Lucian could not keep the hint of a pout from his voice, the forceful reminder of the way he had so often felt as a child too fresh in his mind. He blamed the temptation to wince when the sharp green eyes turned their burning gaze on him on the memory, unwilling to acknowledge the intimidation he felt in that moment.

"Did she box your ears?" Brandon's question was deceptively innocent.

"A riding crop actually."

"Would you like me to demonstrate?" Brandon asked sweetly.

The annoyance in the voice of the man who under normal circumstances had the patience of a saint, and who swung a broadsword with innate ease, tickled the ridiculousness of the moment to the surface, and where they had been willing to tear each other to bloody pieces only two minutes ago, the three men now shared a smile. Friendship could be inexplicable and strange.

7

Safety

Kathryn hesitated in the doorway for a moment. In her five minutes away, the room had filled, leaving her more unsure than she had been before. She recognised the twins with their Celtic good looks and easy smiles, their long limbs arranged artfully in two armchairs flanking the settee she had woken on. They exuded a charismatic power, brighter than that of their Lord, which brought the strangeness of her situation and her surroundings even more to her attention. As she had woken there had been little thought to her surroundings other than a quick catalogue of the dangers and threats to the children and herself. Now, without the girls to consider, she was able to take in the room more clearly, and to her surprise the only description coming to mind was minimalistic elegance.

This was not a room she expected to find in a vampire court. It was not so much the tall windows, science having long since reached the stage where it could produce glass to filter out the spectrum of light harmful to vampires, even at the height of noon; no, it was the utter lack of gothic drama. The steel and glass, the clear lines, the fabrics in hues of sand and beige, the impersonal warmth. It was a single, open-plan room in which a clever architect had distinguished the different areas, a study, a dining area and the comfortable seating area around a free-standing fireplace. This room was designed to be pleasing to all, and intimate to none; more like the epitome of a high-end business hotel. She could almost believe herself far from the vampire court of London were it not for the man, its Master, dominating the area before the fire. Lucian's eyes were on her the moment she stepped through the door, no matter how deep in conversation with a fourth man beside him he seemed to be.

"Kathryn, I wanted you to meet Eric. He is our major-domo and holds all responsibility over the household."

Eric, the fourth man, seemed older; not a vampire but not human either. His pupils were more elongated than round, his skin more green than rosy and his nails more sharp than rounded. This was no human, though the grey in his eyes suggested there were at least some human genes involved in his makeup.

"Milady."

The bow was courtly and there was a gentle calm in him; it felt like a walk in the forest on an autumn day. For a moment, she could smell the fallen leaves, feel the crisp air on her skin, but then she was back in the room, unsure of what she had sensed.

"Eric and his wife Yulia are about to take the children to the zoo. I have asked them to bring the girls up to say goodbye before they leave."

She met the challenge in Lucian's eyes. She saw his expectation, his anticipation of her rebellion at the idea of removing the children from her immediate field of influence. He would be waiting a long time then. She had long since come to terms with what she was, with the danger she presented to the children once there was a supernatural in her vicinity. It hurt more than she could say, but if she had the choice of letting them go with this man to spend the afternoon among the throng of humanity at the London Zoo or have them here with her and three vampires, where they could easily be caught in the crossfire, the choice was easy. They were the insurance policy for her good behaviour and therefore safe, as long as she did what she was told. It would be for the best to keep them as far away from the Lord as possible; as far away as possible from her.

"I am grateful for the opportunity. I am certain they will enjoy the experience," she said.

If either man was surprised by her easy assent neither of them showed it, and any further conversation was made impossible by the sudden intrusion of twin whirlwinds into their cautious tableau.

A kind hand had intervened in the earlier wardrobe disaster, though the red and orange, the yellow and green was no less bright than the previous clothes choices. They barrelled into Kathryn with supreme disregard for life and limb, and her arms closed around them tightly. Anna was slower in following them, more cautious in her approach of any adult, but unlike the twins, she demanded to be lifted into Kathryn's arms whilst the other girls abandoned their older sister for a joyful tumble across the floor toward the other set of twins in the room. Kathryn wanted to hold them back, pull them close, but knew too well that would be a challenge in itself. The girls had finely tuned survival instincts and were generally very good at judging when it was wiser to step away from an adult and when the adult would be inclined to be indulgent. She just had to hope the instincts held even here or that she would be fast enough to divert attention were this not the case. For the moment it gave her the opportunity to hold her daughter close.

"Geht's dir besser, Mama?" *Are you feeling better, Mama?*

Anna had fallen into the German of her early years, instinctively searching for solace in the first language she had shared with her mother. Kathryn answered in the same tongue.

"Yes, Baby. I am sorry I scared you."

The small hand stroked her hair in an imitation of the gesture of comfort her mother normally gave her. It was a heart-breaking gesture, a threat of adulthood approaching too fast.

"That's ok. Uncle Lucian said you were ill, like I was last year, and that you need lots of sleep. We watched over you so that nothing could happen to you."

Her eyes jumped to the man stepping up to them. He just smiled at her.

"Your daughter refused to leave your side as long as you

104

were asleep, which is why we have waited until today for the outing to the zoo."

"Are you coming too, Mama?"

Her arms closed automatically around her child at the hope in that beloved voice, at the obvious reluctance to leave her mother and the clear excitement at the idea of the zoo. They had only been to the zoo twice before, once in Paris and once in Brussels, but both events had imprinted themselves on the hearts of all three girls. It had surprised Kathryn to find that it was not the majestic lions or the exotic elephants which had left the deepest impression, but the gentle red panda. What did it say about those girls that they chose the comfort of the small, ponderous teddy bear over the excitement of the large mammals? And how to tell her daughter to enjoy the zoo, to live those moments to the maximum, without her mother? In the end, she did not have to.

"Not today, Sweetling." Lord Lucian's voice was strangely gentle in the old-fashioned German he used to address her daughter with.

"Your mother needs to rest a little more, but she might be able to take you there herself someday."

His large hand stroked over the little head and came to rest on Anna's back below Kathryn's own arms, providing support as if he was aware of the weakness in her arms. Anna was getting heavy, and Kathryn was tired enough that any attempt at carrying her for more than a few minutes strained her. But, no matter how much aid he provided, Kathryn resented his interference.

"I can stay with you, Mama." There was both reluctance and fear in her voice.

"No, Annie, you go. Who else will tell me what I have missed otherwise?"

The way her daughter turned to the man at her side for reassurance was dangerous.

"You won't leave her, Uncle Lucian?" Anna asked.

"I promised you I would not, didn't I?"

What had happened between her child and this man while she had been asleep?

Lucian took Kathryn's hand as the girls prepared themselves to leave, held it throughout the goodbyes as if he wanted to reassure her, only releasing it in the silence following their exit.

"What day is it?" she asked.

It had niggled at her since she had woken. Something did not add up. Too much seemed to have happened in what she had assumed had only been a few hours of sleep.

He moved back to the settee and took a seat on the light grey cushions before he answered her.

"Today is the sixteenth. You have slept for more than two days. I am afraid my command was stronger than I had anticipated."

Two days. It explained the familiarity between her children and this man. They had been in his care for much longer than she had thought. Only a few hours ago the thought would have terrified her, but she had seen them with her own eyes and had found no ill effects on them. There was nothing she could do and it seemed pointless to worry over time already

106

past. She suspected her own ordeal, now that the girls were safely away, was only beginning.

A strange quiet spread in her. She knew the feeling well, had taken refuge in it too often. She let it bleed away all her fear and reclaimed the cold. The children were safe for the moment, and in the cold she could keep them safe.

"Kathryn."

Sharp, demanding. She knew there was nothing in her eyes as she turned to him but did not know why it made him sigh.

"Come over here."

Obediently she crossed the room, as close to a mindless automaton as she could make herself. It was never perfect, there were always intrusions in the calm, but eventually she could disappear. Her bare feet touched the deep carpet before the settee, its sensuous softness playing over her soles, stroking along the side of her foot. It was warm and indulgent and she pushed it away, shut it out to keep it from shattering the cold. Kathryn stopped before the low granite slab serving as table.

"Luce." One of the twins said, a note of alarm weaving through the word, but the Lord only silenced him with a gesture.

"It's alright. She will lose it quickly enough."

He was beautiful, more so than any other man she had ever seen. In the cold she could see it, could recognise it because there was no emotion attached to the concept. Beauty just existed, as did danger. Neither consumed her nor touched her. Those midnight eyes with the frame of coal-black lashes were simply beautiful. Without interest, she watched him reach for the deep blue pillows, their colour almost matching his eyes. He dropped them to the floor between his long legs. It annoyed her. Something so beautiful should be treated with more care. Then she pushed the annoyance out of her mind so that the cold could become a little bit stronger, a little bit deeper.

"Kneel."

She would have knelt where she stood, her knees bending before the sound of his command had died away, but he pointed to the pillows at his feet. Of course. She knew what would come now, had been used in that way a thousand times by men who had shown her less care. He owned her and had every right to ask her to satisfy him. Still, it was hard to move around the table, hard to take those few steps because, no matter how much she tried to be a cynic, a little seed of hope remained.

His eyes studied her with something close to pity. She did not want him to register the sudden stiffness of her movements, the way she had to fight for the distance. She hated the silence with which the three men surrounded her as she stepped around the table. She even hated the gentleness with which he took her arm to help her down to her knees. She wanted their laughter, their ribald comments, even their insults. She wanted anything which reminded her of who they were.

Kathryn tried to angle herself so that she would be able to see not only the vampire before her but also the other two at her side. It never paid to forget a threat merely because another took precedence in that precise moment. It only seemed to amuse all of them.

"No, little one. I want your eyes on me."

A finger stroking along her jaw, warm against her cool skin, emphasised his point. It was a strange sensation, a line of warmth along her skin. The touch seemed to linger long after his finger had moved on. It licked at the cold and reminded her of the flow of water over pebbles, wearing down their sharp edges with time. The finger reached her chin and held her in place, its strength both a warning and a promise.

She fell into his eyes, and in their wake it was impossible to remain entirely disassociated. His touch broke away the curtain she had drawn over her perceptions. His scent carried on his breath as he leant close, and she could almost taste him on her skin. The memory of the leisurely play of the fourteenth, before her body had betrayed her, was too strong to ignore. The warmth of his body stroked her through the air, sensitised her and took away the chips of ice in her pores. With each breath her mind became less able to ignore her own body, to hide behind the walls of indifference she created with such skill. His destruction of her protections seemed effortless, and she hated him for it.

"You are mine, body and soul. Everything you have known before no longer matters. Everything you have learnt to expect is equally void."

The pronouncement was stark and uncompromising, his hand holding her in place, forcing the unbroken eye contact on her, only emphasised the statement. In self-defence she tried to turn her head, but when his grip on her chin became more firm, she closed her eyes against him. It mattered little;

the declaration of dominance had already imprinted itself on her skin with the weight of fiery chains. As they burnt away at the cold, the constant raging in her mind, the never ending need to fight, calmed. He was right. She was his, both by law and her own promise. There was nothing she could do, nothing she could change. He could kill her tomorrow and no one would oppose him. He could do the same to the children. She was their only protection and she had to live to keep them safe. With steely resolve she opened her eyes and met his gaze. Kathryn did not like the smile that greeted her.

He held her there. The only reality was the man before her as she knelt between his long legs in a cage of his making. There was nothing but him, and with every passing second his very presence superseded every attempt her mind made to skitter away from the impression of his power. All physical sensation but him fell away and she realised this to be the purpose of the room. It was neither too cold, nor too warm; neither too quiet nor too loud. In its simplicity it was safe enough to disappear behind his presence. As the minutes passed, her scattering thoughts reeling in the direction of the children, her fear, the past and future were again and again brought back to the present, to his touch on her chin, her position at his knees, the expression in his eyes, his dominance over her, until her muscles relaxed slightly, settling into the here and now. She felt the slow deepening of her breath, became aware of the even beat of her own heart pushing a languid heaviness through her veins.

"There you are. Just let it take hold of you."

The deep timbre of his voice brushed over her skin like an

110

intimate caress, but it was not enough to break her gaze away from the mesmerising deep blue of his eyes.

"I promise you again, here and now, that you and the girls are safe with me. Safe and protected."

Her natural cynicism, honed through years of flight and abuse, wanted to come to the fore, but there was no space for it. Every atom of her attention was taken up and so it remained a small voice in the back of her mind. Did she trust him? A moment of lucidity threw the question to the surface of her thoughts. Trust was such a foreign concept for her. The thought was discarded as quickly as it had appeared, cast aside as irrelevant and ridiculous. Trust was for the unprepared and stupid, an excuse when the possible danger had not been foreseen. She did not trust him. She saw the danger too well but she had no choice.

He watched her as if he could see every emotion on her face, watched the smallest change in her tension, in her eyes. She knew he would not be able to discern anything of value, her expressions too disciplined by necessity to give away anything. Still, something must have communicated itself to him for the smile he gave her was rueful.

"I see you do not believe me. I can accept that, at least for the moment. But, no matter what you think of me, the rules I will set out for you to follow are for your protection. I expect you to follow them, and there will be consequences if you do not. Is that clear?"

"A blood oath in return."

She pushed the words out before she could think about them. She might not have managed to bargain for their lives, their freedom, two days ago, but she might be able to do so now.

"Another blood oath?"

There was amusement in the words. It galled her more than it should have. Amusement was better than anger after all.

"Absolute obedience to the rules, within my own physical limitation, in exchange for the freedom of the girls."

Kathryn hoped the phrasing would leave her more space, would put a close enough framework around the issue of obedience as to make it hard for him to be too capricious in the rules he established. She could not risk him ordering her to fly every morning and then base his punishment on her inability to follow the rule.

The warmth of his fingers fell from her chin, stroked over her cheek, the sensation curiously tender. She did not understand the sadness in his voice.

"No blood oath. It is too soon after your bonding for me to take more of your blood. So we will formally exchange an oath of honour. Absolute obedience, within your physical and mental limits, for the safety of the girls as they remain under my roof and protection until their majority."

It had been too much to hope that she would get the children away from him. If this was the best she could get she would accept it. She nodded.

The kiss came as a surprise, gone before she had even felt it, a fleeting touch of his lips. Still, it was enough to resurrect his taste on her lips, that intoxication of lemon and spice.

"I, Lucian, Lord of London, swear to protect and cherish

112

the ErGer Kathryn and those she has brought under my protection."

"I promise absolute obedience in exchange for the safety and wellbeing of the girls."

There was no way to match his oath in dramatic effect, so she did not even try, but in her simple words there was no doubt, not even a quiver in her voice.

"Thank you, little one, for trusting me this far."

There was no point in reminding him that she had not really had a choice in the matter; it was better to assert as much power as she could manage, to ask the question rather than simply kneel there and wait.

"The rules?"

The audacity only made him smile again, the faint network of laughter lines at the corner of his lips an innocuous detail her mind noted with fascination. They turned beauty almost too perfect to be real into something more human. Kathryn shook her own mental head at herself in disgust. She needed to stop. She needed to make sure her mind was not running away. This was too important.

It helped when he sat back, sprawled on the sofa in leisurely abandon. Freed from the blue intensity of his eyes she was able to think a little faster, breathe a little freer. Strangely, it meant her mind was less clear.

"Take off your shirt."

The command was soft, still gentle, but there was no question of the steel underneath it. Her hands found the hem of the large, white dress shirt and pulled it over her head without hesitation. She lived under no illusion. It would not have been any protection anyway.

"The first rule: Your life will be restricted to these rooms and our bedroom until further notice. There is therefore no need for clothing. As long as the children are not here, you will refrain from covering your body with any form of garment. The consequence of disobedience will be to be stripped of the garment you have chosen with force and you will lose the freedom to move for a designated time. Is that understood?"

Unpleasant to a degree, but the rule in itself was fairly innocuous, designed more to undermine her mental equilibrium than do her any harm. She could live with that. She nodded.

She did not see the hand coming, did not see him move, it was so quick. His elegant finger tapped her nose – not a painful touch but designed to startle – a move she had observed pet owners do in the park. She felt the muscles of her face begin to tense in a scowl but resisted the temptation.

"The second rule: When asked a question, you will answer verbally, if possible in full sentences. If you do not do so you will be gagged for an hour to remind you of the rule. Understood?"

At the last moment she managed not to nod but to speak.

"Yes, Lord Lucian."

His hand found her chin again, circled it in a touch becoming familiar, as was the sensation of losing herself in his eyes.

"The third rule: You will refer to me by my first name only. When answering a question you may use 'Sir', but in any other situation it is Lucian. Understood?"

She hated him for understanding that she used his title as a way to distance herself and hated him even more for taking that away from her. This man was more dangerous to her than any other because he understood the myriad ways in which her mind escaped and would not let her get away with it. Still, there was only one possible answer.

"Yes, Sir."

She would not give him his name, would preserve what little freedom she could. He would just have to deal with it. His smile turned grim, but he let go of her chin.

"The fourth rule: Every single aspect of your life will be ruled by me, or in my absence, by Kieran and Brandon. You will spend all your time in the presence of one of the three of us. You will eat at our command, sleep when we tell you to and move where we want you to move. Nothing in your life will be under your own control. Each time you do not comply, you will be punished. Is that clear?"

It was harder to assent to this one – so much harder. In a very real sense this rule would put her at his mercy. Without question, he could already do whatever he pleased with her, but only by force. Assenting to this rule meant he could order her to slit her own throat and she would have to kill herself. Her voice was barely more than a whisper when she said, "Yes, Sir."

Because in the end, there still was no choice.

He stroked her then, his hand a warm weight gliding over her head in exquisite gentleness. It was not a sexual caress, not even a sensual one. It was closer to a touch of solace than anything she had felt in her adult life. But she could not trust it.

"One more, Kathryn. Just one more."

What else did she have left to give away?

He leaned forward, surrounding her with his body once more, and she felt the touch of his lips on her hair.

"I don't ever want you to hold back your questions so this is a rule to give you something. We will all answer whatever questions you have, truthfully and as completely as possible, as soon as you ask them."

She knew it sounded like a boon, but it was also very clever. It would force her to speak, to interact with them. Every time she did not she would curse herself for not making use of all the resources to her disposal. A clever man indeed.

"Now to your punishments. If you intentionally disobey any of the commands you are given, you will lose a privilege for however long the person in charge at that moment thinks appropriate."

Now it was her turn to almost raise an eyebrow. Privilege? What privilege?

"As your body and mind are entirely mine, any moment you spend not under my immediate control is a privilege. You might lose the privilege to wash yourself, to brush your own teeth, or to shave on your own."

He continued too quickly for her to really react.

"Pain will never be used as a punishment. I believe you have felt too much of it already in your life. We need to find out if it serves any purpose aside from torture for you but I will use pleasure." She had no idea what he might mean by that. Pleasure as punishment was a concept she could not relate to and was almost certain she would rather remain in ignorance of. For the briefest of moments, she considered asking for clarification, but fear held her back. His question showed her that he was only too aware of it.

"Understood?"

"Yes, Sir."

Her voice sounded empty and she knew she had lost an opportunity to prepare herself. His hand rested on the top of her head for a moment before stroking down her hair. He bent over her, closed the cage of his presence around her once again. She had to look up to him, and for perhaps the first time in her life, she felt genuinely small and breakable. Caught between fear and anger, terror and confusion, she was a ship without anchor buffeted by the storms of emotion. She felt so much and so desperately wanted to feel nothing at all.

She hated the trembling in her body, hated the physical betrayal of her confusion. It had been a long time since her control had slipped this much, had turned her from the doll she made herself into a human. He gentled his voice when he continued.

"Kathryn, do you know why I am setting these rules?" Her eyes burned, the heavy pressure of tears unwelcome and shameful. She struggled for dispassion, but in the end it became only a thin layer over the venom in her voice.

"You want to break me with your rules."

There was deep sadness in his eyes now. "No, little one, I think you have already been broken. Now you can no longer

117

care for yourself."

How dare he! She had been taking care of herself since the day her parents had been murdered and the first vampire had raped her for blood and power. She had taken care of the girls and Paul, but before she could tell him that his finger covered her mouth, keeping her from speaking.

"You have learnt to look after others but not after yourself so I have to do it for you."

It was unbelievable how much she wanted to hit the patronising bastard at that moment.

"Alright, up you get."

The move was unexpected, and as his hands helped her up she was, just for a moment, unsteady. It forced her to lean into him, to borrow his equilibrium until hers returned. As if burnt, she shied from his touch. Kathryn thought she saw sadness in his eyes, but there was no other reaction.

"Bring me the black box over there."

She followed the line of his outstretched hand and saw an intricately carved box on the table across the room. It was beautiful, and so at odds with the room it fit right into the ultra-modern decor. Under her hands, the carvings revealed themselves to be the image of a tree, its branches intertwined and reaching, cradling a multitude of figures and objects. Below her thumb she thought she could recognise a witch's hat, beside it the sleek form of a stylised mountain lion. The box lay easy in her hands, large enough to be substantial and small enough to be easily carried. The size and shape reminded her of the old document boxes used by medieval monks. She felt the eyes of all three men on her as she crossed the room to them, their gazes wrapping themselves around each of her movements.

She halted before the Vampire Lord, offered the box. His warm grip covered her hands and pulled her between the strength of his thighs before taking the box and setting it down against the pale grey of the seat cushion besides him. It was almost disorienting to be the one to look down on him.

"You are very unselfconscious."

He said it with wonder and calculation, a piece of information to admire and to file away for future use.

"The only thing clothes protect is your dignity. Dignity does not concern me," she said.

Kathryn was not quite sure if it was a movement or a sound which drew her attention to the men to the side. They had not changed their position, both still sprawled in their respective seats, a study in relaxed nonchalance, but as she met Brandon's eyes she was caught by a burning rage that lit the emerald green. Any possible fright was washed away as she felt hands spanning her waist and the feather-light touch of a kiss just above her belly button. Looking back down to the vampire before her she felt enveloped in his arms, saw him rest his head against her middle in the gesture of a man seeking comfort. She had held the children too often like this for the mother in her not to react. Without thought her hands stroked over the opulence of his silky hair. She felt the sigh against her skin.

Her rationality re-engaged and her hands dropped away, her mind shocked. She needed to remember who he was. He was her enemy, not some lost child in need of comfort. She could not let him get under her skin or see him as anything other than a force to be resisted. The arms behind her back held her gently, even as he looked up at her. Again, she had to fight the image, though this time there was nothing in her which saw him as anything but a beautiful man. His skin was as pale as hers, the red of his mouth so close to her body waking the heat in her own. Under his gaze she felt a shiver along the path of his breath where it stroked her rib cage, felt it tease the underside of her breasts and wake the nerve endings.

"With each move, with each action you teach us dignity and grace. You are so far above the concern for either you do not even realise it," he said.

Kathryn had no idea how to react. He simply smiled, amusement and warmth tugging at his lips.

"Lucian," Kieran said, breaking the spell. "Your Lady has not had any breakfast as yet and she truly cannot afford missing any more meals."

The arms holding her shook with laughter and the friendly kiss he pressed against her middle as he sat back sounded loud in the room.

"Too true. Well then, Kieran, if you could get the dishes Eric undoubtedly left for her, we can continue to map out the daily routines. Kneel for me again, Kathryn."

She was glad of the order, to return to the position which drove home the vulnerability of her situation. Her knees bent almost gratefully.

"Open this," he said, handing her the box.

Under his watchful eyes she set it on the floor to lift its lid.

Bile clawed at her throat, and only the emptiness of her stomach rescued her from throwing up. Breathing became a chore, the oxygen simply unable to push past the burning ring of terror contracting her throat. Her hands shook on the lid and she felt the sharp edges dig into her flesh until she thought they might break the skin. It was his utter lack of expectation that helped her to step back from the edge of panic. He did not touch her and that helped as well. Minutes passed, minutes in which she simply breathed, her eyes fixed on the contents of the box, but with the retreating terror came the realisation it could be far worse. He gave her the time she needed, never pushing, only speaking when she was able to swallow without the bitter taste of bile in her mouth.

"Take out one piece at a time, tell me what it is and put it in my hand."

Her fingers trembled as she reached into the box and pulled out the first object at random.

"Blindfold," she said.

She held it out to him but he did not take it. She was forced to lay the silken cloth on his outstretched hand, the mere act a surrender in itself. He placed it carefully beside him.

Next Kathryn's fingers touched padded leather, and a jumble of items came from the box when she pulled.

"Restraints – wrist and ankles."

Her voice broke, to her own horror. Just as with the blindfold she handed them over, now moving as quickly as she could simply to get the chore completed.

"A ball gag."

She was very familiar with this. The Lord of Tirana had loved to hear her scream and delighted in finding new ways of getting her to that point. But what he had loved most was to hear her choke on her own screams through a gag – a ring had been the preferred choice for those times when he wanted to fuck her face. He had still been quite fond of the ball. She could see her own hand shake as she handed it over.

"Only one more item."

She knew it was meant to reassure her.

The last item in the box puzzled her. It was black and made of a soft synthetic material, with a pointy end widening in a teardrop shape before it narrowed and then flared again. Her fingers touched the curve in incomprehension. She really had no idea what it was. Her best guess was that it was some form of dildo.

"Do you know what it is?" he asked.

She did not like revealing her ignorance, but her silence was as much an answer as an outright denial would have been.

"An anal plug?" Her voice broke.

His voice remained gentle. She felt his attention taking in the smallest of her reactions, the slightest shift in her posture. His care was not necessary, her horror too overwhelming to hide her reaction. She almost dropped the plug in fear, and only one of his lightning fast movements saved it from falling to the floor.

"Kathryn, look at me."

It was a definite command. He studied her, watched her fear soar then be brought under control, but did not make a mention of it. Instead he informed her of the last aspect of her routine.

"Every day before breakfast you will bring me the box. Each time it will contain a different combination of items. I will use all of them in the course of the day and night. Some will be in there all the time as reminders of possible punishments and some will be new. You will bring me the box, open it, and just as you did now, you will take each one out, name it and place it into my hand. You will give them to me – do you understand?"

She nodded. Hate, burning and painful, rose in her. His hand snaked out and grasped her chin, forcing it up to make eye contact.

"What do you answer?"

"Yes, Sir."

His thumb stroked over her skin while he calmly accepted the hate in her gaze. Then he let her go again to reach for the items besides him.

8

Weakness

His hands found one wrist restraint and he looked at her as if considering. She could not help the small, instinctive jerk of her arms as if she were trying to hide her hand behind her back. She controlled the impulse quickly but he had spotted it, though his chuckle was low.

"I think for this first meal we will not need them. I do not think you are quite ready to fight me again."

What a challenge! She closed her eyes, refusing to let him see her anger. Where was the numbness? She so desperately needed it back.

Kathryn felt his hand stroke along her jaw, sliding below her hair to hold her neck. He started to massage her tense muscles as if he wanted to push the warmth of his skin into her frozen limbs. She refused to let it affect her, let it touch her, desperately reaching for the distance, the cold. Only when he spoke did she realise how close he had come.

"New rule: when I am in the room I want your eyes on me."

It was only a low whisper but it reached inside her, forcing her eyes to open for him. The smile teasing his lips was slow and beautiful, and for an instant she wanted to reach up and touch them.

"That's it. Your eyes are beautiful, no reason to hide them."

Her eyes were brown, nothing special, just as the rest of her lacked any distinction in regards to beauty. She felt a shiver through the link of their minds and saw his gaze sharpen.

"I have no idea what that thought just was, but we will have to deal with it, eventually."

His finger tapped her nose playfully.

"But first things first. Breakfast."

A glance to the side made her realise she had been dangerously inattentive. Not only had Kieran returned, but the low table now sported an assortment of dishes which had not been there before. Their odour made her nauseous.

"Are you comfortable?"

What was he asking? Was she comfortable kneeling on the floor, wearing nothing at all, in close proximity to a man who wanted to suck her blood and who had spent the night intimately linked to her body even though she had no real memory of it? Obviously she was not comfortable. So why was he asking? Was he asking out of a sadistic pleasure in her discomfort? In her mental agony her eyes had dropped from his face to the hollow at the base of his throat. No heartbeat.

125

Of course.

"Such a busy mind. It is simply a yes or no answer."

His thumb travelled softly over her brow and jaw before painting her lips. Gently, with one finger under her chin, he guided her eyes back to his.

"Let's try again. Are you comfortable?"

It was his finger under her chin that kept her from shaking her head, though it was a near thing. She had already started the movement when she remembered the second rule and hastily corrected herself. "No."

His thumb was still travelling over her lips as he grinned.

"No what?"

He wanted her to say his name. So she gritted her teeth and repeated, "No, Sir."

It made him laugh. "I will get you to say my name, Kathryn, before the week is out. Now, why are you not comfortable?"

"Because I am kneeling naked on the floor in front of a vampire!"

The moment the words left her mouth she bit her lip. He had provoked her into snarling at him and now he would have the right to punish her. Instead he seemed to be strangely pleased. His hand caressed down from her chin to her naked shoulder and back, a ceaseless pattern of gentle discovery over skin and muscles that softened under his touch.

"One day you will realise your nakedness is not designed to demean you. Far from it. Until then, I enjoy your body too much to give up the pleasure, and more importantly, the clues every move gives me. Time will let you relax and time will also allow you to become used to my appetite for your blood."

His fingers stroked over her throat and goosebumps rose on her skin. She hoped from fear, but decided not to examine her own feelings any closer.

"As far as your position on your knees is concerned, you could always come up here and sit on my lap."

The grin was almost boyish, his voice teasing. She did not trust it one bit. When she simply glared at him he continued.

"No? What a pity. Well then, why don't you sit more comfortably? Whilst you will spend a lot of time on the floor at my feet, I will not require you to spend all that time on your knees."

She tensed. Was this a test? Would she be punished for relaxing her rigid pose? It had happened before. Again she felt his awareness travel over the surface of her mind and it frightened her more. But if she moved she would be able to see the room and the door which meant she would be able to keep an eye on the other two vampires in the room. They had been so quiet that she had almost forgotten about them, but a vampire was not something whose existence you forgot and remained alive. Slowly she shifted so that she could pull up her legs and hug them, still keeping an eye on all three men.

When she had settled with her knees drawn up to her chest, Lord Lucian shifted in a slow movement. Every muscle in her body locked, tensed and awaited the punishment, but his leg simply came to support her back. He reached over her head to pick up a steaming plate from the low table, and at the same deliberate pace, he lifted a spoon buried in the food and blew on it to cool the steaming mass before offering it to her lips. Kathryn was too surprised to react right away. It was porridge! Simple porridge, with the unmistakeable smell of syrup and cinnamon.

She gave up and opened her mouth for the spoon, ignoring the little voice in her mind that warned of sedatives and poisons. She was simply too tired to care.

The atmosphere around her seemed to undergo a bleeding away of tension she had not even been aware existed. Spoon by spoon the Vampire Lord of London fed her food fit for children and invalids whilst his two most powerful courtiers looked on. The girls were not here and there was nothing presently to fight for, nothing to take care of. She could simply let go and stop fighting the inevitable tide of defeat. Finally the distance returned and even the slow agony of cramps churning her stomach seemed far away. Another bite, then another, then another. She had stopped caring.

"Luce!"

Her own violent retching came as a surprise. The sudden bitter burn of bile barely a warning before her throat was scalded and she began to empty her stomach into the bowl. Her whole body spasmed with such violence it was hard to remain upright. She was dimly aware of arms supporting her, a hand stroking her head in a soothing rhythm. His warmth battered against the cold in her.

Five minutes later she had thrown up the whole meal and found herself sitting on the bathroom counter. A terse voice told her to wash out her mouth before her face was wiped with a soft, warm cloth. When he was done, Lucian dropped the cloth into the sink, and with a heavy sigh, rested his hands flat on the counter beside each of her legs. Her eyes found his in quiet acceptance, too tired to care.

"Kathryn, you really have no self-preservation left, do you?"

Did he expect an answer? She had none.

"Lucian, this is dangerous. You need to deepen the bond." Kieran stood in the doorway.

The answer was immediate. "Not as long as it threatens her health."

"Lucian, this threatens her health!" There was exasperation in Kieran's tone but Lucian's blue eyes never wavered from her face.

"Kathryn, do you know what he means?"

She shook her head, but quickly followed it with a "No, Sir" when he frowned at her.

"You don't show or tell me when your body has reached its limit because you don't know yourself anymore. But your body is now mine to care for and I need to understand it. "This…" a warm wave of awareness passed through her mind, "this is not yet strong enough to give me more than vague impressions. It is a catch-22 situation. Kieran wants me to deepen the mental bond so that I can read you more easily but to do this I have to push you physically and mentally to open to me. I can only do it safely if I can read you. If I take more blood I would increase my awareness of you in the short term, but you are not strong enough for me to take more."

A second, much heavier sigh shook Lucian's frame as he looked at her.

"Well, we will just have to be very careful with you."

He helped her wash her face again, his fingers braiding her hair with practised ease. Returning to the large room he did not set her to his feet again but kept her snuggled in his arms.

"Let's try this again," he said softly.

His arms were warm, their strength curiously comforting, but when he reached for another plate her stomach churned again.

"No, please."

Finally, some sign of alarm managed to reach her. He could not have been pleased with her bout of sickness, but surely he would not make her eat again.

"Three spoonfuls of porridge."

There was no room for debate. His voice showed his complete implacability on the matter. He was prepared to feed her until her body would accept the sustenance. Her head drooped, and with a sigh she opened her mouth.

"Keep your eyes on me," he snapped.

More out of surprise than any thought of obedience, she met his gaze. Surprise which turned to bafflement when the taste of apple and cinnamon exploded on her tongue. It was impossible to suppress the unexpected joy at the treat.

"Your favourite food," Lucian said.

She heard the smile in his voice.

"How did you know?"

"Anna."

Should it worry her how much he had apparently already

learnt about her? Possibly, but as he fed her two more spoonfuls, her eyelashes became impossibly heavy, too heavy to be supported by her lids apparently. She felt her eyes close, almost of their own accord, and she could not help the wave of fatigue gnawing at her consciousness. He told her to look at him, but as he shifted beneath her, she felt him draw a soft blanket over her. It became impossible to raise her eyelids again. A too familiar voice whispered "Sleep" in her ear, and that was all it took for her to obey.

She woke slowly, and confused. She was still on the sofa, still held in the arms of a man, but the green eyes twinkling at her were not the ones she had expected to see. It took her a moment to rearrange her thoughts. Kieran. It should have surprised her to realise she knew which of the twins was grinning down at her but she was beyond being surprised. The title of the journal in his hands might have given her even more cause for astonishment.

"The British Medical Journal?" She could not stop the question bursting from her. She was utterly astounded.

"I thought I might find some pictures of naked women in it but alas it is all boring intelligent stuff." Then he grinned and pulled gently on her braid. "Kitten, I *am* a doctor."

When she looked at him open-mouthed he burst out laughing.

"You cannot have studied medicine!" She was outraged, but not entirely sure why.

"Why not?"

"You would have had to go to class during the day."

"Actually, no. It is possible to do it in the evenings, it just takes longer. You would be surprised how much accommodation for a night time schedule two million pounds in donations buys you."

"I assume your residency was just as expensive?"

"Oh, that took only another two million."

She rolled her eyes. Then she froze. Why was she teasing this vampire? He was powerful enough to be the Lord of London's second and she had never forgotten the potential danger of even a newborn vamp before. Why him? She was intermittently terrified of Lord Lucian but this man did not worry her. She did not trust him at all, but neither did she fear him.

"Such fierce distrust in those beautiful eyes." He grinned at her as if this mattered little to him. "Alright, Kitten, want to use the bathroom?"

She nodded automatically; anything to get away for a while. His voice was still amused but with a slight hint of warning. "You wanted to say something?"

Shit! She had forgotten the rules again. "Yes, Sir."

He helped her up and gave her a light slap on her ass as she moved away. She decided not to make anything of it. At least he allowed her to move away. Her hand was already on the door but his voice reached her.

"Three minutes, Kitten. Then you will be with me again."

She hated his confidence but she knew that she did not have the courage not to return to him in time. Her gaze was caught by the sinking sun when she returned. She wanted to enjoy its beauty but knew it would only delay the inevitable so she turned to the man waiting patiently for her.

The pillow between his legs and the food on the table made what would happen next very clear. He did not even have to tell her to come over. As she stood in front of him his eyes travelled slowly up her body, but it was not a caress, there was no sexual heat in his eyes, he was simply cataloguing her body. It was the look of a doctor noting the condition and imperfections of a body in his care. It made her feel flawed, and she wanted nothing more than to cover herself, but she knew better than to try.

"Kitten, you are a beautiful woman, never doubt it."

It was not a matter of doubt. She had a mirror which told her only too well that he was wrong. She saw him study her face for any reaction. She was not giving him any and she felt his anger rise.

"Kneel!"

His voice had lost the amused undertone and was pure command, and she complied quickly in the hope that she would not incense him more. He softly stroked a stray strand of her hair from her face.

"They have managed too well to teach you to hate yourself. We will have to work on that. Now, let's look at you. You are very pretty as you kneel there but I would like you to spread your legs a little more."

He stroked from her hair over her shoulder and down her arm, waking her body to his touch.

"Cross your wrists behind your back," he ordered.

She knew this position. She had been restrained in it too often to count, though assuming it without the force of biting metal against her skin was almost worse. She felt entirely at

133

his mercy, exposed worse than if he would have just thrown her down and raped her. She knew he saw the anger in her eyes. When he raised his hand and bent close she expected punishment, but he only stroked a finger down her cheek.

"It's alright, Kitten. Hate me if it makes it easier, but even though you might not realise it, this will make it all easier on you."

His eyes held all the pity in the world. She hated him even more for that. She did not want his pity. She had spent the last eleven years evading the efforts of the most powerful vampires on the planet to capture her. Every time she fell, she had picked herself up again and had brought up three children as well as she could in that time. Anger started to rise and she was glad of it.

"Now, when you are told to kneel, you will do so and remain in that position until you are told to change or we change your position for you. Is that clear?"

"Yes, Sir."

She heard the anger and hate in her voice, but he simply ignored it and offered her some bread instead. She wanted to refuse the food, to spit it in his face, but she was bound by her word. So she took the bite, and the ones following it. The bread was good, fragrant and spicy, but it tasted like sawdust.

After only four bites he stopped, deciding not to test her stomach's ability to retain more nourishment. His fingers stroked her cheek, the touch as gentle as a feather.

"So beautiful."

Kathryn heard the door open, heard the distinct snick of the latch and the even tread of shoes. Her eyes searched for the source of the sounds but Kieran grabbed hold of her chin and turned her head back to him.

"I have not given you permission to look away. Eyes on me."

As he held her in place she could hear whoever had entered hesitate at the door. Then the slow measured steps crossed the room. She trembled and hoped Kieran could not feel it as well, but the way he stroked her cheek, soothing and calm, suggested he did. His eyes held hers, let her see his power and feel his dominance.

"The view is staggering," Lord Lucian's voice sounded so close behind her that she almost jumped. The deep voice was breathless, as if he had run some distance rather than merely crossing the room.

"It is, isn't it, Milord," Kieran grinned. "But I assume you would like to have her for yourself now."

"Very much so."

As they exchanged places Kathryn realised that Lord Lucian must have fed, well and recently. His skin was blooming, almost human. His blue eyes caressed her, seemingly unable to lift from her kneeling form before him, but his questions were for Kieran.

"Anything I should know?"

"She has eaten, but as her doctor I would like her to have some more every two hours."

Lord Lucian nodded.

"Any punishments?" She tensed in horror, desperately thinking back if she had made any mistakes or if it even mattered. Would they just punish her for nothing if they wanted to?

"None, though communication is still an issue. I am concerned about her perception of herself."

The wrinkles at the corners of Lord Lucian's eyes drew up in amusement.

"We can deal with that. In time."

Even though he exchanged the words with Kieran, Lucian's eyes never left hers. Now he gave into the temptation to stroke over her hair, to caress the woman before him.

"Thank you, Kieran. If you would give me the box you can go. We will be fine until tomorrow."

"Yes, Milord." He handed the box over, and before departing, pressed a soft kiss on the top of her head. Seeing the box in the hands of the vampire who owned her made the shakes return a thousand fold. But he just calmly opened the box and took out the restraints.

"Your left wrist, please."

"Where are the girls?"

When he gripped her hair this time it was not gentle but controlling. He pulled her head back, stretching her neck almost to the point of pain. It terrified her though she could not hear meanness in his voice, just absolute control.

"You will not prevaricate, delay or avoid following an order. You will comply as promptly as you are able. Is that clear?"

This time there was no hesitation in her answer, she was by far too frightened. "Yes, Milord."

His hand tightened, pushing her a little closer to pain.

"What?" he demanded.

There was anger there. What had she done now? The title! She urgently corrected herself. "Sir."

The pull on her hair relaxed, allowing her neck to move into a more natural position, but he did not let go. His blue eyes held hers as his hand softly massaged her head to ease the sting, and she felt the terror in her mind ease, allowing her to breathe again. Only then did he sit back and repeat himself.

"Your left wrist, please!"

She gave it to him. There was no choice. The cuff was slipped onto her wrist. By slipping a finger between the leather and the cuff he made sure that it would not be too tight on her before holding out his hand for her other wrist. He fastened the second cuff and she automatically returned both wrists to her back expecting him to attach them to each other there. "Good girl!" he said, praising the little pet. He frowned but let whatever he saw in her face pass unchallenged.

"The girls have returned from the zoo and are having their dinner. They will tell you all about the wondrous red panda tomorrow. They have been told you are ill and understand that until you have recovered they can only see you for a few hours in the early afternoon each day. The rest of the day they will be well cared for and *not* your responsibility. You will stop worrying about them."

As if that would ever be possible. His hands were resting on her shoulders, his thumbs stroking in even patterns up and down her throat as his voice dropped and surrounded her like a velvet touch.

137

"I believe I have not yet received a welcome kiss."

His lips were surprisingly soft as they stroked over hers but not as surprising as her own reaction. Her lips opened under his, welcoming the taste, the feeling and the strange familiarity. She felt his lips curve against hers before his hand took a firm hold of the back of her head and the kiss turned from a soft caress to fiery passion. His tongue forced its way into her mouth to demand absolute surrender. To her own horror she gave it to him. When he withdrew she raised slightly on her knees as if to follow him, her lips swollen and wet, her breath coming in pants. His blue eyes were heavy as he let his head rest back, his black hair a cloud of silk surrounding his pale skin, and his too red lips were drawn in the kind of smile a man's face only held for sex or a job well done.

9

Trust

She saw him for what he was – the most powerful vampire in the south of England, the man who held the lives of hundreds of vampires, witches, shifters and fairies in his hands, and now the lives of her children as well. She had no doubt of his power and as she knelt before him, naked and exposed, he left her with no uncertainty about her being in his power.

His nostrils flared and she was sure that he was able to smell the moistness developing between her legs. The smile deepened, a hint of fang clearly visible. She swallowed, but his next question erased all thoughts of arousal.

"Who are the twins?"

"My sisters." Her answer was automatic, not even considering that this could be thought of as a lie. It was not one in her eyes. The girls had been her sisters for eight years, no matter that they did not share a single gene with her. She saw the fury gather in his eyes and tried to stay the coming storm.

"They are my sisters, they have been for eight years; even their passports say that. They know no different and it really does not matter who their actual parents were."

"How did they come to be your sisters?"

She did not know how much to tell him but also realised she would have to tell him some of it.

"They were used in an attempt to make me more amenable. Their mother had been killed, and when I escaped I could not leave them there. So I took them."

"Who?"

She did not understand his question. Who what?

"Which territory's Lord was it? I have reports of most of your movements in the last decade but there are holes. One of them covers a period of ten months approximately eight years ago. When you reappeared you seemed to have found twin sisters. Some suspect that they are your daughters, but as you have never hidden Anna's parentage I assumed there must be something else behind it."

She stared at him. He had researched her. No one had ever gone beyond trying to figure out where she was at that moment. She bit her lip. His eyes were entirely predatory now. "Kathryn, I always plan my campaigns well."

This should have frightened her more than it did. One of the reasons she had been able to escape so often was that they always underestimated her, eventually.

"It was no Lord. I had been stupid. Paul and I were stranded in an Italian village at the Lago di Garda. I loved it there and had managed to get a job at a restaurant. It was at

140

the border between the territories of the Lady of Verona and the Lord of Trento."

"Justitiana and Antonio." He interrupted and she nodded before she continued.

"I thought we were fairly safe. There should have been no reason for a vampire to be around there, close enough to feel my presence. I thought I would pass unrecognised." It had been an easier time then. Her blood call had not been as strong; a vampire would have needed to be within a few metres to feel her. In the last few years, that had changed to a few hundred metres, then a few kilometres. She wondered if she should have tried to enter the city of London differently, if the tunnel would have been safer. But they had been running from Paris and a plane had been the fastest way to get out. His finger stroked her cheek, reclaiming her attention.

"I could feel you from the moment you entered my territory, even before you had reached British soil." He had guessed what her thoughts had been. "Your sisters?" He prompted.

Well, there was not much more to tell.

"A band of rogues came for us. The leader thought that binding me would make him strong enough to control a small territory of his own. They watched me, saw me playing with a little girl and thought I liked children. When they came to get me they killed a whore for her twin daughters. As long as I behaved the girls were treated well."

"How did you get away?"

"Luck. Lady Justitiana had been informed of the rogues and sent some of her court to clean up. They slayed them, but

141

I was locked in the cellar of an abandoned house the rogues had used as a hide-out and so weak that they could not feel me. They left. The girls were with me; I finally broke through the lock and found enough cash in the house to buy passports for the children and get away. Paul had left when I disappeared and I was alone. I was selfish enough to take the children. They were mine already by that stage. I had cared for them, protected them as best I could for five months in that hell. They *are* my sisters!"

The last sentence came out forcefully. He cradled her face. "Shh – I understand." For a moment she wished she could read his mind.

"There are other questions I need to ask you, information I need in order to proceed." This made her tense and suspicious. Proceed with what? He ignored her tension, though under the concentration he had focused on her he must have seen it.

"You did not recognise the anal plug?"

Her eyes dropped to the floor. She was not entirely sure why – she was not shy, definitely not about sexual things, but she did not want to answer a question too intimate for comfort.

"Have you had anal sex before?"

"Yes." What else was there to say? Expectant silence and a raised eyebrow made her add a "Sir" belatedly.

"Did you like it?" His hand returned to stroke gently over her head, like one would a child. Ironic considering the anything but innocent topic.

"No, Sir."

142

Yes, she had been raped anally – been there, done that, didn't even get the t-shirt.

His hand gently found her chin and forced it up again, not allowing her any room to avoid his eyes.

"How many men have taken you at the same time?"

Now there was only pure hate in her mind and voice. "That very much depends on your definition of 'at the same time'."

His eyes had turned expressionless again, hiding his true emotion though his hands remained gentle.

"Have you ever performed oral sex on someone?"

He could not be serious – obviously she had. "Yes, Sir."

"Without force?"

"Yes."

"Have you ever had your mouth fucked?" She understood the difference too well. A thousand memories rose with the terror and her stomach rolled but she managed a nod. There were worse things.

"Kathryn, look at me." He had leant forward again so that his blue eyes were so close. She saw concern and determination. "You will give me a blowjob now. I want you to pleasure me with your mouth and then drink down my seed. Every drop."

She froze as he pulled his shirt over his head and opened his belt. As he snapped his trousers open her hands tensed. He had gone commando under his trousers, and as he bared himself to her eyes she saw that even semi-aroused he was not small. He was beautiful. And he was entirely clean-shaven. She tried to reach for him, an automatic reaction brought short by the bonds around her wrists. Helplessly, she looked at him.

"You do not need your hands."

The deep voice had gone husky, his hands tight on the armrests, although he relaxed them under her gaze. She saw his lips part under the increasing speed of his breath, his throat spasm as he swallowed convulsively; for a moment she felt powerful. She could not keep the smile off her lips. Leaning forward to give a blowjob is less easy than one would assume when your hands are restricted to a position behind your back, but she'd had practice, although she desperately tried to keep those memories out of her head. More importantly, she noticed, he seemed to have had practice. His thighs closed around her to give her just enough support to allow her to free rein without limiting her movements.

When she swept her tongue from the base of his penis to its tip in one move, his shoulders came off the backrest. The power was heady, possibly because she had never thought she might have it. He grew impossibly large as she swirled her tongue over his head before sucking him into her mouth. She felt his moan throughout his body. Rolling her eyes up she watched him react to her movements as she found the ridge running around the head and teased it with little licks.

His face had turned to granite and she knew it was not from anger but desire. She started to suck, only the tip of his cock, but with every pull his muscles seemed to tense a little more until she could see them corded on his arms and shoulders. When she varied her movement with a lick into the slit of his penis at each upstroke his head fell back with a

144

tortured expression. She enjoyed her power and, surprisingly, the taste. The taste of semen had always made her gag long before it hit the back of her throat, but he tasted fresher. There was a strange chalkiness to it, laced with copper and something decadent. He tasted like he felt – like steel smothered in old wine, hard and licentious. She relaxed her throat, and without warning went deep, engulfing him whole with her mouth. It was not easy, but it was worth it when he screamed, his body leaning forward to curl over her.

She could not hold the position for long; she had to come up for air. He relaxed back into the sofa, his eyes closed and his breathing coming in heavy pants. She started to alternate short sucking bobs of her head followed by deep movements. For a second she froze when his hand came to rest on her head, memories flashing to other hands pushing her head down cruelly, ripping at her hair. But he simply started to stroke her head gently, massaging her neck. She glimpsed up at his face and realised that his eyes had not closed entirely. Holding that narrowed blue gaze she started to suck in earnest, bobbing her head whilst her tongue described little circles around the head on the upstroke.

She felt him start to tremble, the hand on her head still gentle but now holding on to her for dear life. She knew he was close, saw it in those brilliant blue eyes that had opened to watch her. The taste on her tongue changed, got sharper, and she prepared herself for his seed hitting the back of her throat. When it did she did not stop sucking, but rather increased the speed, pushing him past concentration and control. His body convulsed on the sofa, every new pull extending his orgasm and drawing a yell from his throat. She was fascinated, loving the feel of his softening penis in her mouth enough that the slightly bitter taste of his cum did not bother her. The yells subsided to moans before his hand gently stopped her movement. She let him slip from her mouth and sat up to admire her handiwork.

This controlled man lay replete before her, breathing as if he had run a marathon, but his muscles had relaxed, his face at peace. She saw the effort it took him to lean closer to her. His thumb stroked the corner of her mouth and then pressed into it, her mouth filling with the taste of his seed again as he fed her a spilled drop; then his mouth found hers and chased the taste. Still pressed against his lips, his hands lifted her to his lap, her knees coming around his thighs in a position reminiscent to that of the first evening. He settled her against the front of his body, the flick of a finger opening the safety clasp of the cuffs. He held her as if she were precious. When the kiss ended he was wearing her like a soft blanket and her hands had somehow come around his neck. Looking into his face so close, she saw the sleepy satisfaction etched in the lines and the languid expression in his eyes.

"Thank you," he said.

She liked it when he spoke with this lazy, sated voice and she gave into the pressure of his hand that guided her head to rest on his shoulder. Like this he was almost safe, physically unable to ask any more of her. When he asked if she was cold she was barely able to shake her head, her body was so tired. Her eyes had closed without her realising and she could not muster enough strength to open them again. She felt no need to sleep, just utter relaxation. As he started to stroke her back softly, up and down, she had no inclination to move. She just wanted to rest there and not think.

She was floating in nothingness when she heard a strange noise, a plastic click, but before she could emerge wholly from her relaxed lethargy the scent of ginger reached her nose and his hands spread spicy-smelling oil over her back, massaging it into her neck and shoulders.

"I will smell like Christmas," she said drowsily.

"Good enough to eat."

His voice had lost its husky arousal, remaining only deep and controlled. The sound reverberated through her, penetrating her muscles and loosening her last few concerns. She could not even react to the idea that a vampire calling her good enough to eat might not be the best thing. His hands wandered lower, stroking over her rib cage and kneading the muscles around her spine.

She let herself drift, simply soaking up his touch. When his downwards movement reached her ass and his talented fingers began to knead her cheeks, she tensed, but under the sensual onslaught of his gentle hands, the tension was short-lived. She soon started to melt into him again, feeling her body give up any pretence of control under the joy of his hands massaging the sensitive skin on her thighs. She did not move, even when his hands began to slowly stroke her inner thigh.

She was warm and safe, and nothing was being demanded of her. She did not have to protect anyone, no decisions needed to be made – she could just float. Her serenity was not even punctured by his hands slowly pulling her ass cheeks apart and spreading massage oil down the crease, rimming her gently. It was only when his finger pushed past the tight sphincter that her tranquillity was disrupted. Her eyes opened to his intent and controlled gaze. Whilst his body was still just as relaxed under her, his mind had clearly recovered and was completely in control. Hers was still too hazy from the pleasure, making it hard to react.

"Shhh – let it happen. Just relax. It does not hurt."

She felt like it should, it always had in the past, but it did not hurt. Her mind could not process the pleasure, the penetration, the utter confusion of the memories in her mind with the reality she was experiencing. Instead of floating, she hurled through an emotional hurricane with him being the only fixed point at its centre. His eyes halted the mental freefall and his solidness under her hands anchored her to the present.

"That's it, Kathryn, hold on to me. I am here. I will not let you fall."

His other hand came up to cradle her head. He brought their brows to rest together and held her gaze as his finger gently pushed into her and withdrew. When a second finger joined the first he started to kiss the little hitches on her breath from her mouth, playing with her lips. Every kiss was deeper than the last, his lips claiming her attention, diverting it from the gentle stretch at her ass, the slow scissoring of his fingers inside her. She did not notice when it was no longer his fingers that penetrated into her, but the tip of a much larger object.

His kisses were addictive, taking all her attention, and when his hand left the massage of her neck to stroke her clitoris in lazy movements, even breathing became a challenge. Her whole being was caught between his mouth feeding on hers and his fingers playing over that sensitive nub. A gentle spiral of pleasure rose in her so that when he pressed a finger fully on her clitoris, the sudden hitch in arousal made her jerk back and something large slid into her ass.

She tried to move away but his hands had locked around her hips, holding her in place. She tried to push against the object, expelling it from her, but he was pressing her cheeks together firmly, making it impossible. She was sitting upright over him, her hands on his shoulders. She could have scratched at his eyes but they were holding her world together. She felt tears streaming down her face but all she could do was breathe and let her body adjust. As she slowly came to terms with the invasion, his hands started to knead little circles into her lower back, relaxing the so tense muscles.

"You are so brave, so beautiful. I know this is not easy. I know it frightens you."

The world came back to her in stages. The warmth of the room, the softness of the chair below her knees and the hardness of his erection pressing against her, all starting to intrude, taking attention away from the feeling of absolute fullness in her ass.

"How does it feel?"

She did not know what to say. She did not want to speak. His fingers moved down, gently brushing the plug in her ass,

149

for a moment intensifying the feelings.

"How does it feel? Uncomfortable," she said reluctantly, unwilling to make any admission.

He smiled but the movements of his fingers stalled. "What else?"

When she did not answer quickly enough his fingers returned to play over the plug.

"What else?"

"Full." She saw the arousal in his eyes skyrocket and felt his cock jerk underneath her.

"What else?" he said, his voice remaining controlled.

His reaction to her hesitation was more acute this time – he pushed her ass cheeks together and pressed her body downwards so that her clitoris rubbed over his cock. The double sensation ripped through her, making the point.

"Owned," she screamed. "I feel owned."

His laughter was joyous and triumphant, filling the room and her head, only stopping when he had pulled her lips down and consumed her mouth ravenously. He was still smiling when he ended the kiss.

"You *are* owned. You are mine – body and soul. I want you to feel me everywhere. I want my cock riding your ass, my seed painting your insides. I want my scent on you everywhere. I want you to feel owned. I want you to feel mine."

His voice was intense, a declaration of intent and victory at the same time. She wanted to tell him that she would not be owned to the core but his hands had rubbed her clitoris against his body with every sentence and her head was spinning. The pleasure spiral rose again as his hand started to tease the aroused nub. His earlier attentions had spread her moisture all over the area and it was easy for him to run his fingers in ever tighter circles around her clitoris. In an attempt to escape the pressure she moved, but he was having none of it. Instead, two fingers of his other hand slipped into her vagina, setting a punishing rhythm of thrusts. She felt the anal plug move inside her in time with his fingers and a strange pleasure rose. Moans were ripped from her throat and she was insensible with sensation.

"Yes, feel how full you are. Let me hear your pleasure."

His fingers moved ever faster, rubbing mercilessly over and on both sides of her clitoris, his other hand matching the speed with his thrusts into her. Then he stopped, and through a desperate sob she heard her name.

"Kathryn."

Her head rolled back on her neck but his voice drew her eyes to his. When he had her attention a smile played over his lips, and with one last thrust he pinched her clitoris and ordered, "Come for me, Kathryn. Scream for me."

And she did – loudly and raggedly as his hands milked the last dregs of pleasure from her.

She collapsed over him, resting again in his arms. She felt the lazy strokes of his hand over her back and the soft kisses on her brow.

"The next time someone asks you about having had an orgasm you can say without any doubt that you have had one. You come beautifully."

She hated him for what he had reduced her to. Her

151

muscles were still weak but she tried to scratch out his eyes. When he caught her hands, she went crazy, hitting him and screaming.

"Stop, Kathryn! Stop it now!"

She heard the words but did not understand them. All she could do was scream insults and accusations, anything to drown out her own fear. She felt his pressure on her mind but was too far gone for him to have any hold on her. She was lifted and carried; she had no idea where to and did not care. Insensible with rage she felt her hands being restrained over her head, her legs forced apart and attached to cuffs at the ankles. She could not move but it did not matter. She was so filled with anger and hate that she could only fight. A warm body came down on hers, covering her, limiting the last bit of movement. Hands imprisoned her face but even restrained like that, she fought and screamed her rage.

"Shhhh, Kathryn, shhhh. Stop it. I am here. You are not alone. Shhhh."

When she did not stop screaming his hand came over her mouth. She bit hard until she tasted his blood and still he did not remove his hand. Instead her head was pressed against his shoulder, just held. It was the lack of air that made her relax, the dark spots in front of her eyes blotted out her fury. She gasped, her body going limp under him. When her sight cleared, his eyes were very serious, his thumbs feathering her cheeks whilst he still held her head.

"Kathryn, calm down. You are safe. Breathe with me."

She felt his breath on her skin but could not bring her own under control. He pressed his mouth to hers, forcing his own rhythm of breath on her. Slowly she adjusted to it, and his taste in her mouth allowed her to calm.

"Can you tell me what made you so afraid?"

She wanted to lash out at him, not with words, she had gone past that, but with every ounce of physical strength in her body.

"Kathryn, I will not accept your behaviour again."

She spat at him. He wiped it off with his thumb and the smile that rose to his lips was anything but reassuring.

"Oh, I will enjoy this." He let his finger run over her lips, pulling back laughing as she snapped at it. Then his eyes turned hot. "Now I get to play."

She was terrified. She had no idea why she had acted so stupidly. Not only had she spat at him, she had *bitten* him. Her body broke into violent tremors when his tongue stroked over her throat, but it did not stop to crush. Instead it travelled further south, halting briefly to tease each nipple, drawing a little circle around both. She knew what he was about to do and with every touch she felt heat and fear. When his fingers slipped into her, she whimpered. Her skin was still sensitive and swollen from his previous ministrations but his touch was soft enough not to cause her physical pain. It was terror that produced silent tears. She felt them fall only to be caught by his caressing finger.

"Why? Why does this frighten you so much?"

She shook her head in one jerky, defiant movement. His thumb stroked over her clitoris, a quick jolt of pleasure which made her body arch. He took it as an invitation to engulf her nipple in his hot mouth, gently lapping at it, not sucking yet but preparing her for the sensation. She wanted to stop him, to push him away but her hands were bound. She desperately tried to keep the pleasure away but he knew her reactions too well. She screwed her eyes shut, trying to build walls against him, and wailed for him to stop.

"Tell me why it frightens you?"

She just wanted him to stop making her feel that way. "You make me into nothing!" she screamed.

His movements stopped, even the fingers on her cheek stopped their gentle caresses. Her body humming with pleasure, her mind was scrambling, and the sudden cessation of sensation jarred to make her eyes snap open. His eyes were close and very, very controlled.

"Kathryn, you are everything! To me you are everything."

His thumb started to stroke around her clitoris, her pleasure spiralling upward. She wanted to shut him out again but his blue eyes held her close to him. She felt the wave rising as her body tightened with each stroke of his finger. Tears ran down her cheeks, fogging her sight.

"Stay with me, Baby. I am here to catch you."

The wave crested. Her body tightened and pleasure swamped her mind, a gentle wind ripping through her body, taking her mind and cradling it safely. He crooked his finger inside her and the wave was no longer gentle. It took over and she became lost again as her eyes fluttered closed, but his mouth descending on hers, demanding entrance and consuming all her fear. And she gave it to him. She felt him hold her together, body and soul. She was too tired to fight, so she let him have her.

She felt him remove the restraints and gather her in his arms. He lifted her into his lap and wrapped a soft blanket around her. She was not unconscious, but in a strange state of calm, floating in safety. And she heard him, possibly heard him for the first time really.

"Baby, you are mine and I will always keep you safe. You will always be mine."

And she cried. She cried for every February fourteenth when her body had taken over her mind and horrific things had been done to it. She cried for the shame, the humiliation and the pain. She cried until she could not cry anymore, until her eyes were swollen closed. Somehow it made her chuckle when she heard the gentle litany he was whispering to her as he rocked and petted her.

"So beautiful. You are so beautiful, so brave, so smart."

The reluctant laughter was swiftly followed by hiccups which somehow seemed to make everything lighter. A hand stroked hair off her face and she blinked at him with her swollen eyes.

"How do you feel?" he asked quietly.

She had no idea how she felt, how she was supposed to feel. Somehow none of it mattered in the least.

"Empty."

Her answer seemed to satisfy him, a kiss on her nose rewarding her for something, but she had no idea what it was.

"Just rest."

And somehow she did, even through being carried to the bathroom and having her face washed. She was carried back to the living room, fed some fruit, and then lain on the settee.

155

It was surprisingly soothing as he sat beside her on the floor, spreading paperwork around, typing on a tablet. She wanted to reach out to touch his hair but something felt wrong with that. Her mind was too relaxed but slowly this realisation, the discrepancy between wanting to touch and knowing that she should not, started to jar. She lay there and thought as reality gradually intruded and her body lost the languid serenity it had held.

Lucian put aside his work to take her hand. She tried to remove it from his grasp, not because she did not want to be touched but because the confusion and fear was rising again. She was not yet drowning but she could feel the ever present tension and vigilance hovering at the brink of her mind. He did not let her take back her hand.

"Hey, the world is coming back, I see." There was regret in his voice. "I was hoping you would get a little more time."

He bent to kiss her hand softly and then rested his cheek on it, his eyes closing. Her other hand could not help stroking the glorious hair that spread on the blanket and it made him smile. But that shared tranquillity could not last. He lifted his head, turning it to kiss the palm of her stroking hand before taking it into his own hand.

"Can we talk?" he asked.

His voice was soft, wrapping around her like a second blanket. It dimmed the pressures of reality and held them at bay. He had asked if they could talk, and although she was not entirely sure if that was really an option, she could at least try to listen. Fourteen years of running, fourteen years of escape and fear and pain. Not once had anyone stopped to talk and listen. Perhaps this was the time. He was waiting for an answer, his eyes telling her that he was not sure what that answer might be.

"Ok," she said. "Let's talk."

The smile passing over his lips was bittersweet, a result of her willingness to talk but still refusing to grant him the intimacy of his name on her lips. Should it frighten her how well she knew this man after such a short time? Probably. On the other hand it also gave her a strange feeling of comfort.

"Kathryn, if you could have anything in the world, what would it be?"

The question made her think. It was clear that he was not looking for a material answer but rather a more substantial, deeper desire. The problem with desires is that they said a lot, often too much, about you. They were also weapons that could be used against you and he had already proven too adept at manipulating her. She bit her lip and immediately one of his hands released hers and reached to stroke her cheek – softly, calming, insinuating a gentle rhythm into her body and mind. Still, the most basic answer was so simple that she could not betray anything, and maybe she could find a way out for all of them.

Her mind was suddenly in overdrive, a plan tentatively raising its head from the calm ruins inside her head, but it would only work if she understood his motivations. She needed to convince him, and she could not do so lying there in her languid state of calm. She pushed on her elbows and felt his stroking hand fall away from her cheek, though she kept her hand in his as she made herself more comfortable.

He tried to stop her from sitting up but she silenced his protest with a raised hand. Looking down at him she realised that no matter how she was sitting, he would always be the one in charge of the situation. She almost rued the suggestion she was about to make, but she also realised that this knowledge of power and control was exactly why she had to make the suggestion. It might be her only chance of salvation.

"Sir,'" she had to take a deep breath before continuing, "Sir, what I would like most, above all, is to be left alone."

The sadness in his eyes was almost heartbreaking. She saw the words hovering on his lips, but she quickly covered them with her finger.

"Sir, please let me finish," she said, barely believing her own daring.

She swallowed, but he just kissed the fingers over his lips and then cradled her hand to his cheek.

"Sir, you have bonded with me and gained the advantage of an ErGer already. There is no real need for me to be here. I could take the girls and live close. You only need my blood and I could provide that. I know you have to renew the bond regularly but I can come here for that too. I can…"

Her voice started to dwindle, she knew she desperately needed to make a strong argument and that she had already bungled it, but it was almost impossible to concentrate with those expressionless eyes fixed on hers. He just knelt before her like a motionless statue, beautiful and cold. However, the coldness might be what would get him to agree. If he was as Machiavellian, cold and calculating as she was counting on him being then this was the best solution. His restraint over taking her blood showed that he was less interested in the feeling of wellbeing it infused a vampire with than the power it could provide. She could give him that without being so close, and most importantly, without having the girls this close to them. He would have to renew the bond periodically, possibly once or twice a month, but he would not need her in house for that. Moreover, even if he wanted to gift members of his court with access to her it did not require her to live at court. She could just come visit from however far away he would let her be.

"I promised not to run and I will not. I do not break my word."

Now she could only hope and wait. His expression gave nothing away. He just listened and watched her. She had no idea if she had read him right. She waited for his reaction and with every second that passed, her body and mind tensed even more. He pressed another kiss on the palm of her hand before letting it go and slowly rising on his knees until he was able to meet her eyes straight on. His hands came around her face, cradling it gently, and her hopes plummeted. She knew what he was about to say before he had even started to speak.

"No."

Nothing more. One word in a tone as unmovable as granite, but she had to try one more time. When she opened her mouth he stopped her, stroking his thumb over her mouth as if to wipe away the words that were bubbling up.

"Let me explain, please," he said. He was still willing to talk; she could work with that.

"There are three reasons why I will not consent to your

plan and none of them is linked to a distrust in your willingness to stand by your word. Firstly, you and the girls would simply not be safe. It has become widely known that the ErGer Kathryn has become my mate and I have too many enemies who will want to harm you and the girls. And so do you."

She wanted to argue but his finger came to rest on her mouth again.

"We could get around that. But the other two reasons outweigh even that one."

He paused for a moment and took a deep breath, almost as if he were nervous about what he was about to say. Still, his eyes were intent on hers, pushing through her thoughts to imprint his words on her.

"Kathryn, you are not particularly good at looking after yourself. I do not know if this is a result of what others have done to you, but you have no sense of self-preservation, no way of looking after yourself."

She wanted to protest, to fight him on it, but he continued before she could marshal her objections into a coherent format.

"Your life centres around the girls, and the moment you realise that they are entirely safe and protected you will lose that. The moment you are not in absolute survival mode something will happen in your mind and you will stop fighting. You will stop fighting for your life and I cannot allow that."

"I have looked after myself since I was twelve years old. Your perception of me is simply laughable." She almost spat the words, unable to remain silent one minute longer. Her reaction had no effect on him aside from making him stroke his lips over hers again in a soft caress. It made her want to hit him. And his eyes told her that he knew it, just as she knew that she would be restrained before she could follow through with the movement. He waited; his eyes challenging her into violence. She saw disappointment when she refused to pick up that gauntlet.

"You are not weak. On the contrary, you might be the strongest woman I have ever met. You are intelligent, loyal, loving and very beautiful, even though you cannot see that. But you need to learn to live."

"So you are telling me that you are tying me up and fucking me for my own good? How magnanimous of you!"

"I could tell you that you need the restraints, but the whole truth is simple. I want you, body and soul, and I will claim every part of you." His eyes were no longer expressionless. They were burning with heat and desire and a dark possession that left no room for doubt.

"I won't let you!"

The conviction in the words surprised her. She had come here expecting to lose herself, not to declare war on the man who held her fate. His laughter surprised her even more. It filled the room and reached her core in a triumphant wave.

"Fight me, Kathryn! I will enjoy every second of it!"

10

Choice

That day became something of a blueprint for the ones that followed. She never left that room, only aware of a world outside through the stories the girls imparted in the two hours she was allowed to spend with them. Anna told her on the first day that it was OK that her Mama was ill and had to spend so much time asleep. From that she deduced that the children were kept in ignorance of her actual position here.

Kathryn had originally been terrified about the treatment of the girls but she soon learnt that their life was just as regulated as hers, possibly more normal than she ever had been able to give them. In quiet moments she admitted to herself that it hurt and made her feel insufficient. She learned that the girls spent time with tutors each day before being taken for outings in the city. What worried her was that they apparently also spent time alone with Lord Lucian before she woke.

Kathryn was entirely aware of the fact that her sleep was not natural. Before dawn he would overwhelm her mind and push her into a deep slumber to remove the blanket from her mind whenever he wanted her to begin her day. She was also aware that she woke freshly bathed, with her hair clean and braided, always on the settee on which she had not normally gone to sleep. In the beginning she was allowed five or ten minutes alone in the bathroom for necessities, but as the days passed, the rules imposed upon her became stricter and infractions cost her more and more time.

The first time she refused food, she had lost the privilege of washing her face, but eventually every moment of her day, every action she undertook was controlled and often taken from her by one of the men. She hated the way her world became more and more restricted, became smaller and smaller. After the girls left she would be ritually handed over to Kieran whose attentions would alternate between reading to her and trying to get her to talk about her life.

After two or three hours, Lord Lucian would return and claim the rest of her waking hours for himself. These were the times she found most confusing and terrifying. He would play with her body in every possible way, but surprisingly never pushing significantly beyond her comfort levels. When she began to forget to articulate her answers he gagged her with the ball gag, but replaced it after only ten minutes with a simple cloth when he realised that her terror and hate of the implement was not abating. He would force pleasure on her, but her orgasms were gentle waves, not mind-blowing earthquakes like the ones of the first day after the bonding.

He never took her blood, but at times she felt him perilously close to sinking his teeth into her neck. The dreaded black box continued to contain no more frightening implements than those introduced on the first day, though they differed in form and material.

The first change came when rather than being handed over to Kieran, Brandon took his place. At first she did not think there to be any noticeable change. She was bid to kneel at his feet and fed as she had been to begin with, but the change came after that. Instead of bidding her to bring him a book from the shelves lining the walls, he pulled out a blue and white picture book, one of those she had used to teach Anna to read French, from his pocket and held it out to her. She had no idea what he wanted from her.

Cautiously she took the book, running her eyes over the cover and the little frog hopping along the white writing inside. It read: "Il était… une petite grenouille" just as it had the thousand times she had read it to her daughter before bed. Her eyes rose to the blonde vampire and she noted his discomfort. What was happening? What significance did this book have? His eyes darted away from hers and he suddenly seemed to be interested in a patch of the carpet at their feet.

"What do you want me to do with the book?" His silence and embarrassment had pushed her into actually asking a question.

"Teach me."

"You want me to teach you French?" The discomfort and embarrassment coming from him was now almost palpable and the answer was gruff bordering on rude.

164

"Je parle le français," he said. So he spoke French, and with better pronunciation than she did herself. Clarification came in his second sentence: "Je voudrais que vous m'enseigniez à lire." He wanted her to teach him how to read.

What to say? She had taught all three girls to read but he was not one of her children; this was an old and powerful vampire. Her hesitation made him raise his hands and she saw such vulnerability there, and shame. She realised that it might be easy to ask for help reading when you are six, but it was much more difficult when you were so much older. But she recognised the gift she was being given. So, just as she had with each of the girls, she raised the book, opened it to the first page and started to read the words to him: "Il était une fois…" And just as she had with the girls she made him search out all the "E"s in the text, and then all the "M"s. She had no idea if this was the best way to teach someone to read, she just knew she had done it like this before. His body surrounded her while he followed her finger as she sounded out the words carefully. She felt his excitement when recognising a letter or word before she sounded it out. Just as with the girls, his patience and endurance wavered after about thirty minutes. He did not stop her as she closed the book at the end of the page and only gave her a heartbreakingly sweet smile.

"Tomorrow again." It was almost a question and she gave it the answering smile and nod it deserved. His raised eyebrow brought her back to her position and situation and she quickly corrected herself. "Yes, Brandon." She did not notice that it was the first time she had called any of them by name.

The afternoon took a further unpredicted turn when Brandon made her rise and threw some clothes at her. She caught them and initially was confused. It was a grey sports bustier and bright pink shorts, clothes normally adorning mannequins in high end sports shops or celebrities in aerobics videos for bored housewives. She had never thought that anyone actually wore anything like this, or at least hadn't since the 80s.

"I am more than happy to help you put those on," he stated.

The drawl and the grin were wicked and left no doubt about his willingness to follow through with his offer. To his amusement, it took her less than ten seconds to pull on both pieces of clothing. He touched the wall and it opened out into a hidden room. There was no doubt about its purpose. This was a state of the art gym with weight benches, cross trainers and rowing machines. Seeing this room and the grinning vampire waving her into it, she wondered whether she was going to hate it or love it.

He bypassed the weight bench, for which she was eternally grateful, and started her on the cross trainer. If she had thought this would be easier, she was disappointed. For the last ten days she had barely moved. Her most strenuous activity had been struggling against the restraints that held her down as her body was being aroused by a myriad kisses. Saying that she was out of shape would be a lie. She would have needed to have been in some sort of shape for that. She had spent more than the last decade undernourished, alternating between bouts of physical abuse and fleeing for her life. She wondered every day if she would be able to feed her children.

Twenty minutes on the cross trainer left her sweating, ten minutes on the rowing machine made her arms shake. He was still not finished with her. While she was unpleasantly sweaty he pulled her out onto a wide mat and tried to teach her how to break a hold, first when being grabbed from the front, then from behind. Her confusion had been pushed so far that she had reached a place of stunned acceptance when Lord Lucian appeared and handed her a weapon.

"A sword?"

His grin was more than boyish, it was mischievous. "Actually, this is a foil, a practice weapon to teach the use of the sword, which today is in the form of the epee, the most common weapon for fencing. You need to learn to defend yourself."

No amount of stunned acceptance could stand up to this statement. She simply had to laugh out loud.

"I hate to tell you this but the days when one had a handy sword within reach when walking down a dark alley are long gone."

Something happened when she laughed, something changed in his eyes; a depth opened, threatening to swallow her whole. It took her breath away and sobered her. She wanted to ask what was happening, but was not sure she had the courage, not because she feared his reaction, but because she feared her own. Suddenly there was a sexual tension in the air, an awareness she did not know how to deal with or even describe. She expected him to step in and make use of this sudden link but instead he stepped back.

"I love that laugh." His voice was almost dry, out of line with the heat burning in his eyes. The next half hour was a whirling mix of commands and instructions about her correct positioning and grip of the weapon. It was frustrating and fascinating at the same time. Should she not have been happy about this? Not only was she learning to defend herself, but he was refraining from touching her with the usual sensual undertones. She was unable to think or enjoy it for too long though as utter exhaustion took over. When she could no longer lift her arms he called a halt to the session and took the foil from her hand. For a moment she could only stand there panting, all her concentration focused on her aching muscles and the need to draw in air. She was almost thankful for the arm that came around her waist and the chest she was pulled against to lean on. She needed help to lift the offered bottle of water and did not even mind that the same hand covering hers also kept her from bolting down the water as she wanted to. His breath against her temple cooled her whilst his soft kisses along her jaw left her relaxed, which said something about the effect the last week had had on her. Instinctively she recognised that his touch did not require anything of her. She could just enjoy the feeling of his strength and care, the warmth of his chest on her back, the scent that stroked her senses and reached into the depth of her mind.

"I smell!" She could hear the humiliation in her own voice, just as she heard the smile in his answer.

"Yes, you do."

With a quick kiss to her neck he released her. "Go soak in

the bath for a while but leave the door open, just in case you fall asleep."

She had only taken two steps before she turned back, not sure why or what she wanted to say. He had not even broken a sweat and his calm strength was more seductive and dangerous than she would ever have thought possible. The last seven days of constant exposure to his blend of gentle control and absolute confidence had been more devastating than the weeks of brutality and pain of the past, nibbling away at the walls she had erected between herself and the world. She knew that he would soon be able to break her more thoroughly than anyone had before and that she was not entirely sure she still wanted to fight him on it.

"Why can you not just be like the others?" He understood her question, she saw it in his eyes and the slow smile stretching his lips; she also realised that she had given away more than she should have with the question, as so many times before.

"Because I choose not to be."

Letting the hot water relax her knotted muscles gave her the opportunity to think over his answer, occupying her mind so much that she could not revel in the unexpected luxury of being allowed to wash herself. He chose not to be like the others. Choice was a concept that had lost almost all meaning to her over the years. She had not even had the choice of where to run to, normally basing her decision on the thickness of her wallet and the schedule of the most convenient means of public transport. Choice meant responsibility, so the question arose: what if she was not responsible for what had happened to her? She might not have been to blame for what had been done to her, but she was responsible for what it had made her, how it affected her, just as every single vampire who had brutalised her had been responsible for what they had become. They had had a choice, as had she.

Her exhausted body was convincing more and more of her cells and synapses to succumb to the idea of letting go and welcoming sleep. Not even her rational mind, which suggested that sleeping in a hot tub was not one of the wisest ideas she had ever had, was able to combat the slow, languid creep of oblivion. A thought rose from the depth of her mind momentarily. Was this proof that she lacked self-preservation? She discarded that thought immediately, her mind was too aware of Lucian's closeness to recognise her sleepiness as a true danger. Her mind was proven right when arms lifted her from the water. With the last impediment to sleep removed, she embraced oblivion.

She woke on the settee, with him beside her surrounded by papers and documents. It had quickly become a habit of his. He would sit on the floor and when she woke he would tell her about whichever of his many business interests he was working on at that moment.

She had quickly realised that through his own work, and as advisor to many of his court, his interests were varied and diverse. He owned a wide range of restaurants and shops, large and small, local and nationwide, and he also held a controlling interest in various financial and legal service providers as well as a theatre. She was almost certain that there was more but she could barely get her head around the problems and decisions he told her about. Nor did she entirely understand why he told her, other than that it kept her quiet for a while, allowing him to finish whatever he had been working on at that time.

She moved her arm and felt the agony of muscle ache. Lucian tapped his fingers against the manila folder in his hand for a moment before setting it aside and turning to her.

"How much does it hurt?" Her wince had already given that away so she saw no reason to hide her discomfort from him as she sat up.

"Bad; amazingly so."

He grinned. "It will get better over time."

She was still rearranging her aching legs into a comfortable position when three large catalogues landed on her lap, the top one bearing the crest and label of University College London. She knew the crest well. One of her secret pleasures had been the job at Gower Street, in the heart of the campus. Every day she had listened to students talk, envied them for the life they had, but also loved the fact that she was able to soak up the atmosphere of learning. In her lunch break she had sometimes snuck into lectures, and pretended that one day she would have a place there. But she always remained aware of the fact that it was an impossible fantasy as unreachable as the moon. Her fingers played over the crest and she allowed herself a wistful little smile. She had already figured out that he had arranged to have her watched throughout her time in London and was probably aware of her lunchtime excursions into the paradise of learning, just as he had no doubt known about her discovery of ginger lotion. With any other man she would have expected him to use it against her in the most vile and painful of ways, but she had learned enough in the last week to know that although he might use it to manipulate her, he would not use it to destroy her.

She looked up and saw that he had put his work away and was now sitting in the chair across from her. He had not allowed her to sit alone without physical contact in the whole time she had been here. Sitting this far away from him, even if it was only two metres, was a new experience, but his serious expression gave her further warning. His clothes were in the same style as those of the first evening: black trousers and high boots which highlighted the strength of his thighs and the length of his legs, the blue shirt which duplicated the colour of his eyes without ever reaching their brilliance. His black hair, held back in an intricate braid, hinted at the otherworldly beauty of that face, emphasising the high cheek bones and the mobile lips. Just as on so many other occasions, he regarded her with concentration and contemplation. Instinctively she knew they had reached a turning point in their interactions and relationship, and that this turning point, this fork in the road, was entirely beyond her control. It should make her angry. It only left her apprehensive.

She raised the brochures in her hand, his eyes never dipping down to them as he answered her unspoken question.

"You need to choose a course and university so that we can decide how best to prepare you for it."

For a moment she thought she might be able to love this man, not because he had recognised her dream and wanted to make it come true, but because of his unfailing trust in her ability to achieve whatever he thought she wanted to do.

"Lucian, I do not even have the most basic qualifications. University is simply out of the question for me."

The surprise and astonishment in his eyes amazed her. He knew virtually everything about her life and was too intelligent not to have made the connection between her age and the lack of education after she had been discovered an ErGer. She wondered if it was simply a question of him having grown up in a time when education was a luxury not a right, and generally a lot shorter. But then she recognised the source of his surprise. She had called him by his name.

"This is why you need to choose your course now. We can then start to prepare you for your A-level exams. I know from the girls that you have spent a considerable time in libraries over the past years and both Kieran and I agree that your basic knowledge is actually remarkable in some areas. I suspect you need less tutoring than you might think and might even be able to start your courses this autumn, rather than next year. I understand that you might prefer an Oxford College to the London Universities but, unfortunately, I have to restrict you to the city limits, for security reasons."

She was unable to take this in. Her mind was getting stuck on the possibility of finishing her education. Her world was undergoing a further seismic shift. A week ago she had doubted she would still be alive today and now there were decisions she was supposed to take about her future. She felt her hands shaking, her mind reeled. Once again it was his eyes, so sure and steady, which gave her an anchor to hold onto. With each breath he held her gaze she managed another foothold in the present, but still she did not know what to say.

"I expect all members of my court to either acquire new skills or further develop old ones. Not all of them chose university but in your case it would seem the best fit."

"Why?" Finally a word she could utter through her astonishment.

"It is in your nature to seek knowledge and you seem to enjoy it. I assumed you would want to develop it if given the chance."

She shook her head. There was no doubt that she would develop her education if she was allowed to do so. But that was not what she had been asking.

"Why do you make them develop new skills?" For a moment she thought she saw some discomfort, perhaps even embarrassment in his face.

"You know, no one has ever asked me before, they simply followed the rule." His fingers steepled in his lap, a gesture that made her grin. The answering raised eyebrow did not help the matter. When her grin changed into an outright chuckle he narrowed his eyes.

"Have you heard of Martin Heidegger?"

"German philosopher. Twentieth century. Existentialist?" She clearly surprised him with her knowledge.

"What do you know of his theory of existence and, especially, mortality?" This time she had to dig deeper than she was entirely comfortable with. She loved reading the existentialists but it had been four years since she had chosen to develop her own education in that direction and was worried that she might have forgotten much.

"He draws on ideas from Husserl, Kierkegaard and Jaspers when he argues that our existence is defined by mortality. Only when we become aware of the possibility of death do we engage in conscious living, in developing and defining our existence in a meaningful way. Only through mortality do we take responsibility for our actions and define our own life and character." And that was his point, she realised. "You think that vampires will atrophy mentally if they are not forced into developing because they lack mortality?"

His answer was slower in coming and she realised that he was more serious about this.

"I don't think humans live a more conscious life necessarily. For the most part they exist without true existence just as most vampires do. They get through each day without ever truly taking responsibility for their actions, without ever experiencing and acting in full knowledge and intent. It is easier for a human who knows that his or her time is limited to combat their inner fear and laziness and truly live because if they do not do something today they might not have a tomorrow to do it in. A vampire has little incentive to step out of his comfort zone. We are often too concerned with survival to face our shortcomings. Before I formed my own court I spent centuries at other courts where the most interesting concern for most people seemed to be the latest fashions and what someone else said over dinner. I wanted to have a different type of court. I wanted to create a place where people could develop and strive for more."

His expression was so intense that it took her a moment to realise that he was also apprehensive. He seemed to expect her to laugh, not to understand. He was a child of the renaissance, literally, she suspected, who had made the eighteenth century Enlightenment his own and now faced the disillusionment of the modern age. For a moment she wondered what it said about her that she understood him better than she understood her own contemporaries.

"Philosophy and law." He had given her one of his dreams, so she told him one of hers. "I would love to study philosophy and law. Or political science. Because I think that no matter how badly the world treats us, we have a responsibility to change it, not just make sure that there is a vaccine for cholera but that our minds don't forget what it means to live with others, to have responsibility for others, to stand up for the weak."

For the first time in thirteen years she heard her fourteen-year-old self speak and was surprised that it still spoke the truth.

The silence that followed was not uncomfortable, it was restful. She had never thought that she would be able to share such a silence again with anyone, had thought that she had lost that ability with adulthood, and sharing it with a vampire seemed surreal. He leaned forward, resting his elbows on his knees. He was almost close enough to touch her but still did not initiate the contact. In the depth of his eyes she saw a gravity which frightened her.

"Kathryn, I will take your blood tonight in a first step to

deepen the bond."

It did not surprise her, did not even frighten her. She had known this was coming. The change in routine had proven that her physical health was sufficiently improved for her to lose some blood. In her mind and body she still felt a deep reservoir of power untapped by the surface link she shared with him and she had always known that he would eventually force the access to that power.

She had no idea what a deeper bond would mean, but over the years she had wondered if a full bonding would mean she would stop existing, become nothing more than a zombie. It was what every vampire had expected to happen, some telling her gleefully that they were "playing" with her before the full bond formed because there would not be enough of her afterwards to make it truly worthwhile. That had frightened her even more than the brutality, but now that the day had come, somehow she was at peace with it. For years the only reason she had fought had been the protection of the girls. Paul would have been only an indifferent guardian for them at best, but this man would not. The problem with the bond was that it went both ways, and over the last seven days she had recognised that there was a core of honour and integrity to this man which would make the girls safer than they had ever been with her. The gravest danger the children might face with him was to be overprotected, smothered in care and affection, but they had had so little in terms of material goods and safety until now that there could be worse things than being spoiled rotten.

"If something happens to me, promise me you will listen

177

to them. You will give them the space to make mistakes."

His lack of reaction showed her that he knew exactly who she was talking about.

"What do you think will happen?"

"I don't know." She broke eye contact, her hands plucking nervously at the blanket over her legs. "I always thought that the bond might just take over... bury me." She shrugged, keeping her concentration firmly on her fingers, seeking out imaginary loose strands. She almost wished the blanket had a pattern, simply because it was so much easier to give her hands and mind something to play with. She even recognised that the thought in itself was an escape in some form, letting her mind ramble and shy away from the actual issue at hand. As she plucked at another thread she realised she was happy to let her mind do that, but he clearly was not. His pale hand covered hers in her lap. It was a beautiful hand, more fragile looking than she had realised, especially considering the strength it held. His fingers were long and narrow, each bone clearly delineated under his pale skin. Her free hand came to trace along the blue shadows of blood. Whose blood was running through his veins today? When he turned his hand to capture her roving fingers, he reclaimed her attention.

"Kathryn, the only thing that will happen is that the link we have will become more pronounced, will reach further into your mind. I will be able to tap into your emotions, to monitor them rather than influence them. I should be able to calm you without using the fairly crude measure of pushing you into sleep I have to resort to at the moment. Also, I will be able to reach you from a distance. Aside from the power I will draw from you, it is not that different from what I can already share with members of my court through a blood bond. I have learned as much as I can from your body, but you are too fragile, too unaware of your own needs to be able to tell me, either verbally or physically, where the true limits of your endurance lie. I need the bond to be able to push further. Rather than it being dangerous, the deeper bond should make it possible for me to protect you."

Protect her? She admitted to herself that this was only what he intended to do. To keep the bond intact he would have to renew it regularly, and as her blood was addictive, the needs of his body and of his people would quickly outstrip all good intentions. He was unlikely to push it far enough to kill her, but there would be no reason not to keep her weak and compliant. There were other ErGer out there, possibly only three or four at the moment, but they were sequestered in courts, never seen again. The only evidence of their existence showed through the continued increase in power of the vampires. But did it really matter to her? The point was that she had come here as a trade for the protection of the girls and that was exactly what she would be getting. She might originally have thought that protection would come from Paul and not a Vampire Lord, but she would take anything. Protection of the girls had become synonymous with protection of this man, and if her blood and body could assure that, she was willing to do so.

His eyes had not left her face, but the only physical contact between them had been his hands gently holding hers. When she tugged on her hand he released without hesitation, not pressuring her by tightening his grip. He made sure that she was conscious of the fact that he had *let* her go, that everything she did was entirely under his control. It gave her the strength to offer her wrist to his mouth and to admit to herself that she was choosing this. His fingers wrapped around it, soft bands of heated steel stronger than any artificial restraint he could have used to hold her, stronger because she had chosen them. Not even as he pulled her closer did he break eye contact, he just softly raised her arm and turned his lips to it, ghosting gently over the vulnerable flesh of her wrist, stroking over the blood vessels starkly obvious in their blue shade under her pale skin. She anticipated the pain of his bite, expected to feel his sharp incisors puncturing her skin before his lips sealed around the wound to drink. When he opened his mouth her body tensed. She felt his teeth, but the gentle scrape did not turn to pain as he pressed a tender kiss on her skin.

"Not like this. I will take your blood, I will invade every aspect of your being, I will demand your submission and you will give it to me when I have taken you past all these civilised concepts. I will not be satisfied until I own every part of you, until you have given yourself to me entirely."

11

Fight

His eyes were burning embers waiting to ignite her mind and body, capturing her attention and holding it so she came almost unthinkingly into his arms. He pulled her towards him and his hands settled gently around her waist, bringing her to kneel over him. Ten days after the first time he had done this he no longer had to guide her knees up on the chair beside him anymore. Her body came naturally into the position he had gently moved her into so often. Even though she did know he had done so on purpose, she still had to challenge him, show him that his manipulations did not go unnoticed.

"I know what you are doing," she said.

But this was a lie. She was so far out of her depth. She was about to sink and it was becoming harder and harder not to care. The bastard. His body was entirely relaxed under her, his head resting back against the side of the chair, spreading his long, dark hair over the red velvet. He looked lazy, his lips relaxed in a slight smile and the normally so sharp eyes half closed as he enjoyed the sensation of his hands stroking in lazy movements up and down her side. She had become so comfortable with this position that not even the feel of the soft denim of his jeans under her naked thighs could make her aware of her own lack of clothes and her vulnerability. She had become used to being naked around him, not really noticing as long as he did not draw her attention to it. She knew all of this was intentional and he forced her to recognise it, taking the ammunition right out of her hands.

"What am I doing?" he said, making it clear that he not only did not mind her being aware that she was being manipulated but that he wanted her to know. And she could do nothing but meet that challenge.

"You hold me like this because you think it makes you appear less threatening."

His only answer was a chuckle that made her mad.

"It won't work," she snapped, not caring if he heard her irritation. She had the feeling he was working hard on not laughing out loud but at least his eyes were now wide open, brimming with mirth.

"It will not work," she repeated crossly.

It did nothing to wipe the grin off his face. "Hmm," he said. Before she could become more annoyed though, he relented.

"Kathryn, this way, the only time you fight me, when you let me see your annoyance, your anger, your resentment, is when you are looking down on me. The fact that you can do this after barely two weeks amazes me."

His words in his dark, confident voice frightened and excited her. He was right. She might still cringe from him but she had lost the bone-deep terror that had made her remain vigilant enough to protect herself and the children by suppressing all possible challenge for as long as possible. Every muscle in her body froze in indecision and she could no longer make sense of it. For once, he did not allow her any time to come to terms with the new emotions or the realisations they brought with them. Instead he reached to the table beside him and lifted a velvet-wrapped package. She was still frozen when he snapped a heavy silver bracelet onto each of her wrists. At first she thought them to be simple jewellery, but she quickly realised that there was more to them than that when she met his carefully blank gaze.

They were too soft. The bracelets looked like simple broad silver bangles, decoration found on so many women, but their insides were soft, heavily padded, distinctly more than normal jewellery required. The second clue was in the cleverly concealed fastenings, almost indistinguishable from the geometric patterns etched on the bangles – the fastenings were not to open the bracelets, they were to attach something. These were very cleverly worked restraints, no less sinister for their beauty. His control was not so good that she did not feel his tension as she discovered the purpose of her new adornment, though his body remained pliant beneath her. In her mind she felt him prepare himself for a fight. It intrigued her that he would allow her this, that he had chosen to face the potential battle.

"They were not in the box." She was not entirely sure why

she said this apart from it being the only thing that came to mind. She had come to rely on the box, to know that whatever the box contained would structure her days, and she had started to adjust her emotions based on that. When he had used the restraints in the box, or the blindfold, she had always known that afterward it would be over. Somehow, she felt unreasonably put out by him not sticking to this silent agreement, more so than she was by the restraints now on her wrists.

"That is because they do not belong in there."

And she understood. These were not transient. They would not go back into the box in the evening – they were as much marks of claiming as tools to subdue her.

"Why?" She could not hide the slight tremble in her voice, but she wanted to know. His hands returned to her waist, to the slow and hypnotic movements over her skin, though his eyes were too hot for calm.

"I love seeing them on you. Love the fact that I can restrain you at any time, for my pleasure." She saw the arousal in his eyes, heard it in the smokiness of his voice and felt it in the hard ridge of his arousal pressing on her vagina through his jeans. There was no doubt about the truth of his words and she would have accepted them, but he was not yet finished with his explanation.

"And you need them. With them you will have the opportunity to fight me, to resist and challenge me without ever risking harm coming to you. You will come to love them too."

She did not want to accept this arrogance as anything but

delusion, could not imagine a situation in which she would not hate the signs of her lost freedom. But she could not tell him that, not now his eyes had dropped to her neck and his smile contained more than just a hint of fang. He had told her that she would bleed for him today and it seemed that the time had come to pay the piper, to make good on her promise not to resist the bond. Suddenly she was frightened. The scars on her neck attested to the fact that she had fed more than one vampire, and most had been more cruel than this man could ever be.

She had no doubt that he would try to make the experience as painless as possible but also that he would bite her neck. Experience had taught her that it would hurt like hell, but it was not the pain that truly frightened her. It was the fact that she had given her word not to fight him in this. She had made this promise feeling she had nothing to lose, believing that she would have to make good on it that night. The fact that it turned out to be a multi-part promise did not change her obligation in her own eyes.

Her word was important to her. Not only had she spend too much time on the outskirts of a society in which promises mattered more than life, but she identified herself through her honour. Most of her life had been outside of her control. Horrific things had been done to her, but at least she could say that, until today, she had never betrayed who she wanted to be – an honourable person. If she fought him now she would lose this last part of herself, but for the first time she was not sure if she could remain passive. For the first time in too long she had an inkling of what life could be like and a small stirring in her mind that wanted to fight for it.

Her body started to tremble as he gently stroked her hair away from her neck, laying it bare to his teeth. Goosebumps rose on her arms, not from sensual pleasure but in terrified expectation. She could hear her own breath, fast and wheezing, and felt in it the little catch she could not suppress. The strokes of his hands remained gentle and sure, trying to calm her in her terror, but her fear was quickly taking over. The bracelets moved when she involuntarily made a fist, and for a moment she wanted him to use them. Before she could even comprehend what she was doing her mouth whispered, "Please." Please stop? Please hurry? Please hold me? She had no idea what she was begging for. Fortunately, he did. She felt his hands stroking her shoulders and slowly down her arms, somehow linking the restraints on her wrists behind her back without her becoming entirely aware of his intent.

"You only had to ask, Kathryn. You only ever have to ask." The movement had brought him close enough for his words to be a whisper on her skin and his eyes were lit with sympathy and controlled warmth. Somehow, it made everything better. She might be lost in all this but he was not and he would not let her fall. The strength of the hand cradling the back of her head took control of her movements away from her. Now that he had her secure she expected to feel the pain of his teeth in her skin and was ready to endure and accept.

Instead he relaxed back into the chair, bringing her with him into his arms, her head tucked into his shoulder, her weight resting on him. She was surrounded by his scent of sandalwood and lemon, and each breath he took stroked over her neck. Her first reaction was to tense more, but there was no bite, only the feeling of soft lips resting against her. There was no urgency in him as he held her close, let her accustom herself not only to his mouth on her skin but to his arms holding her. Soft music wound its way through the room providing her with some distraction as he began to caress her with soft, open-mouthed kisses. His hands provided a sensual counterpoint to the soft jazz as they began to rub her muscles in gentle circles. She was lulled by his movements, the music, his scent, the whole atmosphere; entranced enough not to notice the gentle pressure behind his caresses which adjusted her in his arms, allowing him to gently stretch her neck. By the time he began to alternate the soft kisses with gentle sucking, bringing the blood to play below the surface, he was holding her securely but tenderly. When his teeth finally slid into her skin her mind was so caught in a haze of pleasure that it took more than a heartbeat for her to react. It was not pain making her jerk, it was the lightning bolt of arousal hitting her with every pull of his mouth. A silken rope of fire coiled in her womb, reaching every molecule, every inch of her skin, leaving it wanting and burning. By his third swallow her breasts were heavy and so aroused that it bordered on painful. Her pussy was so wet that she had soaked through the fabric separating their bodies. Two swallows later, even the touch of his hands caused her agonies of unfulfilled sexual need.

She had no idea when he had released her restraints but she found her hands clutching his shirt, not sure if she wanted

187

to push him away or pull him closer as he let go of her. She had never been so confused, so frightened and so aroused in her life. It was almost impossible not to press her mouth to his as she watched his tongue travel over his full lips, removing all evidence of her blood from them. Still her body screamed for an end to these waves of painful desire burning through her. As he cupped her breasts in his hands her screams were no longer silent, her body too sensitised by far to be able to endure the thumb he flicked over her hard nipples. In desperation she ground her vagina against his cock, but no matter what she did she could not find relief. Her whimpers turned to quiet sobs in her throat but she still could not find a way out.

"Baby, you won't be able to find relief until I spill in you."

His voice penetrated her sexual haze and reminded her of the world outside her burning body. She became aware of the hardness of his body, the light sheen of sweat on his skin and the blazing heat in his eyes, a heat that rivalled the waves in her own body. Still he did not move, no matter how much she could see his muscles quiver under the need to do so.

"Help me!" she wailed. She knew she might be ashamed of it later but in the grasp of this heat she was unable to suppress it. His hands were shaking as he unsnapped his trousers to let his cock spring free, hard and fully aroused. Neither of them cared that he was still dressed when he urged her over him. She tried to push down, to speed up his entering her channel, but his hands were rock hard on her waist, delaying all movement. Her whine was animalistic and had no effect on him.

"Beg for it!"

She barely understood, caught between the need to feel him in her and his uncompromising hold as a barrier to this fulfilment.

"Beg me!" The command was as raw as his voice. She could not believe that he was keeping her from extinguishing the painful arousal but there was no space left in her to resist.

"Please!" Before the sound of her voice had even died his hands slammed her body down as he pushed upwards, sheathing himself with her in one glorious movement. It was enough to push her body into orgasm, letting her ride the waves of pleasure that rippled through her.

Her need should have been sated, letting her rest, but he refused to let her go. As the last spasms of pleasure shook her, stroking the still-hard penis inside her, she felt his tongue circle one of her sensitive nipples before closing his mouth around it. With each alternating lick and nip and suck of his mouth he fanned the embers in her to new light, not allowing her even a moment of respite. Her nipple felt huge, swollen and incredibly sensitive when he let go of it to kiss a path upwards. Reaching her lips he devoured her. There was nothing gentle in that kiss. It rivalled in intensity the waves of pleasure of the orgasm rising in her and she could not claim that the kiss was only his. Her body and mind were so consumed with desire that she met each of the thrusts of his tongue with one of her own, duelling for dominance, never letting him withdraw without following. The next orgasm surprised her in its comparative gentleness, its quivers matching the movement of his tongue in her mouth and his hands on her breasts. This time he did not let her come down but continued to thrust through her orgasm, prolonging the demands of her body. She realised that he had still not come and was still hard and large in her.

"Why?" Desperation consumed her with each thrust to rival the pleasure that was breaking down her composure. With each upstroke his mouth played over the corner of her lips, his arms holding her safely in place, presented for his pleasure.

"Because you can give me more, and I want it all."

With every moment she seemed to lose herself more and his hold on her seemed stronger. She needed something from him, and so she begged for a third time.

"Please!"

His full laughter wrapped around her body and mind at the same time. He let himself fall back in the chair and his hands on her waist encouraged her to move on his shaft.

"Take me, Kathryn, take all you need from me." And with a sob she did, allowed her body to overrule her mind and move over him as it craved to. Her whole being concentrated on the feeling of his hard cock moving in and out of her, and the way her body's position changed the pressure points in her. She was still tight around the ridge of his foreskin stroking into her, felt him gliding through her moist heat. As the beginnings of another orgasm trembled through her she felt his fingers around her clitoris, stroking over its side before slipping over it. The faster she moved the harder was she able to rub against him, the stronger the touch on her clitoris, pushing her closer to an explosive climax. When it came it took her senses and laid her bare. She felt him everywhere; felt his heat filling her, his hands holding her upright in a strong grip and felt his hold on her mind insidiously strengthen. It was tinted with something she had not felt in a long time, something she was too scared to analyse further – a feeling that was more than fondness.

Somehow her mind shut down all non-essential communications and let her float, let her rest. It was a strange moment of clarity in its simplicity. She was entirely aware of him lifting her, swathing her into a blanket and carrying her to the bed to rest. She let him hold her and press soft kisses to her brow. His hand came to rest on her cheek, warming her skin before he stroked her hair gently from her face. She noticed that whilst he had made very sure that she would be on top when he took her blood and body, he seemed to have no intention of being in anything less than an utterly dominant position now as he looked down on her. His body was stretched out by her side, her head bedded on his arm whilst her face was gently held in his other hand; she was completely enveloped by him. It should have made her think but she simply could not marshal her thoughts. Faced with his intent gaze she said the first thing that came to mind.

"Why the punishment?"

His gaze did not waver; his expression did not change from the intent and gentle warmth she had become used to.

"I have already promised to answer all your questions truthfully," Lucian said, "but first, answer one of mine."

"OK." The less than formal answer garnered her a quick kiss and a smile rather than the expected challenge.

"Why do you think it was a punishment?" Her mind was still too slow to think, too slow to censor her answer.

"Because I deserved it."

"Why, Kathryn?" It almost annoyed her into wakefulness that he had to ask but she could simply not be bothered.

"Because I am bad."

"Why are you bad?"

"I have to be." This was all clear in the depth of her mind. Everyone punished her for existing so she had to be bad. Something niggled in the place that normally held her rational thoughts but that part of her was still swamped by the emotions that had wiped out thought so efficiently earlier.

"What did you do to be so bad?"

"I don't know." It was a wail and it broke a dam she had not even been aware existed in her. All the terror, the fear and anger, all the hate and feeling of unfairness she had never had the luxury to indulge in, all rose threatening to drown her. There was no way to hold back the flood of tears coming from that lanced wound in her mind, nor was there a way to suppress her litany, until now a shameful secret in her mind which she had spent so much effort on ignoring and now was unable to keep in.

"Why me? What did I do wrong?"

It did not matter that there was no point to it. Why not her? Why should someone else have been dumped with this rather than her? She knew it was stupid and selfish, and that was what made these thoughts so much worse, made them into an affirmation of her core-deep wickedness. His arms came strongly around her, holding her firmly anchored through this sudden storm.

"That's it, Kathryn, let it go. You have not done anything wrong. I have got you now. They won't get to you anymore."

Eventually there were no tears left and no anger, just bone-deep tiredness. The thoughts in her mind had moved from simple awareness of a lack of control to a rational clarity regarding herself. She had done nothing to deserve this life.

"I did not do anything." It was not quite a question but not a sure exclamation either.

"No you did not." His lips found hers in a gentle touch. "And every time you forget that I will remind you of it."

Her eyes were heavy, swollen and captured by his blue ones.

"Kathryn, I love you." She should be annoyed at this blatant lie. But her mind was too calm for anger.

"That makes no sense." She declared without rancour instead. His grin was boyish but a little sad.

"I know, Baby. I know it makes no sense, but it is still true. You are an amazing woman; warm, loyal and courageous to a fault. I will gladly spend the rest of our lives teaching you to love me back."

"You cannot love me."

"Why not?" There was a smile in his voice.

"Even I don't like myself." That startled a bark of laughter out of him. An echoing laughter made her realise that there was someone else in the room with them. Kieran sat at her feet, his back to the wall, relaxed, just looking at her with a smile. Somehow she did not mind his presence there. Lucian's chuckle brought her attention back up.

"Kathryn, to say that you do not like yourself is like saying that the sun is slightly warm. You punish yourself constantly and we work constantly to make sure you cannot actually go too far." It was not true. She did not punish herself and wanted to set the record straight, still without anger. But he never let her speak, simply ignoring her attempt.

"Baby, I know you do not realise that you are punishing yourself but whenever you reach the ends of your endurance, when you reach your limits, you push harder rather than stepping back. You hate yourself so much that you have built a wall between your mind and your body. You need to learn to communicate with your own physical needs again."

She did not want to understand what he was saying, wanted to avoid the implications. She tried to turn her head, to escape his too intense gaze, but he held her in place. It made her angry.

"What if I do not want to?"

His smile turned predatory at that. "You will not have a choice."

She wanted to scratch his eyes out but had to content herself with a glare. She could not help challenging him.

"Really? I am not afraid of you anymore!" To her own amazement that was true. She might fear what he would do but she did not fear him anymore. His laughter was warm and full and loud as it reverberated through the room.

"I am serious, I am not afraid of you anymore!"

"I know." He whispered it against her mouth, accompanying it with a soft kiss. She felt the smile on his lips as they met hers and she had to admit to herself once again

194

that she simply did not get men.

He moved back enough to give her the space to look at his face, though he never let go of her.

"I promised to answer your question," he said.

She knew which one he meant but was not sure if she wanted to know the answer anymore.

"Kathryn, it was not punishment. I wanted to show you what the bond actually is. It is an exchange. Just as my body demands your blood, yours craves the pleasure I can give you."

Somehow he had found one of the problems she had only been vaguely aware of as being an issue. The bond had always been this frightening doom which would take everything from her and now he claimed that she was getting something in return, though she was not sure she wanted it. His steady gaze did not allow her to escape as she started to squirm under him. He shifted his weight to hold her in place, catching her chin in his hand. Despite being exhausted, mentally as well as physically, she erupted into a frantic struggle. She hit him, tried to kick him, even scratch at him but to no avail; he quickly caught her hands and pressed them into the mattress before reattaching the cuffs. The anger flamed higher and higher, egging her on.

She felt his presence in her mind and knew that he could push her into sleep at any moment and that he chose not to. Instead he let her fight, and the control he held drove her even more insane. She found her arms restrained above her head, her body held securely under his with one leg immobilising her. No matter how much she tried to buck him off he did not waver. As she started to tire it was almost comforting. She understood the lesson – he would not let her hide from reality. He would not let her run but he would be there to hold her when she faced it down.

"I don't want it." She told herself that they were tears of rage on her cheeks, but she could not say what exactly it was she claimed not to want. The bond? Definitely. The pleasure of his touch? That proposition was becoming a more difficult desire to deny. The unwavering protection of his presence? She did not even want to think about that. With the deeper bond she felt his bittersweet sadness in her mind as well as seeing it in his eyes.

"That's alright. It will get easier in time," he whispered.

He held her like that, unable to move, restrained by the cuffs he had put on her and the weight of his body. His breath stroked her face, inviting her own to follow its rhythm. Almost instinctively she followed that invitation and as she drew in his scent with each breath she felt herself relax into his control. In the end it was Kieran's soft voice which broke this intimate spell.

"It might be time to call it a night and head downstairs."

Lucian did not react at first other than by letting his lips stretch into a quick smile. It was almost as if he wanted to preserve this moment of quiet, but then he raised his head with a sigh and a wry chuckle.

"Kieran is caught between his duties as your doctor and my second. He does not like it when I sleep up here."

This made her tense. She had stopped considering these rooms to hold any threat, and the sudden realisation that there might be reason to worry made her uncomfortable, especially with the girls an entire floor away.

"What threat?"

Even though her question was directed at Kieran, it was the man still holding her who answered.

"No, there is no true danger. He, actually all of my court, does not like it when I am taking the day-sleep up here as the defences are less extensive than they are down in the sleeping quarters of the court. They are just being overprotective."

The thought occupied her enough that she missed the exact moment when Lucian unsnapped her restraints and swung her up into his arms. The suddenness of the movement made her wrap her arms tightly around his neck, and his mischievous grin was proof perfect of her suspicion that he had intended just that. As he headed to the door, a moment of worry rose in her.

"Where are you taking me?" Somehow this room, her prison, had become more of a haven and the sudden possibility of leaving it worried her. At the door he waited for a vigilant Kieran to precede them and took the opportunity to bury his nose in her hair.

"I am taking you downstairs, as I have every morning for the last ten days. This time you are just awake for it."

"Why can I not stay up here?" They had now reached the elevator and the thought of leaving the girls, even though she was separated from them by a ceiling, worried her. His eyes caught hers.

"Kathryn, you will spend the rest of your nights in my arms. I will not let you sleep away from me. I cannot."

She heard the implacability and need in those words. There was no part of him which would allow for argument or any other outcome. He would not be willing to have her sleep away from him when he was most vulnerable. She had to look away to break the sudden tension. The only possible distraction was large, blonde and looking at them with an annoying smile.

"So, Kieran, are you here as my shrink or his bodyguard?" She might as well face the issue head on. The smile turned into a sparkle in his eyes.

"In there," he said, indicating the direction they had come from, "I am your shrink and doctor. Out here, I am his bodyguard."

She was only mildly interested in her surroundings as the elevator sped down, but she was curious to see the court halls again. The night she had come here she had not been able to take them in with anything resembling equanimity. She remained disappointed. The elevator opened to the long hallway in front of the room she had been taken to that first night so her curiosity remained unsatisfied in respect of the wider world. Kieran left them at the door with a quick, friendly kiss to Kathryn's brow.

"Why do you make them touch me like this?" she asked as soon as the door had closed. "I know that you will want to share my blood with them, that you will want to widen the bond to them, but why the suspense, why not just get on with it?"

His answer came calm and unruffled.

"I want you used to them before they take your blood.

You are terrified enough as it is and we are in no hurry. I want the additional security of their bond before you begin to leave the building but until then we can take this slowly." He set her back onto her own feet, making sure that the movement let her body slide sensuously along his, although his eyes held more amusement than arousal.

"But if you think that these two would not take any and every opportunity to touch a beautiful young woman, you have missed an essential part of their character." He gave her a gentle push in the direction of the bed before turning away to pull his shirt over his head. "Go to bed, I will be there in a moment."

The room had not changed since the last time she had been there and for a moment she wondered if it should frighten her. This was where she had lost her freedom, and been so terrified, but as her eyes wandered over the warm tones of the decor, she felt a curious sensation of relaxation and cold. The fire was banked but a winter chill seemed to emanate from the high stone walls and travel up through the bare soles of her feet. A shiver racked her body.

"Kathryn, get under the covers."

She heard the impatience in his voice and it needled her obstinacy into existence. In the past she had always feared for the girls and chosen compliance, but now that this threat was removed, obedience became harder to bear. Before she could do more than glare at him though, she felt herself being lifted and, after a moment of breathless weightlessness, bounced on the soft surface of the bed. The bastard had thrown her halfway across the room with enough control that she landed safely in the middle of the mattress. As she sputtered in outrage, he had the temerity to laugh, loudly and deeply, filling the room with an unbridled joy. It was hard to remain annoyed with him in the face of this abandon and she did not even try. Instead she chose to crawl under the heavy down blanket, its weight and warmth creating a haven around her.

She watched as he folded his clothes, endearing in its unexpectedness, before he moved through the room to extinguish one candle after another until only the embers in the fireplace remained. With each light doused the shadow images on his skin changed, altering the definition of his muscles and limbs. He was breathtakingly beautiful, but for the first time, she had the opportunity to study his controlled strength without any distractions. His skin was so pale that it shone like the moon in the disappearing light, revealing its absolute perfection – there truly was no mark on him, no scar or sign of his life prior to turning. This anomaly bothered her. It was rare for someone to grow to adulthood without some signs of life drawn into their body, even if they lived a sheltered life. If not battle scars, then at least the signs of childhood scrapes or sports injuries tended to show in places. Lucian had none of these, his skin was truly untouched. It puzzled her, and in the twilight of the morning, she was able to simply ask for information.

"You have no scars," she said.

He had blown out the last candle, and in the near complete darkness only the white flash of his teeth gave away the smile he held when answering.

"No, I was unmarked in any way before I was turned."

"How is that possible?"

"I was a sickly child and well protected, never having had the chance to play rough. My father was an affluent trader in Granada and I was the apple of my mother's eye. I was very vain, interested more in clothes and fripperies than any young man should be." The quiet amusement so clearly directed at that long faded youth he remembered was audible in his tone. Before she could enquire more she felt the bedspread move and his body slide into the warmth beside her. The sudden cold draft made her huddle closer into the mattress and he pulled her against his warm body. Her body encountered the warm steel of his as his limbs adjusted themselves around her. There was nothing sexual in the feeling of his shoulder under her cheek, his arm around her waist or the long line of his body along hers – there was only a strange comfort and familiarity.

"How old were you when you were turned?"

"Seventeen."

This surprised her – he did not look that young. If he had still been human she would have thought him to be in his very early thirties.

"Baby, we still age. The speed with which our bodies change simply slows with the level of power we develop. In the first few years most of us age almost as fast as humans."

This was news to her. With his hand stroking a hypnotic pattern through her long hair she allowed herself to consider this new information. It was surprising, not in its actual content but more because it made her realise how little she actually knew about the culture she had been running from for the last decade and a half. She had no idea that the ageless appearance of a vampire was in any way connected to their power levels. What else did she not know? What else had she missed?

"So the younger looking a vampire is the more powerful?"

"Not necessarily. He or she might simply have been recently turned, just as an old vampire might simply be so old that he or she has aged despite their high power levels. But as a general rule it is wiser to be careful with younger looking ones, especially if you think they are older than their physical age proclaims them to be."

His voice was a soft whisper in the darkness, the warmth of his body soaking into her bones like a drug.

"How old are you?"

She felt his smile on the lips that kissed her brow. "I was born sometime in the 1380s."

His "umpf" was exaggeratedly pain-laden as she levered herself up using his stomach as support for her hand.

"You are six hundred years old?"

"Just over, yes." He had the audacity to laugh!

"Just over?" Her voice was shrill and set his laughter off even more. She was one step away from pushing him out of the bed, already imagining the satisfying thump it would make if she dared to do it, when he caught her in his arms. Suddenly, their positions were reversed and she felt his body tower over her. There was still laughter in his voice but it was joined by a dark pleasure, underscored by the feeling of his erect penis against her groin – not entering her, not even demanding entrance, but reminding her of his body and the pleasure he could give her.

"I am an old man. I may have to prove to you that my age will not mean I cannot keep up with you."

She froze, her body lost in the confusing mire of arousal, fear and need, followed by that innate self-preservation instinct that makes humans withdraw from a reality that becomes too overwhelming. She knew that feeling well and welcomed the protection it gave her even as her body readied itself for his penetration. And still she could not suppress the wince. Her body had undergone a lot of strain already – sensual and physical – and no matter how pleasurable the act might be, she was sore. He must have seen her involuntary reaction to the pain, for all he did was stroke his lips over hers in a gentle movement.

"One day I will show you how your body can forget the pain through pleasure, how I can gently tease you into ecstasy." His lips spoke the words against her cheek, a softly knowing caress. Then he let himself fall to his side again and pulled her close against him. She felt him in her mind and knew he was getting ready to overwhelm her body into sleep. Instinctively she protested, mentally pushing against him.

"I can go to sleep on my own."

Only when she heard his answering whisper in her mind did she realise that their bond had deepened to a level where mental communications would be possible.

"No. I will hold you safe, body and soul." And with that he enforced his command and led her into deep sleep.

12

Elves

She fit into his arms as no one had before. Was it the genetic imperative which made him feel this way? He doubted it very much. She was all he had ever wanted. The sensation of belonging he felt more every day had nothing to do with her blood or the power she allowed him to access. It was intimately connected to her. She was a woman worth fighting for.

Lucian breathed in her scent, the ginger and cinnamon overlaying her own personal bouquet, and tried to ignore the nagging worry in his mind. He wondered how much longer he would be able to isolate her from the rising pressures of his world.

Today had been a meeting of the parliamentary subcommittee and it had left him so unsettled that not even the body of his ErGer held safely in his arms could calm him.

"You met with the other humans."

The voice was cold and hard. It slithered along his spine with a quality too alien to be recognised with the paltry range of human emotions. Lucian took the time to place Kathryn gently among the green sheets of his bed, covering her still too-thin limbs with the quilt in an attempt to keep her body warm. Only then did he turn to the mirror and the man leaning against its frame from the inside as if it were a turret window.

He was tall, his features human and alien alike, with large green eyes, slitted like a reptile's and just as hypnotic. The iridescent hues of green and blue shimmered over the pale skin, mirrored in the long silken strands styled in a simple braid less intricate than was the Elven's usual habit. The wide robes did not hide the power of the warrior's body, nor did the languid posture disguise the innate readiness of the man.

Tolkien had been right when he gave the Elves pointed ears, but he would never have been able to portray their teeth. The human subconscious would not have been able to see them as anything than the predators they were. Their teeth were more like those of a large cat than that of a human, complete with incisors closer to those of a vampire. Lucian always thought them to be proof of the Elven claim that vampires were an Elven construct. No matter how young, how innocent they portrayed themselves, those teeth were a constant reminder that they were a threat.

This Elf was a young man, but still bore the impression of timeless age, of centuries lived. Lucian knew little of the true age of the Elves, or if all of the High Elves shared the impression of ancient existence within their young forms.

This Elf was the only one he had ever met, the only one he would ever meet, for each supernatural court only held the anchor to one of their number. The day a new Lord took power he, or she, linked their very existence with its counterpart from the other side. Scientists had it right, there was no magic in this world, but through the link with the Summerlands it could be brought in. Looking into eyes so far removed from human perception of right or wrong, Lucian wondered if the trade was worth it.

"My Lord."

He bowed, a politeness hovering carefully between a greeting to an equal and the deeper gesture due to a superior. In the eyes of the Elf he saw the amused recognition of the ploy.

"What did your humans want?"

To the Elves he was as human as all those beings whose lives were so fleeting. Sometimes Lucian wondered if the seeming inability to see a distinction between human and vampire was not a studied insult. He was too wise to call the other on it, though.

"I am not altogether certain of their intention. They showed me a list of my court members and wanted me to tell them if these were all the members."

"Were they?"

Lucian turned to light one of the candles, not because he needed or even wanted the light but to buy some time to think before he answered. "There were fewer names than actual members, but more than I thought they knew of. The depth of their knowledge leaves me uncomfortable."

That last comment was a calculated risk. The Elven Master was not his enemy but neither was he his friend. The terms were too human, too normal to be applicable to the Elven. It was a risk to let him see the weakness in Lucian's position. A risk and a test.

"Ah, your complacency has been shaken, young friend."

There was satisfaction in the voice of the other, and Lucian was almost offended by the amusement in those overlarge green eyes.

"I had already begun to wonder when I would have to break in another human conduit but it looks as if there is still time for you."

Lucian swallowed twice, a precaution to help him hold back the anger he felt and rethink the words he was about to say. It was never wise to give an Elf the upper hand by showing them anger. They rarely understood the cause of it, though Lucian sometimes doubted the veracity of the claim.

"I assure you, My Lord, I am not willing to step down as yet."

There were too many teeth in the answering smile for it to be comforting.

For a long moment, the two simply looked at each other, one leaning against the frame of a mirror, too relaxed, too nonchalant for him to be anything but posturing; the other in a room of gentle darkness, warmed by a woman whose presence he had only just learnt to bask in and who was still far from realising her importance. Neither of them spoke.

Lucian's knees gave way in a wave of pain which bypassed his brain and penetrated his pores with needles of agony.

Breathing became painful, each movement a renewal of torment. Black flecks danced in front of his eyes as he knelt there on the floor, his arms barely strong enough to keep him from completely collapsing. It was not the first time he mused about the fact that even pain has a scent, independent of sweat and tears.

"I was wondering if this would still work now that you have found an ErGer."

The tone was mild, almost disinterested. Lucian had to think hard about every move necessary to even raise his head, let alone to make his limbs cooperate with the ambitious plan to rise to his feet, but he would be damned if he would kneel for the amusement of the Elf. For a split second, as his knees threatened to buckle and the room spun in front of his eyes, he was torn between the urge to vomit or faint, but any vampire becoming a Lord had long since collected ways to deal with the aftermath of mental control used to hurt and subdue. A Fae, even a High Elf such as this, was hampered by the uncomprehending nature of their cruelties. Stronger vampires taught new ones obedience with all the knowledge and intent of humanity.

"I can feel the bond you share with her but you make no use of it to protect yourself from my touch."

Lucian had learned to remain quiet in these conversations, or at least inscrutable, even if his body trembled under the strain of recent pain and his shirt was soaked by the red tinge of his own sweat. It was far wiser to appear as if he was trying not to give anything away than admit he had no idea what the other man spoke off. So he let his calm gaze meet the alien one, hiding all the pain, the concern and the fear behind a mask of mild emptiness. Another skill every vampire learned early on.

"My Lord, is there anything I can help you with before our monthly meeting next week?"

There was satisfaction in seeing the anger in the other's eyes. It was rare to see the Elf show that much emotion. Lucian did not let it shine through his own eyes, but he refused to lower his gaze. It was necessary to remind the Elven Master that he, Lucian, was not one of his minions, no matter how much power the other might have over him.

"You have a traitor in your ranks. Deal with it!"

The mirror went blank, leaving Lucian no opportunity to respond to what amounted to an order, no chance to remind the other man again that he, Lucian, was more an equal than a servant. Lucian was too exhausted to care. He allowed himself to give in to his buckling knees and sat heavily on the edge of the bed, his hand searching for Kathryn's under the heavy quilt. She might not be conscious but her mere presence gave him a measure of solace.

When she stirred in her sleep he realised that his mind had reached automatically for hers, had taken the newly formed path without conscious thought in his need to share. With a smile he soothed her back to sleep and instead travelled along an older, well-worn path to find his seconds.

"Kieran! Brandon!"

He had an impression of fire and books, of shared laughter and wine, and knew neither man had found his bed yet. Their awareness surrounded him with strength and support.

"What did the old bugger want?"

Brandon's mental voice was as calm as his physical one, though it was harder for him to withhold his true emotion in this form. Few, even among the members of a court, knew of the link between the Fae realms and the Lords of the supernatural courts. In his own court the knowledge was limited to his seconds, his major-domo and a selected few. There were reasons for this. It was long understood that fairies took their power from belief – and human belief is a powerful thing.

Centuries ago, before even Lucian's memory, the Fae had used this world freely, fighting their battles for power in the Summerlands by proxy, through the devastation of human armies. The practice had not been so different from that of humanity in the era of the Cold War, but when Elves were pulling the strings there was an added level of cruelty.

No one was entirely certain what had finally turned the tide, or if the tide had turned. Shortly before Lucian had been turned, an accord had been bartered. Neither side of those vying for dominance in the Summerlands would directly affect the human world anymore. The Supernatural courts which had, prior to the accord, been little more than refuges for those too weak, too badly connected or defended to stand against the tide of constant war raged by the High Elves, became doors between the worlds. A Lord held the link connecting the Summerlands to the human worlds, allowing the lower Fae and those humans who, over time, had acquired magic through interbreeding with those from the Summerlands, to pass and exist, protected from both sides, humanity and elves.

With the disappearance of the High Elves and Higher Fae, magic slowly withdrew from humanity, kept alive only by the trickle held through the vampire courts. So the Lords of the supernatural courts had become the most powerful members of the supernatural races in this world and the jailers of the High Fae, holding the line against a renewed intrusion of beings too powerful, too unemotional to be allowed to play with the fate of mankind.

The High Elves rarely interfered in the machinations and happenings of the supernatural courts anymore. They had grown distant in their dealings with humanity, even with those weaker Fae choosing the human world over the Summerlands. Lucian's interaction with the Elf Master was limited to monthly meetings, rarely spanning more than a few minutes, and which he was certain were designed solely to satisfy the strange curiosity his counterpart seemed to harbour for human ingenuity. Over time they had spoken more about the uses of cars and computers than the political or social realities of a world so changed the Elf would no longer recognise it. So what had he wanted?

"I am not certain," he answered.

"Did he ask about the other courts? Or other Elves?"

Kieran's voice held the tension they all felt when it related to the High Fae. No one wanted a return of the Fae influence over the world.

"He asked about the subcommittee meeting today and warned me of a traitor in our ranks."

The growl vibrating through the link from Brandon was

vicious and expected. Brandon was too much the straightforward warrior to deal well with betrayal of any kind. Kieran ignored his brother's outbreak.

"Do you think there is a link between the sudden human interest and the Fae?" he asked.

Lucian took a moment to think, letting his mind range in the comfortable silence of their exchange, even though it had been a question he had been considering for far longer, for weeks now.

"I had almost convinced myself there was no link before the High Elf's visit. Now I am no longer certain."

He almost felt the way his friend turned the information around in his head.

"All our information indicates that it is Carlisle who is the one cooperating with the humans." Kieran was certain of his spies.

"The two are not mutually exclusive." Lucian sighed.

"What do you think it means?"

Lucian was not entirely certain which of the twins had asked the question. It happened on occasion when the two men's minds were particularly aligned. It mattered little to his answer.

"Carlisle's court has been a concern since its creation. I have never known if the Elven Masters of these recent courts have simply been slower in opening their lands to access to this world or if these are newly formed power bases in the Summerlands. Carlisle wants the title of the High Lord of the British Isles to be revived for himself. It might be purely his own ambition or perhaps something more."

"An attempt to consolidate power for his Elven Lord?" It was easy to forget that Brandon was not only a supreme fighter but also a superb strategist.

"Possibly."

"But why now? Carlisle has been making noises for decades but has not accrued any more support over the last year."

"I don't think he was intending to show his hand quite yet. The meeting today seemed too haphazard, the threat too ill-conceived. What have they achieved by showing me a list of court members other than warning me of a traitor in my ranks? Something forced their hand before they were ready."

Lucian's gaze flickered to the body curled up in the bed beside him, the light of the single candle caressing skin only just beginning to lose its sickly pallor.

"Kathryn."

Who had said her name? Had it been himself or one of the other men? No matter, it was true. She was the only thing which had changed for them.

"With an ErGer as a member of your court, many of the lower Lords will be vying for your protection." Brandon's voice was thoughtful even on the mental path.

"So Carlisle pushed the humans into a pre-emptive strike before you have had the chance to settle into the new situation. Even had you forced Kathryn's compliance from the beginning you would still be dealing with the pressure the sudden increase in power would bring with it. With your bond still vulnerable, the threat is even greater." Kieran's tone was expressionless.

"The blood exchange today has settled the bond. The flow of power is now even, though I have not experimented with it as yet."

"You are in control of the bond then?" Brandon's voice was as careful as his brother's. For a moment Lucian regretted that he had taught the two men to be cautious when it came to demands on his ErGer but he was only too aware he would not allow anyone to threaten her.

"The bond is safely established, further supplemented by a blood bond. I can use and control the power coming from her, but I am still only receiving a small amount. Her shields are still formidable and she is only beginning to drop them when pushed. There won't be any sudden waves of power spilling over the court and hurting them, but at the same time there is also very little change in my personal levels of power. The power of the court currently filtered through her is still held behind her shields."

"Do you think Carlisle wants her?"

A blunt question and one that needed consideration. Perhaps there was no Elven conspiracy. Possibly it was a question of the simplest explanation being the best. Maybe the haste in which the human's had reacted was based on Carlisle's desire to unite the other Lords for the purpose of acquiring the position as High Lord, with the added bonus of stealing an ErGer in the process, and no Fae hands were involved at all. But Lucian did not think so. Without a doubt, Carlisle would be happy to take Kathryn if he could get his hands on her, but there was another issue to consider.

"The Elf asked about her, even tested the power of the

Summerlands link to see if I would use her."

"Use her how?" Brandon's question was exactly the one he could not answer.

"I do not know. He thought I would be able to protect myself against his influence through her. When I did not he seemed amused. But how, I do not know."

"Neither do I. I have done as much research as I could, but I know you have too, Lucian."

Kieran had always been a scholar, and if he was not able to bring light to the Elf's comment then there was nothing to be done for the moment. He just hoped they would figure it out as Kathryn relaxed her shields. Without it coming back to haunt them.

"What now? We wait?"

Brandon hated waiting, hated letting the enemy come to them rather than taking action himself. Lucian played with the hand of the sleeping woman, tracing the lines of the fragile bones where the skin stretched over them.

"For now, we sleep. Tonight we prepare. I want first level emergency precautions in place including basic surveillance on our most vulnerable members."

"Do you want those children attending human schools to remain at home?"

Lucian had to think hard about that. His first reaction was to draw those most vulnerable into the court and build a fortress around them. But sometimes a fortress is more vulnerable than a straw house, at least if the straw house stood among many other straw houses.

"No, leave them in school but keep the schools under

surveillance. Only a few of them have as yet been identified by the government and I would prefer not to remove the protection anonymity grants them this soon. Tonight I would like to go over the information we have in light of a possible Elven connection."

He left the other two men with this thought, knowing only too well both were as disquieted as he was. But as he extinguished the candle and pulled the unresisting body of his ErGer into his arms, he also knew that the peace her presence gave him would not be shared with them; not yet at least.

13

Decision

Something was wrong, really wrong. She had no idea how she knew this, but she did. She had woken, still in Lucian's arms, but surrounded by the dim light of hidden lamps in the ceiling. Their light was harsher than the candles she had become accustomed to, more intrusive, but it had not been their light that woke her.

From her estimation the time was still early enough in the morning that even Lucian's hibernation cycle would be hard to break, let alone that of the other vampires in the building. She knew little of the habits of this court, but just as with most courts, the lower floors were probably restricted to vampires during the "out of office" hours between four and noon. So there should have been no one moving around to wake her, especially not through the suggestion of sleep that Lucian held on her. As she slipped out from under his arm she felt his sleeping mind surrounding hers, a comforting weight encouraging her to return to sleep.

The problem was that not only had something woken *her*, but the disturbance had clearly triggered some reaction in the house to lead to the lights coming on at a time when there should be none. It was impossible to go back to sleep without finding out what was going on even if it was just a malfunction. The girls were in the building and Kathryn's sense of responsibility had raised its head. At that moment she might be the only one on this floor who was physically able to react easily. She was surrounded by hibernating vampires at their most vulnerable and she had some responsibility to find out if they were in danger. She might not be entirely clear on their status in her world, but she needed to know if there was the potential for harm.

Her lack of clothing presented the first barrier to her endeavour. Looking back to the bed and the prone body under the bedspread reminded her that using the sheet toga-style was out of the question, no matter how much she would enjoy the opportunity to study his naked form. A flash of sleepy amusement surrounding her mind made her realise that she might not be as divorced from him in this state as she had thought. Wariness rose, but in reality the realisation did not change anything. She needed clothes.

The chest of drawers loomed ominously. She knew what lay in the top drawer and was certain that no piece of clothing in there would be of any help in concealing her nakedness. But there were four other drawers below that and at least one of them should contain some form of usable garment, so why was she reluctant to open them? She admitted to herself that she was not entirely sure she wanted to know what other possible surprises the chest might hold. The surprises contained in the box he offered her each day after waking, surprises she knew originated here, in this drawer, were enough for her, although she knew that in the spectrum of toys of pain and degradation whatever he had brought her had been mild. She remembered the whips she had found in here that first night, remembered the pleasure he had felt, the anticipation. And still, until now, he had been careful with her, had watched her every move, her every reaction, and though the last few weeks had felt violent to her, they had not been. Not really. Her mind had been turned upside down, the outline of her world redrafted, but without brutality, without true pain, without harm coming to her.

She was entirely too aware of how much control that had taken from him. What would happen when that control snapped? When he abandoned the care and caution with which he treated her? A man did not own a drawer full of sexual torture instruments because he admired the handicraft going into their production. He wanted to use them, and probably use them regularly. What would happen when the novelty wore off for him and he took out his toys? She had been whipped too often to doubt that she did not like it.

None of this mattered. She was bound to him by her word, and no matter what the future might hold, she needed clothes now and her squeamishness was not helping to solve that problem. Resolutely she grabbed the lowest drawer and pulled, surprised to find her jeans and shirt, neatly folded, in it. Somehow they made her smile. She had not thought she would see these clothes again and it brought home to her that two weeks ago, when she had worn them last, she had not expected to survive long enough to wear them again. The cheap fabric of the shirt was almost abrasive as she pulled it over her head but the well-worn jeans slid over her legs like a memory of times past. They might not have been good times, but what they had been were fighting times. She had donned her armour, just as when she had come here, and was ready to find out what was going on.

Her next hurdle was the door. She had heard the locks snap shut when Lucian touched an area of wall beside the door, but rationality suggested that safeguards would be in place to protect the leader of the supernatural court of London. At first glance there seemed to be little difference in the texture and visible make-up of the wall besides the door but as she ran her fingertips over it a rectangle lit up. Not sure what to do she tried to press it as she would have a button, but only when she flattened her whole hand against it was there a change. A line of red light appeared and scanned her hand before releasing the door mechanism. As if in a dream she reached for the door handle. It opened. She had not believed that he would trust her to stand by her promise to stay. The realisation froze her in her tracks and she had to pause for a moment with her hand against the wood of the door.

Over her shoulder she saw him sprawled on the bed. She could see the elegant line of his exposed arm and shoulder stretched over the space where she had been asleep only a short time ago, his face curiously vulnerable in repose, the

220

dark eyelashes and hair a stark contrast against the pale skin. His vulnerability was brought home to her acutely when she saw this strong body lie there motionless, caught in the defencelessness of his race at dawn. Not only had he exposed himself to the possibility of danger by sleeping with her in the room, but that the danger was quite as real as her wakefulness proved. She hoped, had to hope, that it was a mistake, that he had not given his life into her hands to this extent intentionally. It was easy to deal with the fact that her own physical and mental health was under his control; she was not sure she wanted to deal with the emotional implications of him having handed that power over to her. She welcomed the feeling of unease that distracted her from these considerations and drove her out the door. Nothing scared her more than emotional confusion.

The hallway outside the door was lit by artificial light and it was empty. Nothing seemed out of place in the long hallway or the myriad passageways leading from it. Still, her disquiet rose with every moment she spent in those long, wood-panelled passages, among old art and antique furniture. Every time she passed one of the solid oak doors she paused for an instant, listening for any sound, any evidence that the occupant was stirring. But all remained eerily quiet, a silence deep enough that it was hard to avoid the comparison to a grave.

It was more by chance that she managed to find her way back to the hallway in front of Lucian's room. Here the feeling of disquiet bloomed into a sensation of worry bordering on fear, but there was nothing to give her any indication of where it had come from. On her right stood the doors of the elevator that would be able to carry her upstairs where she could investigate further, but she felt uncomfortable about leaving the vampires down here, especially Lucian, unprotected. She had checked the door to his room several times through her search but it had remained unlocked. She found a similar panel to lock the door from the outside and placed her palm against the sensor, holding the image of it in her mind and pushing it against the walls of his. She had felt no awareness from him since the earlier flash of amusement, had no idea if she could reach him in any way, but at least she felt she had done the best she could. With that thought she entered the elevator and activated it by allowing another panel to scan her hand again. High-tech vampires indeed.

The apartment upstairs was just as quiet and deserted. After a quick visit to the bathroom she resolved to find a way to the floor where the girls stayed and check on them first. It was interesting that she had not panicked right away and felt a need to check on them. Even now she was relatively calm regarding their safety. It brought home to her, more than anything, how much she had handed the responsibility of their safety over to Lucian. She might wonder if he had sufficiently protected himself or even her, but she was in no doubt that the girls were behind a phalanx of protection so stringent that an army would be needed to get to them. She found the door leading out of the penthouse – and stepped into pandemonium.

The door led out onto a gallery overlooking the lobby of

the floor below, on which a standoff between a large number
of policemen and black-clad security personnel seemed to be
in progress. At its centre, one well-dressed and imposing
figure was screaming at another whilst a third man was held
to the floor by four policemen. She did not know the man on
the floor but the man who was the target of the screaming
was Eric, Lucian's major-domo. It would have been
surprisingly satisfying if her presence had any effect on the
situation. Unfortunately, everyone seemed oblivious to it, and
she had no idea if it would help the situation. For a moment
she considered returning downstairs and ensuring that the
lower floors were secure, but the immediate danger seemed to
be to Eric and, potentially, to the girls on the lower floor. She
had made those downstairs as safe as she could. Now it was
time to see if she could do something here. Whatever the
reason was for the police demanding entrance, it was
happening on the floor below her, not in the cellars. She
chose the staircase that would bring her out closest to the
doors to the lower apartment as she descended to the lower
floor, listening and trying to make sense of what was going
on.

Eric was repeating himself calmly. "You cannot enter here,
Sir, without proper authorisation or permission by my
employers, who are currently unavailable to give said
permission."

The other man was having none of it, his face unpleasantly
red over the well-cut black suit. "I am investigating a
kidnapping. Information has led me to suppose that the
victim is being held here."

A kidnapping? Here? This surprised Kathryn. She knew that the top two floors were limited to Lucian's personal household, accessed only by a select few. He had assured her that apart from Eric and his wife, the twins, himself and her, only the girls were allowed access past the ground floor, and in the time she had spent here there had not been any evidence to the contrary.

But it was not the accusation that rubbed her the wrong way – it was the demeanour of the stranger. Too much sly aggression towards someone whose nature was too warm, too timid to stand up to it. Eric was fey, or at least mixed blood, and held the illusion of a human appearance well enough, but he was meek in character and so shy that she had voiced concerns over his ability to keep her boisterous girls in check. Still, he showed surprising backbone in the way he denied the visitor access.

"Sir, I am sorry, but you will have to return this evening to wait for Lord Neben's return. I cannot grant you access without his permission."

"You have no choice." Disdain dripped from every syllable and the large man moved forward as if to bodily push Eric out of the way.

"Kidnapping? How horrible! Of course we are happy to provide support and help in whatever way we can within the requirements of the law."

Why did she speak? Why did she feel the need to step in to defend Eric? One second there were too many emotions and then there was only one: he was one of hers, hers to protect, hers to care for. He was a member of her court. His eyes were

224

cold and met hers implacably. She could almost see the wheels turning.

"We have received information about a young woman, Kathryn McClusky, and her three daughters being held against their will here by the CEO of the company, Lucian Neben. We have come to investigate these accusations." His tone was challenging, as were his eyes. But the reaction she felt from Eric was more drastic. The man cringed with fear, almost jerking into her path as if to keep her from coming closer. And suddenly she understood. This was her way out. She had given her word not to take any action to escape but if she told this man and the police that she was a captive here, or even simply said her name without disabusing him of the idea that she was a captive, he would carry her and the girls off without her ever having broken her word. There was still a good chance that they would break into the vault and carry Lucian off to prison, potentially killing him in the course of the arrest through sun exposure during hibernation, ridding her of the bond. She would be free without ever having broken her word and Eric knew this. His tension, and that of the security personnel, was due to her being a threat; not physically, but a very clear legal threat. It was their loyalty to Lucian, and their distrust of her, that had caused the tension.

She felt a wave of relief coursing over her. It validated her instinctive rejection of the thought that she could betray Lucian. This man had manipulated her and forced her into coming to him, into agreeing to link her mind and life to his. He had forced her body into sexual acts she could not think about without blushing, had badgered and pushed her into

225

eating, sleeping and even bathing. He had invaded and taken over every aspect of her life, had forced her to kneel at his feet, but no matter what he had done, no matter what he was promising to do in the future, her fight was with him and it was her fight. He had given the girls his protection, and even though he might have done so in order to keep control of her, the care and thoughtfulness he showed in his interactions offset this potential mercenary motive. But there was another dimension. As ruthless, as hard and manipulating as this man might be in his actions, he was also intensely loyal, honourable and protective. She had seen him pour over the proposal for a little corner shop one of his vassals had presented to him for comment with the same attention as he devoted to the million-pound projects of his own business. She had heard him discuss the needs of a single father in his employ with the same seriousness as he devoted to the security concerns Brandon regularly brought to him. He was devoting more attention to those than to security. And she had seen him distract Helene when her overabundance of energy threatened to disturb everyone else, without a thought for dignity or distance. For all of that he deserved the loyalty of his people, and hers. Her trust and obedience was a completely different matter.

"Fortunately," she said, addressing Armani-man. "I should be able to clear up this misunderstanding. I am Kathryn McClusky and I can assure you that I, as well as the girls, are here entirely of our own volition."

She could almost feel the breath of relief travelling through Eric and the assorted security personnel, although the man she had spoken to gave her a dark scowl instead.

She met his annoyance with calm assurance, trying to portray the image of absolute confidence. It only seemed to deepen his glare. She had no idea where the staring contest would have gone had Eric not, clearly deciding that she was less of a wild cannon than he had thought, broken it by informing her of the as yet unexplained background of the situation. Apparently at barely eight in the morning, Armani-man, whose name turned out to be Robert Owens with the Crown Prosecution Service, had appeared in front of the building brandishing a warrant that allowed him to search the premises of Neben Enterprises. When he tried to enter the upstairs and subterranean spaces he had been informed that these were not under the possession of the business, but the personal property of Lucian Neben and therefore excluded from the warrant. Citing the case of a kidnapping as an emergency, Mr. Owens had insisted on entering the premises. When refused entry by the deputy chief of security, the man restrained on the floor, he had accused them of subverting the course of justice. That was the point at which Kathryn had appeared on the stage.

There was a wide range of worries fighting for dominance in Kathryn's mind. She could hear the movement below where a second contingent of police was already searching the business premises. Why? And why was this man here? His suit was too well cut, too expensive for that of a simple lackey, and it seemed strange that anyone higher in the pecking order would accompany the delivery of a warrant to search premises. There was no one in her life who could have

227

put enough pressure on the justice system to prompt such a high level attention to her supposed abduction. This did not even touch on the question of who had given her name to the Crown Prosecution Service.

"Eric, I assume you have contacted Lord Lucian's attorney?" The moment the title slipped out she could have kicked herself. His title was that of the nocturnal court, not the outside world. It was interesting that Mr. Owen reacted with barely concealed anger rather than surprise at her slip.

"Yes, ErGer, he has been informed and should arrive any minute." Eric was no better at swallowing non-human titles it seemed.

"Well then, Mr. Owens, may we dispense with the crudeness until he arrives?" She gestured to the still man at their feet, hoping that she would be able to remove the danger of escalation first. It worked. At a nod he was released. "And I am sure you would like to tell your colleagues to leave the business premises. We can wait in the living room for the attorney to arrive to check the warrant. Can I offer you a coffee?"

She hoped her strategy would work. She had declared that she was not a victim held against her will and therefore there was no reason for the warrant to be carried out, but she was also certain that, as her supposed abduction was a mere smokescreen, there was every possibility that Mr. Owens would dig his heels in. For the moment she needed to remove the officers from anywhere sensitive material might be stored. She was banking on Mr. Owens being willing to wait and try to milk her for information instead. She was also counting on

Lucian's attorney being able to get them all out of this, if she just managed to buy him enough time. For someone who had never been part of a team she was counting on others surprisingly extensively. Her gamble paid off and met an unexpected problem at the same time. Mr. Owens was quite willing to follow her upstairs for a coffee and to call off his hounds. The impediment to her plan came from her own side when the deputy chief, recovered from his near arrest, informed her that he could not allow her to go upstairs alone with Mr. Owens for security reasons. For a moment she had some very impolite thoughts regarding testosterone. She knew she had no more than a couple of minutes to sort this before Mr. Owens got off the phone with his minions so she negotiated the compromise that his people would be in the hallway outside the upstairs penthouse and she would leave the door open. Both were unhappy with it but they were at least able to live with it. She supposed that this would be the best she could get.

On her way up she wondered how Mr. Owens would play his cards. What he tried to discover would hopefully give her an idea of what was going on and provide valuable information for Lucian when he rose. She did not have to wait long for the conversation to leave the ever present British opening of the weather. They had barely taken seats on the sofas upstairs, facing each other across the glass coffee table, when Mr. Owens asked the first question – clearly meant to pry, if not disturb.

"ErGer? It sounded almost like a title when Lachlan addressed you with it." Lachlan? Oh yes, Eric's last name –

the intentional disrespect Mr. Owens displayed by refusing to use the man's title annoyed her almost enough to answer without due consideration. It almost hid the fact that he was fishing for information. She might not have been prepared for this if she had not noticed his study of her scarred and exposed neck and the overwhelming stink of garlic emanating from him.

She was certain he would be wearing a cross under his shirt. She knew that again and again there were suspicions among humans and conspiracy nuts who set out to prove the existence of vampires, but they were rarely at this level of government. She wondered if she should shake his composure by mentioning that neither religious symbols nor garlic were an efficient deterrent. Instead, she stretched her arm along the backrest of the settee, ensuring that the exposed skin of her lower arm and hand came to rest in the pooling sun there. His eyes followed her movements greedily and she saw them widen in surprise when there was no adverse effect on her skin. So he was looking for vampires here but had come without any concrete knowledge. His body language showed that he had decided that she was no threat after seeing her in the sun and therefore was entirely ignorant of the fact that sun was only harmful to most vampires after the fledgling stage when they had fallen into hibernation. Or that all the glass in the building was treated to filter ultraviolet rays of the relevant harmful bandwidth.

"Merely a nickname." Her voice was even and non-committal. She doubted that there was any chance that this man knew what an ErGer was, especially after having displayed such overwhelming ignorance as to the nature of vampires. He let the topic drop.

"The scars on your neck are horrific," he said. A statement no doubt intended to make her feel uncomfortable and ugly. She could live with that.

"Yes," she said, revealing nothing.

"An accident?" Clearly he was not about to let this slip. Did he believe there to be a weakness where there was none?

"An attack," she said.

He shifted in his seat to lean forward, a bloodhound on a cold trail. "Who attacked you? I will be happy to bring them to justice."

"It was wild animals." Deadpan. The moment she said it she realised she had made a mistake. He had offered his help, at least in his own eyes, and she had shown him up, embarrassed him and polarised the situation further. She should have been more careful but she had become caught up in the verbal match without giving enough attention to the fact that they were not playing a game.

"You have three daughters here?"

She did not want him to inquire into the girls and it was impossible for her to suppress her instinctive start at their mention. Her only chance was to cover it with banalities, to divert and deflect.

"I have two sisters and one daughter, all of which are in class just now. May I ask who informed you of my supposed abduction, Mr. Owens?" But it didn't work. This man might be ignorant but he was not stupid. He had found a weakness and was not about to let it, or her, escape.

"They are home-schooled?"

"For the moment. We are planning to enrol them in a new school after the summer. We have been moving regularly and it seemed easiest to allow them to acclimatise to the new city before subjecting them to a new school." She knew the girls were being taught a wide range of subjects, had seen the curriculum and discussed its content with Lucian, but she had never enquired if any permissions for home-schooling had been acquired. The children were her weakness and she had left too many cities under the threat of social services, rather than the vampire threat, for her not to be aware of the precariousness of her situation.

"Do your parents agree with the home-schooling?"

She could not help the terror that was coursing through her. This was exactly what she needed to avoid. Eight years ago she had bought fake papers for the twins which named them her sisters, but nothing could change the fact that her parents had died fourteen years ago in a supposed home invasion and the girls were only ten years old. If anyone ever bothered to check then her fraud would be discovered and she would lose the girls. Her hand had balled into a fist on the backrest and she had to force herself to relax it.

"Our parents are long dead." If she was lucky he might attribute her reaction to pain connected to memories of her parents. She was never that lucky.

"I am sorry. When did they die?"

"The girls were still babies; they are almost teenagers now. It was a burglary gone wrong." There. That would hopefully be vague enough.

"You must have been very young."

"Yes." If she said as little as possible she might get through this. She met his eyes calmly, surprised by the cunning fanaticism she could see burning in their depth.

"I am surprised that you were able to care for the children. I am not sure you display the right level of maturity for their care. An association with a man like Mr. Neben could be argued not to be in the best interest of such young, impressionable minds."

She understood his threat. He was about to force a choice on her and there was nothing she could do to avert it as he leaned into her personal space, resting his hand on her leg.

"It is entirely reasonable that were you coerced into coming here. You would have been unable to keep your sisters away, though it might be hard to explain to a court why you would subject them to a man of such depraved morals without coercion. It would be even more difficult to explain their lack of schooling."

Here it was. Either she gave up Lucian or this man would take the girls and argue in court that she was not capable of caring for them. And he would win. She had done all she could over the years to care for the girls and although she had managed to ensure their health and happiness, their education had suffered. In some ways they were far ahead of their peers, but in some subjects, such as mathematics, they were not. The twins were barely able to hold their own against children two years younger than them in these subjects and whenever they attended school it was normally in a year group younger than they were. While she knew that home-schooling to a curriculum wasn't compulsory, she also knew that a formal investigation by social services would cost her the children based only on that it would bring to light her fraud, proving without doubt that she did not have a genetic claim on the twins. He left her with no choice, and the victorious smile on his lips said he knew it. It was as if his hand on her froze her in place with a suffocating certainty of mental anguish, of his enjoyment of this moment of absolute and utter defeat.

She had faced men like him many times before, men who enjoyed the utter destruction of someone they perceived as weaker than them. She kicked herself for having underestimated him. In a matter of just two weeks she had forgotten what it meant to constantly fight, to constantly be afraid. She had felt protected here, safe and able to consider a world in which every step was not fraught with danger. It all came crashing down around her now, and through the curtain of hopeless tears she looked at the man who was reminding her of what she was. A means to an end; always just a means to an end.

"But neither Mr. Neben nor any of his employees coerced me into coming here or into bringing the girls with me."

Saying the words was almost physically painful but she knew it was the only way out. If he took the children now she would lose them, but if he removed Lucian from his rooms in a state of hibernation he might die, and with him many of his court, all those too weak to have broken the Sire-bond. Even those independent of him might not survive. His death would destabilise the city and possibly even the power relations between Vampire Lords, leading to a fierce battle for dominance. And power battles among vampires were rarely civilised. Most had taken Machiavelli and built on his advice when it came to preservation of power. A new Lord would, first of all, establish a power base by killing all those formerly loyal to Lucian and those of no interest to him. She was almost certain that neither Eric or his wife, nor the twins would survive that. Lucian's death would mean that her own bond would be broken, but it would also mean that she and the girls would be on the run again. Lucian had declared them part of his household, had put them under his protection, and that meant that any new Lord would hunt them down to eradicate the link and ensure his dominance. In the vampire world it was not only the Lord that lost a fight – it was his entire court with him. It was the most effective impediment to constant power struggles; the consequences of losing were simply too great. But if a power vacuum was created through the removal of Lucian by a human, a power struggle would be inevitable.

This was not the only consideration that led her to oppose this man whose victorious smile had faded to an expression of utter disbelief. She admitted freely that had he threatened the girls she would have chosen them over Lucian and his people, and damn the consequences. She generally did not believe in the good of the many outweighing the good of the few, especially if the few were children. But he had not threatened them, he had threatened her. He would take the children now, and the pain would be heart wrenching for her and them, but in the end they would be safe and she would move heaven and earth to get them back. So would Lucian.

There was not one moment of doubt in her that the Vampire Lord of London would bring all his considerable influence and power to the table when it came to reclaiming the children. Through the tears that ran unchecked down her cheeks, even though her hands were shaking and her body felt like ice, she met his gaze and let him see her resolve and hate.

"So you are a whore who would sell her children." Finally the ugliness of his voice matched his intent. It was almost a relief. His words could not harm her; she had been called far worse too often for it to hurt. But when he stood and menacingly leaned over her she had to lock her muscles to keep from cringing away. She saw the desire to hurt someone clearly displayed in his eyes. "Well, I will go and get the little ones then." The threat, so expected, still frightened her. For a moment she thought she had misjudged him again, that his desire to harm could be a danger to the girls. She needed to provoke him into an act of rashness towards her, some expression of violence which would allow him an outlet for his feelings before he saw the children, but any attempt was forestalled before it could come to fruition by a polite cough from the door.

Mr. Owens turned, snarling at the noise, but then froze, although the figure in the door did not suggest any threat. It was an old man – old enough that Kathryn's grandfather would have appeared spry beside him. He was diminutive, short and frail, even for someone of such advanced years, but still this gentleman caused her unwelcome visitor to straighten and stiffen. Belatedly, Kathryn remembered her manners and rose to greet the new arrival, telling herself that this man, friend or foe, had at least given her a reprieve.

"Sir, can I help you?"

Where the hell was Eric? She had no idea what to do. What could a vampire captive do when faced with threats by the police and the necessity to engage in polite conversation with a complete stranger? Before she could even step past Mr. Owens to greet the gentleman she was waved off impatiently.

"Do not trouble yourself, young Lady. There is no need to stand on ceremony at all. I am your legal representation and entirely at your disposal."

Her own speechlessness was nothing in comparison to the sudden tension in the man at her side. Owens had not only gone completely still but his eyes, so full of disdain and disgust only a matter of seconds ago, were as cold and still as those of an alligator. Yet, when he spoke, his voice had returned to its cultured and bland Oxbridge accent.

"Lord Edge, it is an honour. I had no idea that you still practiced."

A Lord? Kathryn had no idea if this meant anything for the situation so she just stayed quiet. She had long since discovered that you could learn more by listening than talking. The old gentleman also took his time with an answer, traversing the distance between door and the settee with measured steps before setting down his old-fashioned briefcase and snapping its clasps open with a loud snap. It made Mr. Owens jump, and with his back turned to the man, Lord Edge winked at her. It did much to settle her before he turned to Mr. Owens and let his eyes travel slowly up the immaculate trousers and overpriced shirt. The moment in which he turned from old man to lawyer was almost visible.

"I still represent some select clients personally, even since my retirement from active practice. And of course *Edge, Straw and Holbein* have represented Neben Enterprises since its inception. I can therefore assure you that a veritable army of my younger colleagues are at this moment hard at work downstairs to clear up this misunderstanding." His voice was deceptively soft, honey over steel. A caution clearly too subtle for the other man.

"So you are representing Mr. Neben, not Miss McClusky. If you would please give me a moment I will be happy to return..." Mr. Owens voice had shown relief when he spoke but Lord Edge's raised hand halted his speech before he could finish the sentence.

"I am sorry if I left any room for confusion, young man. I should have clarified that I represent both Mr. Neben and his new wife."

In the first moment she had no idea how Mr. Owens reacted to this announcement as she was too consumed with her own stunned surprise. To pretend that they were married might solve a lot of problems now but would backfire quickly. It was too easy to disprove. But it might, just might, buy them enough time to get the children away.

She felt Lucian strongly in her mind, surrounding her with waves of reassurance and the suggestion of calmness. He clearly did not want her to lose control of her composure or to protest the marriage declaration. It made her furious, absolutely furious. Who did he think he was! She did not mind the marriage lie. The idea of marriage had never mattered to her. As a little girl she had never dreamt of it, not even before she had found out that she was an ErGer. She had dreamt of love, of someone who would go on adventures with her, discover the world and fight injustice and dishonour, but she had never dressed up her dolls to play wedding. In the years of her constant flight marriage had never even merited a wistful thought. There was no sentimentality attached to the concept in her mind. That was not why she was furious, why she wanted to wring his neck. She was furious because he dared to patronise her by thinking she might be so dim-witted as to protest here and now, in front of an "enemy". She was so occupied with her anger that she only half heard the conversation of the other two men.

"*Wife.*" Mr. Owens did not yell and still the incredulity in that one word made it reverberate loudly in the room.

"Wife. The marriage was registered two weeks ago. The romantic date of February fourteenth. I am sure you understand why a man with Mr. Neben's standing did not want to make the date public knowledge."

She had to hand it to Mr. Owens, he put away that knowledge and dealt with it – though he needed a millisecond to adjust, his cold eyes fixed on Kathryn, boring holes into her as if he wanted to singe her skin with his gaze. She met his eyes unflinchingly.

"The children—"

Lord Edge again did not let Mr. Owens finish the sentence.

"The adoption papers have been filed."

This almost made Kathryn twitch until she realised that

this also had to be a ploy to buy time. Then she realised that even if it turned out not to be it would not change anything. In very real time Lucian was their guardian; at the moment more so than her. Again a wave of reassurance stroked around her mind, stronger now.

"There is no judge who would allow a man like Neben to adopt a child." Mr. Owens' voice had risen in volume and tone and the disdain in it increased Kathryn's ire. She might stand by and have him call her a whore, but Lucian did not deserve that tone, no matter what he was. But before she could say anything Lord Edge's silky tones intervened.

"A man like that? Whatever do you mean? Mr. Neben is a successful business man of high standing. Or do you have information contrary to this?"

Suddenly Kathryn understood. She had taken it as given that Lucian as a vampire would be unable to stand against the law openly, but he did not have to. For Mr. Owens to take the children now, when they were the wards of a well-known businessman and his wife, he would have to admit that he thought this man to be a vampire, and even in today's world of vampire enthusiasm he would be laughed out of a court room. He might be able to take them later when he found out how often they had moved, and most importantly how their documentation was blatantly fake, but for the moment he would have to leave without them and without any papers obtained by the search. For the first time in the last half hour Kathryn was able to take an uninhibited breath again. She allowed herself a smile as she met his icy gaze. They still had no idea what this man wanted, why he was truly there, but for the moment at least, the girls and the court were safe.

Mr. Owens left without another word to her. Kathryn's mind was still assimilating information and setting out an action plan for the near future. Unfortunately, what might be possible was very much dependent on the amount of time they had just bought and on Lucian. By the time the hallway door closed behind Mr. Owens her whole body was shaking.

"He will be back for the girls," she said. Her voice was strangled and Lord Edge's smile turned quickly.

"Milady, please sit down. There is no need for alarm."

His incomprehension of the situation agitated her more and opened the doors to the panic she had suppressed. The feeling of Lucian's calm increased around her mind but she was too far gone to relate to it. She was rushing into another panic attack. She needed all her strength to push the words out through the rising tide of terror but she had to make the lawyer understand.

"The twins' papers are fake." She didn't even consider the possibility that there might be any ethical or legal issue involved in telling the man that she had committed forgery. It only mattered that he needed the information to begin an attempt to protect the children. His quiet laughter shocked her out of her terror-induced stupor.

"That matter has long been taken care of and does not have to concern you. There may be other issues, but strategic responses have been set in place for the possibility that someone might come for the children legally."

She looked at him uncomprehendingly. What the hell did he mean? He took her hand and stroked it gently.

"Not to worry. Lord Lucian had the police reports regarding the death of your parents dated forward by five years when he looked into the matter eight months ago. He also made sure that the relevant personnel have an interest in forgetting the exact date. Only interviews with neighbours might lead to some questions but it is unlikely that anyone will go to that much trouble if there is no indication of foul play. If the worst comes to the worst we can happily blame foreign record keeping on changed dates. British courts are often happy to believe in the inferiority of foreign records. I believe you acquired birth certificates for the girls stamped in Romania. We should be able to play with that. And most importantly, with that many contrary pieces of evidence, we will be able to stretch out any proceedings, if there will be any, which I very much doubt."

It was very interesting that the one thing that stuck in her mind was the timeframe. She had only been in London for three months.

"Eight months ago?"

"Well, yes. That was when he contacted me to consider the possible avenues we would have to guard against and informed me of the need to change the dates."

Eight months. She had still been in Switzerland then, had not even settled in France from where she had come over to London. Suddenly she realised how far back her life had been controlled by Lucian. Had the hunters who found her in Switzerland and in France been sent by him to force her into coming to London? She had no answer and was not sure she wanted one.

14

Possession

She had switched off the lights and lit the candles again. Sitting on the red sheets waiting for the infuriating man to wake up she enjoyed the intimate comfort of the soft light. Something had happened upstairs after Mr. Owens had left and the revelations had come to an end. Her mind had become fogged, incapable of concentrating on anything but a need to return to Lucian's side. Lord Edge seemed curiously unperturbed by her inability to concentrate on him and had simply patted her hand gently and allowed her to leave. Eric had wordlessly held the elevator door open for her and accompanied her downstairs. Her mind had only started to clear when she reached Lucian's side, though as soon as she settled Indian-style on the bed beside him, a bone-deep tiredness settled into her. It was almost impossible not to lie down and return to sleep but she was lucid enough to realise that it was Lucian who was trying to pull her under and she simply did not want to comply. She was too confused and troubled to relent. When the pressure to rest became overwhelming she pushed against what she knew to be Lucian and felt the pressure recede, though what she perceived to be his attention did not waver.

As her mind cleared she was amazed by the texture and structure of their bond and his state in hibernation. In theory his body should force a period of inactivity on him, a period in which he was utterly helpless and lost to the world; a state close to death. Still, she felt him alive and awake in her mind, perhaps not as utterly 'there' as she felt him on occasion in wakefulness, but still 'there' enough to affect her. It was only when she took his hand into hers that both of their minds calmed, allowing her to clear her thoughts, but whenever she tried to think of the girls and the danger to them she felt her mind skitter away. She worried that she had turned into one of these women incapable of facing problems, but even that thought was taken from her. She settled back onto the question of hibernation, seemingly an acceptable topic for her consideration.

To her knowledge the length of hibernation was as dependent on the strength of a vampire as it was on the rate of melatonin production. The vampire's body, changed through the virus, required melatonin for rejuvenation and healing, but the disadvantage lay in the need to shut down the physical demands on the body in order to stockpile enough for the day. The best time for this was during the hours of sunlight as the increased melatonin production also made a vampire vulnerable to certain wavelengths contained in daylight. A vampire had to recharge his melatonin levels at regular times but, realistically, there was no need for him, or her, to do so at daybreak. The only stipulation was that the period of rest remained uninterrupted for the required time, making hibernation almost impossible to break. She had never considered that the wide slew of mental abilities a vampire held were little affected and that their hibernation seemed to be an entirely physical act. At least that was the conclusion she had drawn from the influence Lucian seemed to retain on her mind.

What did this mean to her? Two weeks ago she had been sure that by this stage she would either be his puppet or dead. It had turned out to be neither. Her bond linked her to him, allowed him to influence her. Control her? She was not so sure about that. He had tried to calm her down, to divert her thoughts away from certain topics, but she was aware that she could resist his suggestion. Was this because their bond was in its infant stages or because he had allowed her to do so? Would she ever know? Her life had taken a turn so unpredictable that she was lost; the only fixed point was the man whose hand she held. She would never have thought it possible that she would be in the situation where the most important question had become 'could she trust a Vampire Lord?'

But she was too honest not to admit that it was not a question of choice. This consideration was not based on the fact that she was held captive by him. She knew too well that something in her was broken, possibly beyond repair. The question was not so much if he was trustworthy, no matter how much she wanted it to be, it was if she was capable of trusting him and she had no answer to that. She had felt him start to wake at various stages in her thought processes, had felt his attention on her. How much of her thoughts could he follow, how much could he read in her mind?

"I don't trust you." Her eyes met his, wanting him to see the truth of the statement in her eyes.

"Do you want to?" he asked.

She felt the world hang on her answer. It would signify the beginning of an unknown road and give away more of herself than the statement had. Was she courageous enough to take that first step? A future was tantalising her with its possibility of even existing. It was hope that made her say the words. A fool's hope possibly, but hope had been for so long the only companion of her mind.

"Yes, I want to trust you."

He did not smile at her answer but joy radiated from him as he rose on one elbow to cradle her face.

"Then you will learn." Each word a quiet confidence, a gentle caress. And with it she allowed him to pull her into the warmth of his embrace, to settle her into the hollow of his body, surrounded by his scent and touch in the darkness of the room.

In the warmth of his arms her mind relaxed enough to allow her to consider the life she found herself in. Under the hypnotic caress of his hand gently stroking her long spine, the even rhythm of his breath over her face, she was able to let go of the emotional battering of the earlier situation and let rationality take over. She realised that she had, almost subconsciously, gone through the usual steps she needed to take to flee the city – what needed to be taken, how to muddy her trail – just as she had done countless times over the last decade and a half. It shocked her that she had almost made the decision to run with the girls, no matter what that would have meant for their long-term survival, or her promise for that matter. It had just been second nature to her, the way she reacted to threats.

Looking at the deep blue eyes in front of her she saw the knowledge of her potential flight in them, though there was not the condemnation she had expected. He was so close, his body turned to face hers, a long warm line along the length of hers, soft skin over hard muscle. She felt the relaxation and warmth through her clothes, curiously unaffected by his nakedness, only conscious of the intimacy of their position.

"Did you set it up?"

The moment she asked it she knew that she was being stupid. She had been forced to recognise and choose a life with him over a life without, uncertain of what that life would look like. She had been given a way o t, with the incentive of a threat to the children, and she had consciously chosen him. The situation had played into his hands but it was stupid to assume he had set it up. She lived under no illusion that he was not Machiavellian enough to engineer a situation in which the same choice might be forced on her, even using the children as long as they remained unaware of the situation, but he would not have involved a high ranking human official. He was a manipulative powermonger, not foolhardy. He did not even bother answering her question but others had to be addressed.

"Who is Mr. Owens?" She decided to start with the most current issue and work her way back from that. In some way, she was aware she was testing him, seeing if he would answer her questions truthfully.

"He is a barrister with the Crown Prosecution Service, a rather high level one."

The sparseness of the answer was a challenge in itself.

"What was he doing here?" She liked the quick smile and the sparkle in his eyes. It made him look more human and so much more dangerous to her. His hand abandoned its rhythm on her back to gently stroke a strand of hair from her brow.

"A simple power play in our negotiations with the government."

At this her whole body tensed, fear rising, and breathing became difficult. Government attention was never good, not for vampires and not for runaways who forged papers and stole children. Immediately he pulled her closer, feathering her face with gentle kisses until she was able to breathe normally again. When she had calmed he spoke.

"Kathryn, it was just a standard power play, nothing to worry about. I would be more worried if, at this stage of the proceedings, they had not tried some intimidation tactics. Though we will have to see who gave them your name. I am uncomfortable about that as it might hint at a leak in our own ranks. But it is overall nothing entirely unexpected. We will deal with it."

"What do you mean 'negotiations with the government'? What negotiations?" She was unwilling to be diverted from this point. He would be able to deal with the issues in his own ranks, most likely had for centuries, but the overall threat of governmental action against them threatened them all, her and the children included. The supernatural community was too aware of history, the inquisition and witch burnings being the most notable incidences, to be comfortable with too much official attention.

"The new government has approached us regarding registration of supernaturals. As the representative of the supernatural community I lead the negotiations from our side. Neither them, nor we for that matter, want it to become common knowledge that we exist but, due to the whole vampire craze, for the first time in history the government perceives that we have less to lose than them, and that makes them uncomfortable. So they are trying to limit the danger to them should we decide to take a lead. This is not the first time a human government has tried to pressure us and it will not be the last."

Her hands had cramped into fists against his chest and his words did nothing to relax her. "Yeah, the last few times ended in burning!"

She could see he was surprised at her vehemence.

"Kathryn, you are human in their eyes. Even if the situation were to escalate, you would be unaffected by possible repercussions."

"You bastard!" She was so unbelievably angry by his callous brushing away of her concerns, especially because she did not know if she could make him see her point. Her concern was not only for herself, or even the children, but for the wider implications, the potential deaths and sufferings of so many too weak to defend themselves. It was always the weak that suffered. That made the threat very real for she was one of the weak, and no matter that she was human, in their eyes she would not be human enough. He had no concept of weakness. She tried to push away from his touch, too angry to suffer the intimacy, but at her first movement he turned from gentle confidant to dominating male, rolling to cover her body with his, capturing her resisting wrists with his hands. In the blink of an eye her situation had changed dramatically.

"Tell me!" He insisted.

His gentle tones had deepened, entered the space in which there was no leeway for prevarication. He had taken absolute control, and her whole being comprehended it when he touched her like this.

Suddenly his nakedness was no longer innocently intimate but erotic. Her mind was unable to comprehend the mixed signals, the rapid change occasioned with only a look, a change in voice. But he was not pushing her, not forcing his will on her, simply making her aware of his dominance.

"Tell me!" the absolute confidence in his voice should have pushed her to comply but she was too smart, or too scared, to tell him the most important secret.

"It will be the weakest ones that will suffer if the government decides to hunt again, not you, the ones that make the decisions."

His eyes were serious on hers, searching for something; she did not know what. She relaxed her body, trying to defuse his need to control her, making herself appear as compliant and submissive as she could. Though he did not show any outward sign of it, she knew he was annoyed at her response. Her mind started to race frantically to remember anything she may have said to annoy him, but he did not give her the time to think.

"Kathryn, remember when you said you wanted to trust me?"

He waited for an answer and there was nothing she could do but nod. His mouth descended onto hers, but before he touched her, he whispered against her lips.

"This will be your first lesson." Then he took her breath with the softness of his lips. He invaded her senses with touch, and smell, and taste. Took her attention and scattered it under the onslaught of sensation so that her internal warning bells only started to chime when he removed his hands from her wrists and she found them immobilised.

The warning bells chimed louder as he sat up and allowed her a good look into his face, into his eyes. What she saw there was absolute resolve.

"Leaving aside that you have just insulted me by assuming that I have no interest in protecting those under my care, let's turn to a problem we seem to encounter again and again. Let's call it a failure in communication."

His tone was deceptively mild and she realised that she had just accused him of something that in his world could have been taken as a mortal insult. She had no time to even consider the apology he deserved before his hands gripped her shirt at her neckline and, in one smooth movement, ripped it apart. She could not contain the whimper escaping her but he simply continued in a conversational tone.

"Now, it might very well be that this shirt held some sentimental value for you, but then, I would not know about it, would I? Because you have never told me so." His hands came to rest on her rib cage, warm and strong, holding her without pressure. It caused a strange warmth in her belly and a flutter of nervousness in her mind. "Which is exactly what I will call our communication shortfall. You are very sparse in the information you give me voluntarily."

His hands stroked gently to her back, and in a practised move she felt her bra open. Could he see the fear she felt?

"There is no doubt at all that you are fulfilling your promise by not lying to me, but as you keep most things to yourself you are hardly challenged on this point."

Two further quick yanks allowed him to throw the remnants of both shirt and bra to the floor beside them. Leaning over her, bracketing her with his arms resting on each side of her head, he turned into a menacing shadow over her. Her breath had sped up at his first touch but now became almost too fast to fill her lungs. He lowered himself onto his elbows, catching her face between his palms. His eyes, full of power and control, reached into her to touch her very core, inexplicably calming her with his presence. Almost instinctively she adjusted her breathing to his, taking air into her body, tasting his essence with each deep breath.

"The reason why you are not talking to me is because you have learnt too well that information is power and you do not trust me, or anyone, enough to give them power over you. Unfortunately, the bond does not allow me to read your thoughts and never will."

The relief she felt over this almost made her miss what he said next.

"And the fact that you have never asked about the extent of the bond is a good example of the communication shortfall. Two days ago I would not have dared to do what I am going to do, to push you past the silence into beginning to trust me, because you have no idea where your limits lie and you will not communicate enough with me to allow me to learn about your thought processes. But now, although I might not be able to know your thoughts, I can feel your emotions enough to disperse with the caution of the last two weeks, especially as your physician is happy with your physical recovery. So let's see where we might start."

In sharp, short movements he stripped the bed of pillows and blankets, leaving her bound on the dark red satin sheet. She wanted to be terrified of him holding her there so effortlessly but she could not. She was nervous and more than a little scared of what he might do, but she realised in that moment that she had lost her fear of him. The gentle smile with which he checked her wrist restraints, ensuring that she could not hurt herself on them but was still securely held, made her realise how firmly his mind surrounded hers. She felt tendrils of awareness permeating her mind, tendrils that had not been there before he took her blood. She felt unaccountably cherished.

His hands stroked with firm pressure along her arms, her flanks, waking her skin to the warmth of his touch, weaving a net of sensation over her body and mind. When he reached the waistband of her jeans he dipped his fingers underneath the fabric. A challenge? Definitely. It made her aware of their position and intent before he unsnapped the buttons one by one. She understood the message. He was daring her to resist, to fight the slow removal of her jeans. But as his hands stroked over her butt and along her long legs, taking the denim with them, she lay caught in passivity, caught between a desire to risk all, here and now, and the shadow of experience. She was almost paralysed in indecision, between wavering impulses and the threat of the unknown. He made good use of her passivity by robbing her of the last of her clothes and loosely attaching ankle cuffs to her legs. Then he knelt at the foot of the bed, his hands resting firmly on her calves, a gentle massage of her tense muscles the only contact point, and ran his hot gaze over her body.

"Baby, you have no concept of how beautiful you are." His voice was almost a reverent whisper echoing through the dim cavern of the room.

"You are the beautiful one." She had not intended to say that out loud, had not intended to think it even. Her lack of control worried her less than it should have.

"Feel what I feel, Kathryn. Feel how beautiful you are for me." She could feel his pleasure as a low level buzz in the back of her mind, a blanket with sparks of heat. It was hard to believe that this was his reaction to her.

"I have scars."

His finger played over the white line on her thigh, a knife scar, old enough to have faded.

"I cannot find them ugly." His gaze was so serious it was

hard to doubt him but she still managed it. And he was too attuned to her not to realise that.

"I cannot find them ugly because they are simply part of you. They are part of the woman that is you. And you are a magnificent woman."

"They made me what I am, you mean!" She heard the bitterness in her own words. He held her gaze as he bent forward to run his tongue in a long, even sweep over the slight ridge on her skin. And with that one movement a sudden heat bloomed in her.

"No. I believe you were that person long before your nature as an ErGer revealed itself. I do not believe that our core changes with what happens to us, it simply defines what we will do. These scars have not turned you into the warm, intelligent, loyal and honourable woman you are, though they might sometimes hide that woman from view. I will happily spend the rest of my life enticing her to come out and play."

The image of him kneeling there, at the foot of the bed, candlelight playing over his naked skin, brought the image of a tiger ready to pounce to mind, but his eyes dispelled that idea. There was no wildness there, just controlled intent and a powerful will. This was no animal feeding a sudden hunger but a man with an endless thirst for her.

"By the end of the night you will trust me with every thought in your mind without censor or restraint." It was a dark promise and a provocation, a dare.

She expected him to crawl up the bed but instead he rose to relight the flames in the hearth and add some more candles to the room. His movements were smooth, utterly secure in his skin, certain of his form in a way she envied. The envy was quickly overtaken by a fascination with the promise of sensation. When he turned, his long, silky hair fell over his back and she could almost feel the smooth strands stroking over her own skin. As his hands cupped the small flames she felt their heat caressing her limbs, and as he knelt at the fireplace she imagined the feeling of his strong muscles holding her. Heat pooled between her legs and she felt herself go damp. It surprised her. The last two weeks had left her almost constantly damp, but her body had never reacted to the mere sight of this striking man moving around. As he placed the last candle on the chest of drawers she saw the long lines of his back and firm globes of his ass in the stark contrast thrown by the firelight. An unfamiliar temptation to touch, to run her fingers down that back, to kiss the two dimples over his butt made her pull against the restraints. She must have made a noise for he half-turned to her, examining her face with his all-seeing blue eyes. What he saw must have pleased him as it stretched his lips into a knowing smile.

"I like that you like what you see."

That arrogant comment almost made her forget about what he was doing, but nothing could make her ignore the opening of the top drawer, the contents of which had been all too clearly imprinted on her mind that first night. She gasped and all relaxation left her body. He turned fully to her and, whilst collecting various items from the depth of the drawer, he held her brown eyes in a constant reminder of who was there with her. It did not help. Fear and trepidation erased the warmth he had built before. By the time he returned to the bed, dropping various items on the sheets besides her body, she was shaking.

He calmly straddled her, and as he leant forward to take her mouth in a deep kiss, his long hair curtained them in a world of their own. His kisses were deep and addictive, a leisurely play on her senses, an instant aphrodisiac. He took his time to taste and feel every last corner of her mouth and only let up when both their lips were swollen and sensitive.

"That's it. I want you to be only aware of me." There was a wicked light in his eyes – wicked, aroused and full of gentle laughter, a combination more desirable than anything.

"First, I will narrow your world so that your busy little brain cannot take you away, and then I will play with you. The rules will be simple. I get to do whatever I want and you have to take it. If you tell me something I do not know and cannot find out any other way, something secret and intimate, then and only then will I give you relief."

She did not understand what he meant but her confusion was quickly overtaken by alarm when he covered her eyes with a soft cloth. She did not like the limitation to her sight even though he had blindfolded her repeatedly over the last two weeks. It made her tense, and increased her awareness of both his touch and his taste. She felt his lips stroking over the cloth, gentling her into the darkness. She was surprised when his hands slipped under her shoulders and he made her upper body more comfortable – she had not noticed the discomfort from her muscles, but he had. He had noticed the increased tenseness and adjusted her body to avoid it. That realisation was terrifying and reassuring in equal measures.

She felt him get off the bed, though his hand remained a calming pressure on her skin at all times. A gentle pressure was laid over her torso, just under her breasts, and as it tightened her body was further immobilised by what she realised was a strap. A second strap followed the first just over her breasts. Both straps were tight but not painful, smooth lines of warming leather on her overheated skin.

"I am just making sure that you cannot move suddenly and risk hurting yourself." His voice was an anchor in her world, a deep note of calm in her rising nervousness. It almost failed to stave off the waves of panic when he gently lifted her right leg and bent it to attach a thigh cuff to the side of the bed, leaving her exposed. She tried to struggle but he had ensured that her range of movement was already so limited that any resistance was ineffective at best. Quickly he attached a second cuff on her other thigh and tightened the ankle restraints, leaving her laid out on the bed, restrained and open, her legs parted and bent, entirely helpless and accessible to his touch.

"You have no idea how beautiful you are like this — splayed for my desire, unable to resist the pleasure I can give you." It was his voice that kept the rising panic at bay. She felt the bed dip on her side and knew he had come to kneel beside her, but the first real touch was a soft kiss on her belly, a loving touch more than a seduction. Then his hands began to play over her in gentle caresses and soft massages, touching her everywhere without a pattern that would have forewarned her. One moment his hands were playing along her flank, over her hipbone, the next they circled her wrists above the restraints, reminding her of them, or massaged along her thigh. But he never touched her pussy or let even the gentlest movement play over her breasts. This absence made her skin there hungry and sensitive to him, more so than he could have done with hands or lips. She started to burn, inside out, every cell of her body reorienting itself to him, her mind consumed entirely by the expectation of his touch. Her ears followed his movements, her nose noticing his scent over that of the fire and her own arousal. When his lips engulfed her nipple in wet, hot sensation, a strange sound was torn from her, a sound somewhere between a moan and a cry. His encouragement became a caress of its own on her sensitised skin.

"Sing for me, Kathryn. Let me hear your pleasure."

He took his time with her breasts, sucking, licking, never pushing her endurance but centring all her attention on his mouth over her nipples and his hands roving over her body. Only when she felt both her breasts swollen and heavy, her nipples taut and engorged, did he let up. Her breath was panting and as he sat up, removing his hands from her, she whimpered from abandonment, not pleasure. Every aspect of her demanded his touch, his scent, his voice – him.

His dark laughter rose to engulf her.

"Shh, now. We have only just started. I am here, always at your side. Remember that to get relief you only have to tell me something intimate, something I cannot guess or reason out for myself. A secret of your heart." As he spoke she heard the sound of a bottle opening, and the smell of peppermint permeated the room. She felt the touch of a cool cloth over nipples, leaving behind a slight wetness, nothing else. She was distracted from the new sensation by the hand gently stroking along her thigh to her vagina, a teasing touch cumulating in a finger stroking along her labia, collecting the moisture at her entrance and spreading it along the length to circle once over her clitoris. Then she felt a second cloth stroking along each side of her engorged clitoris, not touching directly but applying something to the skin around it. And suddenly there was a burn – a warming of her skin first but then heat in ever increasing intensity. The sensation was soon joined by a cold burn around her nipples, like ice prickling on her skin. The combination was entirely overwhelming – neither pain nor pleasure but all-consuming in its intensity. She wanted to writhe, wanted to escape, but was held firm by the restraints. Her body was winding tighter and tighter, desperately wanting relief, wanting to be filled. When his fingers stroked down to her entrance she whimpered, but after a lazy circle they travelled further, coming to rest on the tight rosette of her anus. She had worn a plug often enough over the last two weeks for her nerves to be deliciously sensitised there and for his finger to slip into her easily. It was not the penetration she wanted and the change in sensation pushed her away from the precipice of her looming orgasm without allowing her relief. He started to move his finger, penetrating deeper with each push, allowing the burn around her nipples and clitoris to take over again while still fanning the fires of her orgasm. Somehow, his finger was not enough, and when he started to replace it with the narrow end of a plug she almost moaned in relief. The burn as he pushed the plug into her, stretching her anus over the wide end of it, almost pushed her over, and would have if he had not removed the oil from around her clitoris, quickly and carefully without touching the sensitive nub, at the same time. She sobbed in despair, unable to take the torture any more. His lips found hers in a gentle kiss.

"Remember, Kathryn. Tell me a secret and I will give you relief."

She needed it badly. "It makes me feel good when I hurt."

At this admission his fingers found her clitoris, and with a simple rub of his index and middle finger on either side he let her fall into pleasure, let her come screaming under his control.

She did not notice when he removed the peppermint oil from her nipples but she became aware of his feathering kisses on her face and the absence of the blindfold as she regained her breath. His hands were still playing over her but now in a calming, loving rhythm. She caught his intent eyes.

"The pain makes you feel good because you feel you deserve it, that you deserve punishment for something?"

Something had cracked inside her and she could not deny him the answer to the question.

"Yes."

He held her gaze and stopped all movement, making absolutely sure that all her attention was on what he was about to say.

"You are mine. The only person who gets to decide when you need punishment is me and you will leave the responsibility for that decision in my hands."

She knew this should not matter to her but somehow his

words settled something in her, soothed an unknown pain, and suddenly she could breathe easier. She felt the relaxation in her own body, felt the corners of her mouth almost stretch into a smile and saw the answering smile on his face. His hand came up to stroke her hair away from her face and he allowed himself a sweet kiss.

"So, where did we stop? Let's see how long you can hold out this time."

Oh God. He was not done yet. She would not be able to survive this.

"Keep your eyes on my face at all times." She saw the stark possessiveness with which he gazed at her breasts, the almost painful desire displayed as his hands cradled them reverently. Seeing his expressions completely unguarded was almost as arousing as feeling his touch on her skin. But this was nothing compared to the image of his mouth surrounding her nipple, his surprisingly dark lips stark against her pale flesh. She felt his mouth starting to work over her skin, licking and an ever increasing sucking motion robbing her of reality. She knew that her face was open to him, that she displayed her pleasure on it. It seemed to make the passion in his eyes shoot sky high.

The shared gaze wove a link between them that surpassed even their bond. It was a silent language of sensuality. When he lifted his head to blow on her wet aureoles, she felt a new spike of lightning travel directly to her clitoris, and his wicked smile showed that he knew what he was doing.

"This might be uncomfortable for a moment."

In her absorption she had missed him reaching for

something beside them, but as he lifted it in his hands she recognised the nipple clamps. When he had used them for the first time on her they had frightened her witless, having acquired scars from some while under another's care, but she had grown used to them. Instead of the blood and agony she had expected, he used them so lightly that she had only felt warmth at their removal. This time though, he tightened them past the level she had become accustomed to.

"I believe I have neglected your breasts shamefully until now."

The sizzling heat in her nipples interfered with her rationality, but that blatant falseness stirred something playful in her. This man was obsessed with her breasts, rarely missing an opportunity to touch and fondle. The temporary amusement hid the sudden sting as he loosened one of the clamps slightly. As he turned to the other breast she was lost in the gentle pressure and pull on her nipple which heated her blood and made the orgasm rise again. Almost absentmindedly she noticed him pick up a strange egg-shaped object from the bed and hold it in his hand whilst beginning to play along her rib cage with kisses and nips. He allowed his sharp incisors to scratch over the skin of her stomach, not breaking the surface but reminding her that this was not just a man but a powerful predator. It had a curious effect on her; exhilaration and arousal with an edge of fear and danger. That it did not make her panic told her something about the way she had come to trust this man. But he was not done playing over her body, and with a quick readjustment he settled between her legs, nuzzling the soft skin on the inside of her thigh.

"I pity humans that their sense of smell is so limited, that they cannot smell the intoxication of a woman's arousal. I have never felt anything remotely like the drugging quality of your scent before. I love your taste even more."

His voice was dark and raw, a deep well of need expressed in tone. She should have been prepared for the long, firm lick along her cleft, but nothing could prepare for the absolute heat, the slight rough feeling of his tongue on her sensitive flesh. For a moment she thought she would come, that he had miscalculated, but just as suddenly as his tongue began to play over her he stopped, and waited for her to settle back from the edge. She moaned.

"Please!"

"Please what, baby?"

Something smooth and roundish was pushed into her and she realised that it was the egg, warm from his hand. It distracted her from his question, but the sudden sting of his teeth nipping her thigh brought her attention back.

"Please what, Kathryn?"

She did not know. She could not concentrate anymore, could not relate to words, or rather could not tell the difference between thought and word.

"I don't know." Her voice held desperation and confusion, her mind only held heat.

"A secret. Just tell me a secret." Something started to buzz inside her, an even but gentle vibration, heating her body but still holding her orgasm at bay. She could not keep her head still, had long since had to give up looking at him, her eyes closed tightly against the rising need in her. She felt the vibrations inside her travel from her vagina to the plug in her anus and back, stroking her nerves with feathery touches that were too light to give her relief. And she needed relief so badly.

"Tell me." His voice was intent and demanding, and there was nothing left in her to resist. She screamed.

"I hate you! I hate you and Paul and even the girls sometimes."

She felt the vibrations end as the egg slipped from her just before he seated himself deep inside her in one almost violent thrust. He stretched her, warmed her and filled her in a way that was enough to bridge her defences and make her come. Her body convulsed around his hard shaft, her inner walls rippled against his unyielding flesh, consumed by fire. This time he did not wait until she had come down from the high, but as her convulsions softened, he pulled the nipple clamps off, and the sudden pain and pleasure drove her into another orgasm. With every lick with which he soothed the hot skin of her breasts he caused another shudder in her vagina, every aspect of her being was connected to him, controlled by him.

When her vision cleared, his face was hovering over hers. Sweat made his skin shine in the light of the flames and each muscle stood out in sharp contrast. He was unbelievably beautiful. He was also still fully hard inside her.

"You are allowed to hate us, although I believe your feelings are closer to anger than hate. And that is allowed too. I have turned your world upside down and taken all you have managed to hold onto. Your brother has betrayed you too often and even the girls have been a constant danger to you. You are not a bad person for being angry on occasion, and no one who has ever seen you with them would say that you do not love them unbearably." For a moment she could see herself through his eyes and it was alright. Then he started to move, leisurely and restrained; a reminder that he was still inside her and her world heated again, though tears were running down her face.

"I cannot," she begged shamelessly. He gently kissed the words from her mouth, but she could feel the fire below the facade.

"One more thing, Kathryn. I want one more thing from you." Then he stopped and fixed his eyes on hers. "What do you feel for me?"

The question shocked her, and she was about to blurt out an answer, something along the lines of anger and hate, but he twitched his powerful hips, slamming into her and driving every thought from her mind. He knelt back, and as one hand started to play with her clitoris, so sensitive as to border on painful after two orgasms, his other hand removed the plug from her ass. She knew exactly what he was planning to do as he withdrew from her and grabbed for a bottle of lubricant but she was too far gone to react. The burn of his penis breaching the tight muscle of her anus drew a sob, but it was not from pain but from utter surrender. His movements were slow but inexorable, giving her body time to adjust but never halting the possession. His eyes were on hers, looking deep into her soul, not missing anything.

"You are mine. Every part of you is mine." Stark

possessiveness was audible in his voice and with each movement he imprinted the knowledge on her mind. A low vibration started in her again and she realised that he had reinserted the egg into her channel whilst she was preoccupied with the stretch of his penis in her ass. When she felt his balls against the skin of her cheeks she felt utterly taken, and she realised that there was no part of her she was not giving him, would not give him. He leaned forward as he started to move, covering her whole body in his shadow. Looking up at him she did not feel threatened, but safe. As his body covered hers, so did his mind.

"I love you!"

It was not him who said the words this time, it was her and it was true. She loved him, maybe because of the bond or perhaps because he had forced it on her over the last two weeks, or even because he had been willing to coax what he could have taken with force. It did not matter; she loved him. She had never thought that the man buried deep in her, the man so desperate for relief that his arms shook, could smile so sweetly. It was sweet and joyous, as was the kiss that followed. But neither of their bodies was willing to be denied and the urgency of his need could not be restrained any longer. With a groan his kiss turned ravenous and his movement lost its moderation. As the vibrations in her intensified sharply, his fingers found her clitoris and pinched. Pleasure swamped her and took everything, even the connection with him. Dimly, she was aware of his penis twitching in her, filling her with heat as his body bowed over her with a shout, but then there was only blackness – deep, velvety blackness full of warmth.

She was floating in a warm lake of life, his body still linked to hers, covering her in a blanket of sated vampire while his hands stroked her head gently. There was no way she had the strength to open her eyes and, most importantly, had no need to. There was no need to be vigilant. She was his. She floated on that knowledge. His breath had returned almost to normal and his penis had slipped from her body when he finally moved. He gently removed the straps and restraints, massaging her limbs until her circulation had been restored to normal. She felt him wipe her body and swathe her in a warm, fluffy blanket before he lifted her from the bed. The movement should have caught her attention, made her open her eyes, but she was too languid to react in any way. She felt him take a seat close to the fire with her safely cradled in his arms but her only reaction was to snuggle closer. She thought she heard someone enter the room, thought she heard him talk, though what it was about she did not register. Her senses returned slowly, gradually, and she thought that a significant time had passed until she finally opened her eyes to look at him. The first thing she realised was how relaxed he looked, how his normal expression always held so much controlled tension. His head was laid back against the red velvet of the upholstery, his glacier blue eyes closed as if in sleep, although she knew he was awake. His lips had relaxed in the beginning of a smile and somehow she knew that this was their normal, unguarded state.

He must have felt her move for his eyes opened to meet hers, still heavy-lidded and restful. The beginning of a smile took its course and developed into a full expression of gentle joy.

"Hey you." He sounded almost drunk, but her voice was no better when she answered.

"Hey."

His smile broadened, and for a moment she did not understand why, but then she did. Ordinarily she would not have answered such a pointless greeting, would have held back any form of communication for the times when it was unavoidable. His hand came to cradle her head, to support her as he readjusted her in his arm, allowing her a more upright position and settling her head firmly against his shoulder. She was alright with that, felt no need to move away or even control her own position in his arms. A playful finger ran along her nose to its tip before he kissed her brow.

"I love you, Kathryn." He had said it often over the last two weeks. Until now she had felt it to be a ridiculous statement, and she was still uncertain with it, uncomfortably aware that the deep knowledge through the bond might be influencing him. But she was also aware now that she loved him, no matter how impossible it seemed after such a short time.

"Can you say it again?" Lucian asked.

She wasn't sure. She truly did not know if she could admit the words, but her mouth spoke them without consulting her inhibitions.

"I love you." The smile was heart-stopping and demanded in its vulnerability that she qualified, "I don't know if I can say it again."

He pulled her even closer, bedding her head into the crook of his neck.

"That's alright, baby. It will get easier."

She was not sure about that, was not even sure if either of them would feel the same tomorrow or next week. This was still all too new, but she knew that she did love him, and come fire or flood, her life was intertwined with his. Most importantly, she was glad of it, no matter the traitor in their midst, the dicey negotiations with humanity, the way he turned her life upside down or her secret that could destroy them all.

15

Future

Hours had passed. She had spent them in turns asleep, playing with the girls, who had remained oblivious to the earlier upheavals, and eating, always under the watchful eyes of Lucian, Brandon or Kieran. The need to deal with the outside threat had led to her self-defence lessons and her talks with Kieran, which she now easily identified as the vampires warped perception of therapy, being set aside for the day.

She had even been wearing clothes since she rose. Her hand stroked over the fine weave of the shirt Lucian had given her, his scent intermingling with hers. It was softer than any of her own clothes, softer and far too large, its folds caressing her skin with every movement. She should have felt like a child playing dress up with an adult's clothes from the way she had to roll the sleeves up to be able to use her hands, but the shirt made her feel anything but childlike, especially when she felt the touch of his hot gaze on her. She knew her attire had more to do with a mark of ownership than a desire to replace the shirt he had torn. The thought did not frighten her.

What had happened to her? Her fingers painted the path of a raindrop as it slid down the window pane, collecting other drops, shedding some, on its way to the bottom. Kathryn had always been so certain her life was developing in a clear, immutable path towards defeat. Now she was confused. He had captured her, blackmailed and subjugated her; exposed her to what many would consider depravities – and he had given her a freedom she had never known before.

The window glass was cold and soothing against her brow as she leaned against it, her mind caught in a strange state of confused clarity. It did not matter what others thought, or what her fears dictated to her. She might never be able to overcome the terrors and the lessons of her past, but one of those lessons had been to make the best of life at any moment in time for there might never be another. She had now been given the glimpse of a possible future in which there was a tomorrow, a next week, a next month, and although they also held dangers, these were less immediate than any others her life had known, and that was the best she could hope for.

Her mind, with all the determination and desperation she had developed over time, did not intentionally dwell on the man whose warm mental embrace cradled her very existence. Some dangers were too confusing to face before there was any need and the realisation that she had begun to trust him was too frightening to think about.

Her breath fogged the glass before her and before she had even thought of it she had drawn a large A into the condensation. A for Anna. Another topic better avoided for the moment. As the drops smeared her writing she smiled at a thousand memories of other letters on windows, in her own hand and the hands of her sisters, her daughter. It was curious how some small pleasures never changed. A yawn broke her concentration, the renewed warm air covering the letter under another layer of condensation.

Kathryn was tired almost beyond belief but with a mind too clear to sleep. Behind her she heard the ebb and flow of male voices as Brandon and Lucian debated and discussed the necessary security measures. Suddenly she remembered what she wanted to ask.

"Why did I wake up?"

Her voice was clear against the backdrop of the deeper conversation behind her and broke it like a sword cutting silk. For a moment she thought they would continue owing her an answer, another secret among so many in a world she only now discovered she knew nothing of at all.

"The wards alerted you," Lucian said.

Kathryn turned from her consideration of raindrops and their patterns to frown at him. It was not an answer designed to enlighten her, and his grin was no more successful in avoiding her ire. He must have seen her rising irritation for he continued.

"I keyed the wards of the building and court to resort to you when I, Kieran or Brandon are not available. It is standard procedure regarding most of the emergency alarms.

Initially the alarm will link to the person of first contact. In the case of an intruder alarm, that would be Brandon, though both Eric and I would receive a ping. If there is no reaction or if the alarm bounces off, as it does when we hibernate, it would resort to the next person in the list. First Kieran, though he was out too, then you, and then my head of daylight security, who you have not met yet."

"You keyed me into your defences?"

She could hear the stunned disbelief in her own voice and did not begrudge him his smile this time.

"Of course."

Her mind could not wrap itself around this answer. It had not been four weeks since he had brought her into his court by force. Two weeks ago she had still seen him as a monster and even today she was uncomfortable with seeing him as anything but her enemy. And he had given her access to the most important part of a court's buildings – its defences.

In her frozen astonishment she paid no heed to his stepping up to the window and leaning beside it. That in itself was a frightening development but she was too stunned to consider it.

"When?"

His hand had risen to play with a strand of her hair, the long fingers stroking it behind her ear in an intimate gesture lacking any erotic sensuality but holding so much warmth.

"Hmmm?"

The sound was a question; one clearly stemming from a mind otherwise occupied. The fact that it was the play of his fingers through her hair which seemed to be this occupation only annoyed her further.

"When did you key me into the defences?"

His eyes were laughing at her, though his features were a study in serious contemplation. Why did his humour leave her with the overwhelming desire to stamp her foot like a three year old?

"I keyed your mental pattern into the wards when you were asleep, the day after Valentine's Day."

He laughed at her wide-eyed disbelief, a sound full-bodied and free. It wrapped around her, vibrated along her skin, teasing and playful. It made her angrier than she had been in a long time. How dare he.

"Are you crazy?"

The careful control in her voice did nothing to hide the fury under her words. It seemed to impress him little. Although his laugh died away, the smile on his lips remained, unhidden and gentle. It only poured oil on the fire of her anger.

"How dare you! How can you risk the wellbeing of your court by adding a stranger to the defences? You did not know me. You still don't. How can you risk so much?"

His face sobered, his eyes capturing her in a gaze so intense she felt it to her toes. The hand which had played so absently with her hair shaped itself to her cheek, took away any chance to avoid the soul-bearing demand of his eyes. Caught between the cold window and the heat of his intensity she heard his words, not only with her ears but with her soul.

"You think I do not know you? I might not know yet what your favourite colour is but I know you, I know what matters.

The woman who spent her life taking care of three children, two not even her own; the woman who is still able to smile in the driving rain is no danger to my court. The woman who yells at me for risking the wellbeing of people who would have brought her to me by force had they found her before would not invite harm to those who have not taken action against her."

She wanted to deny it, wanted to yell at him, to tell him that she would have broken the defences leaving all open to harm, but she could not. He did know her. No matter how stupid it made her, how little modern life was able to account for her brand of honour, as long as the children were not threatened by it she would not have ignored a potential threat to innocents just because their Master had imprisoned her. Even at the risk of her own life.

He watched the emotions on her face and she knew he saw every thought, every doubt.

"Oh, I am certain you would have fought with all your might against someone who wanted to harm you or who threatened the children, but you would never do so unprovoked or simply stand by whilst an innocent is hurt. It makes you who you are, who you have chosen to be, and I admire you for it more than I can say."

He was too observant by far, too good at reading her every emotion, often before she knew what she felt herself. It made her feel safe, in a strange way. It was in that moment she realised that all her protestations, all her careful reasoning was shot to hell. She did trust him not to harm her without reason.

She felt herself relax into his hold, his hand softening to the weight of her head. It was instinctive, an intuitive relaxation of her guard after days in which confusion and worry had battered her mind with relentless force. He seemed as weary as she was, his brow sinking to hers, resting in the twilight of the never-sleeping city at their feet.

"What am I?"

The question was little more than a whisper travelling on the shared breath between them. It held the essence of all the fear, all the vulnerability of the last few days, distilled and expressed. Had he laughed at that moment she would have withdrawn into her shell, but he was too good a hunter not to recognise the moment of grudging surrender.

"What do you mean?"

His voice held even less volume but still managed to surround her with the soft cadence of his strength.

"Does the bond make me simply an extension of you? Is that why you coded me into the defences, why you took it upon yourself to make me part of your court, and your business?"

There was no anger in her, just interest. She had left anger and suspicion behind, caught in the confusing miasma that made this man. His body was a warm presence along hers, shielding her against the room without touching her. His hands cradled her face so gently as if she were made of porcelain, and still he had proven today he had more confidence in her than anyone else ever had.

His breath gently moved the fine hair along her face, the caress pulling at her, fanning a hidden desire for touch. It was so easy to simply relax into him, to let her body close that small distance between them. Her eyes closed in calm acceptance, in a restfulness she rarely felt. She felt the whisper of a kiss on the tip of her nose. He gently let her head come to rest against his shoulder, his arms slipping around her to support her body against his. She felt his heartbeat like a living drum under her ear.

"You are you."

Kathryn was not certain she was satisfied with the answer, not even sure it was the answer to the question she had been asking. In the circle of his arms, his scent lulling her mind, she felt safe enough to accuse him.

"You want me to be dependent on you."

He chuckled, his arms tightening with the sound.

"Yes. I want you to trust me enough that you feel you can depend on me. And I admit that I would love to be as necessary to you for every breath, for every heartbeat, as you are to me."

She started. "I am not—"

But he did not let her finish the sentence.

"I know you are afraid of the power the bond has over you but you have no concept of how it is for me. It is an all-consuming need to hold you close, to know every aspect of your being, to protect and touch. I have to touch your mind as it is almost painful when I am not."

When she turned her head up to look at him she saw that his eyes were roaming over the city rather than looking down at her. There was raw need in his expression but also calm acceptance; and a joy incomprehensible to her. Eventually he looked back at her.

"Everything you do is designed to undermine my independence." Kathryn said.

It was an open accusation and its only effect was to make him smile.

"Yes."

No excuse, no prevarication.

"It is not healthy."

The words were spoken more as if they were a mere trial run, a hesitant use of a concept she was not sure was even applicable. His raised eyebrow was gently mocking but he ignored the irony of a health lecture.

"Were you human, it might not be. Were you human then forcing you to depend so much on me when you are so vulnerable would be dangerous, but neither of us can escape the bond. Were you human it would take years of therapy before you might reach a stage where you could trust another with your wellbeing. As an ErGer you have no choice. You are mine."

She settled her head back on his shoulder, her brow nestled in the crook of his neck in a position which had become a comfortable habit over the last few weeks. Her mind was too full to make sense of his words.

"I don't trust you, not as you want me to."

Trust was such an inexplicable concept. So many forms, all nebulous and hard to define. She could trust, could believe in his intentions, but he wanted something more. She knew he wanted her to give herself to him, to let go and allow him to rule her life without the constant reticence, the constant holding back. Kathryn doubted she would ever be able to do so.

"No, you have not learnt to trust me yet."

His voice remained calm even in the face of her provocation. It disarmed her without giving her solace. She felt her muscles tense, a gradual return to her normal state of vigilance. When she tried to move away from him his fingers spanned her wrists in a gentle reminder of the bonds she wore under his care, and with this single movement he appeased the rising tide of fear in her, placated her inner tension. It was frightening in its simplicity and she realised that he had already conditioned her into surrendering to him more than she had foreseen. Her mind might not trust him but her body did.

"I am sorry, Kathryn."

Sorry for what? Sorry for capturing her, sorry for holding her and breaking all the rules she had thought were immutable and clear. Sorry for turning her world upside down and leaving her with nothing to stop her freefall? She doubted he had meant any of these. Her hair moved softly under the quiet touch of his lips.

"I am sorry that the outside world is intruding when you are not ready to face it yet. I wanted to give you more time, more space to settle, but I do not think I can do so now."

She heard the regret, the remorse in his voice, and a paradoxical part of her wanted to soothe his sadness. But what could she say? How could she explain to him she had never expected there to be a future so that now, suddenly with one in sight, she was utterly lost. She had spent fourteen years in flight, her memory prior to this life of constant fear and readiness being only of a human life. Her experience with supernaturals was rudimentary and had been brutal, her knowledge of supernatural politics non-existent. He was afraid he could not keep the outside world at bay. She did not even understand what the outside world was. How could she tell him any of that?

"It will get easier, you know."

His voice was gentle but that was no hint of what he was talking about.

"What will?"

His broad palm stroked her head, coercing her with gentleness rather than force to meet his gaze. His eyes were dangerous. They told her too much, opened him to her too widely so that it became ever harder to see the enemy in him. His tongue flicked out to lick over his lower lip and her gaze was instantly caught, drawn.

"Sharing will get easier."

He bent closer, his lips starting to play along the side of her mouth, a teasing touch intended to entice not plunder.

"Trusting will get easier."

She loved his taste, the sensation of his soft lips on her skin. Dissatisfied with the access he had to her lips, the teasing temptation of his mouth so close but still just a fleeting touch, she tilted her head, tried to catch it with her own.

"Feeling..."

This last word was almost lost in the kiss, almost lost against the confident claiming of her mouth. But before he could take her mind with his passion her hand came to rest on his chest, and to her surprise his mouth rose from hers after only a gentle touch. She searched his expression, his eyes – for what she did not know exactly.

"What do you want?"

"I have all I want." His answer lacked conviction.

"Do you want to be the Lord of the British Isles?"

Even she knew that over the last few years a competition for this defunct title, the leader of all supernaturals in the British Isles, had arisen and that he was seen as one of the contenders. But he only shrugged.

"Not if we can live freely and without interference. I can barely keep up with the concerns of the London court. I am not sure if I want to broaden my responsibilities, especially right now, when I would prefer to concentrate on you."

"But?"

For there was a 'but' in that sentence. Her perceptiveness garnered her another smile.

"But there is government interest, the strength of which is more serious than any in the last few centuries, and we might not be able to afford an internal power struggle. I am not sure how far I would trust the other aspirants anyway. And there is you. The stake in the game has just risen. With an ErGer under my protection I become more powerful and more vulnerable at the same time. So there are arguments for forcing the decision now rather than later."

"Will you?"

She was still surprised he was discussing this so openly, without any consideration for the secrecy which had to be part of his normal behaviour. No one held the position of the Lord of London, and was a contender for the High Lord, without a keen sense of stratagem and the ability to play his cards close to his chest. And still he answered any question she asked.

"That will depend on the outcome of various developments over the next few weeks. I need to gauge the severity of the governmental threat against the stance of the other national courts. I need to see how our bond develops and, eventually, how you interact with my wider court. I also need to find the traitor in our own ranks and make an example that will dissuade any repeat of disloyalty."

The last was said with sufficient venom to make Kathryn realise that the Lord of London held some old-fashioned attitudes regarding loyalty, and most likely the punishment for betraying it. But she also heard pain, deep and cutting, a wound on his heart. She understood the feeling. The first time Paul had betrayed her something had broken in her. She had thought she would bleed to death from it and only the children had kept her from giving in then. She could not heal the wound. She could only hope that finding the traitor would help. But she could try to make it easier until then.

"You own a variety of whips."

It was meant as a joke, but the wicked smile on his lips as he bent to kiss her again made her wonder about that. Then he stepped back and shook her world once more.

"Now, let me tell you about Elves."

"Elves?" Was he serious?

"Elves."

ABOUT THE AUTHOR

In "real" life, I am an academic with degrees in Political Science, Economics, Philosophy and Law and an insatiable desire to confound, baffle and disconcert my students. Someone once suggested to me the reason for my stories lay in the desire to offset the tedium and rationality of academic life. He wasn't an academic or he would have known better. It is best to use research against tedium, students to offset the rationality and an unlimited supply of stress-balls for the faculty meetings. The stories? Well, they are just for me – like a mental manicure.

I also write a blog on Feminism and Erotica – come talk to me at www.christineblackthorn.eu

OTHER SINFUL PRESS TITLES

PEEPER by SJ Smith
BY MY CHOICE by Christine Blackthorn
SHOW ME, SIR by Sonni de Soto
THE HOUSE OF FOX be SJ Smith

For more information about Sinful Press
please visit
www.sinfulpress.co.uk

CHRISTINE BLACKTHORN

Lightning Source UK Ltd.
Milton Keynes UK
UKOW06f0640160816

280781UK00016B/369/P